Party Favors

Party Favors

NICOLE SEXTON

with

Susan Johnston

THE LYONS PRESS

Guilford, Connecticut

An imprint of The Globe Pequot Press

The Lyons Press is an imprint of The Globe Pequot Press

Designed by Sheryl P. Kober

Library of Congress Cataloging-in-Publication Data
Sexton, Nicole.
 Party favors / Nicole Sexton with Susan Johnston.
    p. cm.
 ISBN 978-1-59921-459-7
 1. Fund-raisers (Persons)—Fiction. 2. Women in politics—Fiction. 3. Campaign funds—United States—Fiction. 4. Washington (D.C.)—Fiction. 5. Political fiction. I. Johnston, Susan, 1971- II. Title.
 PS3619.E985P37 2008
 813'.6—dc22

                                                                2008011177

Printed in the United States of America

10 9 8 7 6 5 4 3 2 1

For my parents Marlyne and Joe
who paved the way to my every adventure.

"I've always said that in politics,
your enemies can't hurt you,
but your friends will kill you."

—ANN RICHARDS

A Note to Readers

Nicole has worked in the political arena for over fifteen years; this story was inspired by what she learned and experienced during her numerous jobs in the fundraising industry. That said, *Party Favors* is a work of fiction and all of the names and characters portrayed in this book are products of Nicole's and Susan's overactive imaginations. Any resemblance to actual events or persons, living or dead, is coincidental. Although some real institutions, historical events, and political figures are name-dropped, all are used fictitiously.

Gray Two is So Not Tall

*E*verything about the dinner had to be absolutely 110 percent fantastic. First and foremost, I needed to look amazing, which I did, in my most conservative, but still va-va-va-voom, belted, black silk YSL suit accessorized with a stunningly bright turquoise Hermes scarf, since I'm Southern and able to pull off risky wardrobe choices with my colorful bursts of personality.

Second and even more important, my staff needed sharp eyes, fast hands, and tip-tip-tippy toes. Majority Leader Ivy's historic three-story brownstone was not only filled to the gills with one hundred of my top-tier Team Victory donors, it was also bursting at the seams with irreplaceable antiques curated by his refined, intelligent, and Parisian wife, Genevieve. I'd instructed my junior staffers to stay in service overdrive: "Donors will be drinking; sloppiness is bound to ensue. I need all eyes on the relics. Thank you." My pre-party pep talk had been taken to heart. The young ones were zipping around, unseen and unheard, effectively anticipating the accidental bumpings of Mrs. Ivy's precariously placed artifacts.

Third and most critical of all, I needed happy donors. A happy donor equaled cash money green. An unhappy donor equaled bye-

bye Senate seat. These Team Victorys were my most privileged, most pampered, most jaded, and hardest to impress givers. They hadn't ponied up fifty grand per couple just to meet Majority Leader Ivy or his wife. Most already knew the six most powerful senators, those in Leadership, I'd secured specifically for the evening. They weren't even there to chat up President Gray or his grumpy, grumpy V.P. who cursed people under his breath and always showed up with a badly bonked head or sprained ankle. No, my Team Victorys weren't interested in handshaking. They paid to see the house.

Donors *love* themselves some houses. They will pay out their a-double-s to see if there's a hamper with dirty clothes, if the fridge is covered in family pictures. They will do everything in their power to sneak a glance at that marital bed. Nosy, nosy, nosy. Since taking the job that catapulted my career from little old me to Big Money Babe, I'd become D.C.'s version of Robin Leach, offering check-writers a glimpse of the Republican Senate's "champagne wishes and caviar dreams." For a hefty price, of course.

Big bucks meant big donors expected big parties to big-time rock—there'd better be A-list entertainment, free-flowing top-shelf booze, plentiful hors d'oeuvres plus a catered sit-down dinner, unfettered access to politicians, and there absolutely, no doubt about it, had to be a click line. Because clicks are donor crack.

Every donor, no matter the size of their wallet, wants a picture of themselves smiling with Someone Important. Even if they are Someone *More* Important and they already have fifteen identical pictures, they will stand in their cocktail dress or tux, waiting like an anxious kid braving a monster roller coaster.

The click line itself is just a cleaned-up carnie trick, a frenetic hurricane of pushing and smiling and shaking and flashing and clicking and pulling and pushing and smiling and go, go, go, go, go, go until every last donor has had their twelve seconds with a Hot Shot. It's ludicrous. Not the slightest bit glamorous. And yet, if I'd ever even *suggested* throwing a fundraiser in D.C. sans click line, I would have been run out of town as a heretic.

Which is why, in a house full of priceless museum treasures, I had one hundred donors and all my staff squeezed into the well-carpeted, less fragile, "books don't break when they fall" library. I'd vetoed the conventional, tacky blue velour pipe-and-drape backdrop and opted instead to put Majority Leader Ivy and Genevieve on a toe mark in front of their mahogany shelves filled with leather-bound tomes. My donors were beyond happy. They were click-crack wild, high from the unprecedented inner-sanctum access. Their clicks would appear more personal, more intimate, more real. They'd frame the photos and non-chalantly prop them on baby grand pianos, on mantles beside the oblig-atory posed "whole family wearing white on a Cape Cod beach" shot as if Ivy and his wife were just that: family. This was overdose material.

Despite the increasingly claustrophobic conditions in the library, my party was running like a well-oiled machine. I flitted about the room making sure donors had drinks, staffers were strategically placed, and the senators were schmoozing with civilians and not one another. All I needed was for President Gray to arrive. Where, oh where, was my little Gray Two?

Genevieve caught my eye and motioned me to her side. She whis-pered her forgetfulness softly in my ear, "J'ai oublié son nom," know-ing my childhood in New Orleans afforded her both the discretion and privilege of her native tongue.

I whispered back, "His name is William, William Sifkin."

Genevieve nodded and greeted Mr. Sifkin like a long-lost friend. I stepped back slightly and wedged myself awkwardly into a tight hall-way between two open pocket doors, discreetly whispering names when requested and smiling, always smiling. I had no idea I was standing in the Presidential Hold.

In a shuffle so swift I had no time to yelp, Advance jostled me backwards and slid the pocket door in front of me entirely shut. I spun to find myself tit-to-tat with Gray Two, the pocket door behind him already closed. And tit-to-tat isn't easily done with me. Though petite in stature, I am, as Mom politely describes in mixed company, "generously endowed."

From the light spilling under the doors, I could see President Gray smiling his shocking white toothy grin. He snickered nervously through his veneers, as seemingly startled by our inadvertent "Seven Minutes in Heaven" as I was.

"How are you tonight, Mr. President?" I hoped my question might lessen the outrageously uncomfortable physical awkwardness of being pressed together like sardines. Neither of us could even lift our arms to shake hands.

The president continued snickering. "I'm fine, Miss Sachet. And how are you?"

"I'm fantastic, sir." Which was such a lie. Just because Secret Service had no qualms about stuffing me in a closet with the leader of the free world didn't mean I had the time to stand around chit-chatting with the man. Outside our spontaneously constructed confinement, there were donors needing appeasement, senators sniffing out dollars, staffers expecting supervision. Heavens to Betsy, Genevieve needed names! I tried my best to remain calm as my brain overflowed with potential emergencies. "I hope they let us out of here soon."

President Gray shrugged and the movement pulled my suit sleeves up over my wrists, where they stayed since I could not readjust them. He said, "Welcome to my life," and we fell into a long, strained silence.

Stuck. Minute One.

It struck me odd. The president was so not tall. Maybe, *maybe* he had two inches on me. Yes, I'd met him before, numerous times, but never this up close and personal. It was always a walk-and-talk, or a nod in passing, or an approach while seated, or a surrounded-by-staff situation. I'd spent more time with his uncle, Gray One, when I was a Ray of Hope. His uncle had been a tall man, impressive. This Gray had amazing, TV worthy, shellacked helmet hair but wow, was he a shorty. His height, or rather lack of it, made him seem much less . . . well, presidential. I thought better of commenting aloud and bit my tongue.

Stuck. Minute Two.

The rhythmic inhalations and exhalations of the president's breathing lulled me into a much-needed meditative state. In the year since I'd moved back to D.C., I hadn't had two solid minutes of nothingness. Ever. I was always on the run, in chauffeured cars, dashing from meeting to meeting, party to party, while simultaneously typing e-mails, returning voice mails, and multitasking in a haze of utter distraction. Two minutes of stillness? That meant I was either asleep or dead. I closed my eyes and allowed my breathing to deepen and enter into my lungs not as hurried huffs but as long, slow draws of life.

Stuck. Minute Three.

Old memories and long-suppressed emotions bubbled up from my core; a molten brew of fiery anger, disappointment, and confusion. This president had tricked and used people I adored. This president had lied to the entire country just to save his own hind end. This president had built his entire career on a long series of shady deals and broken promises. What in the world was I doing locked in a closet with this awful man?

Stuck. Minute Four.

I could not stand one more second of my forced confinement. I gritted my teeth to stop the questions rising in my heart from spilling straight out of my mouth: How did I let myself get so deeply embedded? Why was I raising $95 million for senators without a full understanding of their platforms? When had I stopped believing in candidates and started counting chairs? Worse than that, when did I stop caring whether politicians were actually good people? Everything had moved so fast. I'd gone with the flow of life, and life had taken me to the top of the Hill. My values, my integrity, my personal beliefs, I'd pushed them deep into a closet and now I was literally standing in that closet, face-to-face with the blue-suited, helmet-haired, white-toothed shorty that symbolized my self-betrayal.

How did I even get here?

Part One

REMEMBER

One

Winning Won't Save You

*M*om will tell you it all started with Little Miss Valentine, my first "get out the vote" campaign. Little Miss Valentine was an annual beauty contest held in Miss Bonnetemps' kindergarten class to raise money for the spring tree plantings at Margie Watters Day School in Metairie, Louisiana.

I was nominated along with Sandy, Neci, and that red-headed Heather that none of us liked. Each of us had a Styrofoam cup with our name scratched on it in black magic marker. The boys would put their leftover lunch money in the cup of the girl they wanted to win. Whoever raised the most money won the contest and that girl would get to wear a tiara.

A tiara. Lord have mercy, I wanted that tiara so bad I could taste the shiny metal on my tongue during lunch and dinner. I sang songs extolling the virtues of tiaras while Mom bathed me before bed. In my prayers, I added the tiara to my list of blessings and requests: "Dear God, please bless Nana and Mom and my sister and Papa, wherever he is now. Lord Baby Jesus, please bless me with the tiara and please don't ever let me get married and I don't want children. Amen."

On a day not long before, Papa had driven me to school (which was strange, because we only lived seven blocks away and I usually walked with Mom), kissed me goodbye, watched me walk into the building, then sat on a swing at the playground, crying. Me and my friends watched from the windows as he slumped in the swing, swaying gently back and forth, back and forth. I couldn't see his actual tears—his face was covered by his long sandy-brown hair—but his shoulders were shaking.

The mean old Heather blurted out, "Your dad's got problems."

I wanted to crawl under a rock and die. I prayed a secret prayer: "Please, God, make him leave." Which he did. And then he never came back home. And that's when Mom started crying.

Now, Sachet women are famous for three traits: (1) generations of dark-haired baby girls (no sons) named after famous movie starlets; (2) our radiant smiles; and (3) our prodigious, unstoppable crying jags. Family lore had it that Mom entered the world with a full head of flowing black curls, crying smoky-eyed tears. Inspired by her dramatic arrival, my Nana, Ava Gardner Sachet, named her only child Hedy Lamarr. Bearing the weight of her glamorous namesake, Mom became a pageant queen and an underwear model for the Sanger Harris catalog. (Hey, Cindy Crawford modeled underwear for Dillard's, so judge not.)

My sister, Sophia Loren, resembled Mom in every way, but I'd been born the "blonde sheep" of the family, the first fair-haired child in four generations. Mom refused Nana's request to name me Shirley Temple and the compromise left me Temple Leigh (as in Vivien), though everyone called me Tee.

As a good little Sachet girl, I quickly learned that a smile with bright eyes and a slight, bobbing nod made people like you, smile back, and say yes. I also learned that crying was an art form. There were tears for sadness, tears of affection, tears for laughter, and tears for love. I had not mastered the form but even at five, I understood Mom's midnight tears were salted with pure heartbreak. Papa was gone.

I thought maybe winning Little Miss Valentine might help. Maybe if I won, the newspapers would run a picture of me and Papa would see it and come home. I fell asleep each night to the lullaby of Mom's muffled whimpers and dreamt of tiaras twinkling in the moonless sky.

It didn't take long to figure out that my platinum-blonde curls and chubby cheeks were only going to go so far. The boys wouldn't just hand over dimes willy-nilly and they'd only pay for one thing: kisses. So I gave kisses. I gave kisses on the jungle gym, kisses behind the coat lockers. I snuck kisses across the construction paper, glue, and glitter of our creative arts table. I kissed Curtis Q., who had a crush on Mom. He closed his eyes and said, "Pretend you're your momma," so I jutted out my hip and acted sophisticated, even though I knew he wasn't looking. I even kissed gross old Harley who ran around with his eyelids turned inside out. (Who would have ever guessed he'd turn out to be a Louisiana Supreme Court judge?)

I tried my best to sneak kisses on that short seven-block walk home but Mom held my hand tightly and wouldn't allow me to squirm away. It was just like lobbying in D.C.: You could kiss to get your way, but only if no one was watching.

Red-headed Heather won the tiara. She climbed the monkey bars with no shorts on under her skirt and let the boys lay on their backs to watch. Clearly, kisses couldn't even begin to compare to panties. I was runner-up. They gave me a sad little chocolate bunny when all I wanted was that glittering tiara perched atop my head.

Thirteen years later, I'd be crowned Miss Orleans on a stage in the ballroom of the Canal Street Doubletree Hotel. I'd wear a fire-engine-red dress with a big white bow on my behind, sewn by a flaming

Mardi Gras costume designer who fancied me a reincarnated Marilyn Monroe. But at five years old, I only knew Papa was gone, Mom still cried herself to sleep, and Heather got to take the tiara home.

That night, I bawled as I had never bawled before. Bulbous, rolling tears that glistened and hung on each cheek. Moaning gasps for breath that caused my little ribcage to heave in sorrowful spasms. This, this was a Sachet breakdown. Sensational and wonderfully cathartic, it was transcendent. I became a true Sachet girl.

Mom will tell you it all started with Little Miss Valentine. She will tell you that was the first time I wanted to be in the limelight, the moment I discovered I loved being the center of attention. She will tell you that a little kindergarten beauty contest taught me the good comes with bad and the bad comes with good, and they're always intertwined no matter what you try to do to separate them. She will tell you that the power of popularity and convincing boys to give me their money and jangling those won-over coins in my Styrofoam cup simultaneously titillated, intoxicated, and broke my heart.

And she'd be right.

After Papa skipped town, Mom reclaimed her maiden name, stopped modeling, and got a full-time job in a hospital gift shop. During the day she sold flowers, candy, and stuffed animals to nervous visitors. But in the evening, Mom studied for her real estate license and launched Sachet Connections, a roommate-finder service, out of our garage.

After five long and exhausting years doing both, Mom came home one day and announced she was quitting her job at the hospital and putting those full-time hours and all her energy into expanding her own business. She rented an itty-bitty office in Jefferson Parish and heard about a real estate conference in Georgia. She thought if she went, she could build alliances with other Southern entrepreneurs to take her business to the next level. Unfortunately, my sister never paid attention to price tags and had just paid a small fortune for her prom gown. With the new office lease, no full-time job, and no alimony checks showing up from Papa *ever*, Mom had backed herself into a corner. She was going to cancel her flight to Georgia until Sophia threw a hissy fit.

Sophia was five years older than me, fifteen, and dating high school boys. I worshipped the ground she walked on. If she would have allowed me to glue myself to her hip, I would have. Sophia taught me the word "independent" and I started using it all the time. "I'm going to be independent." I didn't know what the word meant but my sister preached for me to be it, so I tried my best. Sophia was convinced the Georgia conference was the answer to all Mom's prayers. She stamped her tennis shoe on the ground, shook her ebony curls, and did her best Nana impersonation. "For the love of your children, get on that plane!"

Turned out Sophia was right, just not in the way she expected. Mom did get on that plane in her sage-green suit and straw hat, and when she returned six days later, she was married to Gil Matthews, a guest speaker at the conference and the president of a big bank based in St. Louis.

Mom walked into our sitting room holding hands with an older man. She was giggling the same way I did when Sophia tried to teach me how to French kiss a pillow. "Gil, these are my daughters."

He was big, barrel-chested and tall, with the shiniest silver hair I'd ever seen; it glowed like a halo around his rosy-cheeked round face.

He wore a crisp blue-and-white seersucker suit with a flashy pink tie. And pink was my favorite color. I loved him immediately.

Sophia was not impressed. She crossed her arms and protested, "I'm not changing my last name!" It upset me to see Sophia angry, because this man made Mom laugh. That was all that really mattered. In probably my first and last act of defiance against my sister's omnipotent influence, I stepped forward to curtsy and present myself. I barely stood as high as his elbow.

"Pleasure to make your acquaintance, sir. My name is Temple Leigh Sachet. But you can call me Tee."

The man bowed formally and offered his sizeable hand. "Tee, it is a pleasure to meet you. My name is Gil Matthews but you can call me whatever you like."

I grabbed three of his fingers and shook as hard as I could. Deal.

While it was fine for Mom to elope with a stranger, she, like Sophia, was not okay with us changing our names. We were Sachet women and her business was called Sachet Connections. Mom's maiden name stayed.

Mom was also unwilling to uproot her daughters to a new city. From the day we met, Daddy Gil began flying to New Orleans on Thursdays and flying back to Missouri early every Monday. He was madly in love with Mom and gladly arranged his life around us.

During the week, Sophia, Mom, and I lived the dysfunctional chaos of a single-parent, all-girl house, the three of us always on crazy diets. Mom was a Picker and Talker, consuming only what she could nibble during breaks in conversation while on the phone, though, when drastic measures were called for, she was a big fan of the Cabbage Soup Diet. Sophia was partial to the 10-10-10 schedule: ten bananas the first day, ten hot dogs the second, and ten boiled eggs on the third. She swore it never failed to cut ten pounds. I myself was, in

Mom's words, "too young to worry about such things." Still, I wanted in on the action. I was convinced that popcorn was weightless and if I stood up while I ate, I wouldn't gain a pound.

Daddy Gil would arrive on Thursday evening, clap his hands, insist Mom get off the phone, and make me sit at the dining room table, and we'd have a meat and a starch and a vegetable, just like Beaver Cleaver. If you came to our house on a Tuesday night, you'd have thought we were nuts. If you came on a Friday night, you would have thought we were the model American family.

Since Daddy Gil's work was up north, his weekends with us were filled with hobbies, the first of which was flying. After getting his pilot's license, Daddy Gil bought an airplane, which led to a series of Cessnas he jokingly dubbed the Sachet Fleet in Mom's honor. Mom wasn't a big fan of the thought of falling thousands of feet to her death. She decided Daddy Gil needed a new, safer hobby.

We lived three houses down from the Lake Pontchartrain levee, so Daddy Gil took up boating. He bought a twelve-foot blue whaler and hitched it up to a trailer ball on the back of his big yellow Cadillac we called the Banana. We all piled in and stopped at Kentucky Fried Chicken to pick up a bucket of chicken and a six pack of Cokes. He drove us to the boat launch and submerged the Banana halfway in the water but the boat wouldn't come off. Finally somebody yelled, "You need to unlatch it!" We should have known right then and there to head back home.

Daddy Gil unhitched the latch and all of a sudden the boat swooshed into the water. The three of us scrambled to get the chicken, Cokes, and ourselves in while Daddy Gil attempted to stop the Cadillac from drowning. Finally, we were all in, soaked, and ready for our first trip. Then the engine wouldn't turn over. And that's when Mom had had enough.

The boat started drifting, drifting, drifting. People on the launch were yelling, "Do you have a rope?" Nope. "How 'bout an oar?" Nope. The Pontchartrain Lake Patrol pulled up in a tug and started towing us in. Daddy Gil put his feet up, popped open a Coke, and dug into the chicken. Mom went totally ballistic. "Gil! What are you doing?"

"Hedy, I figure this is the only boat ride I'm getting today so I'd better well enjoy it."

After that Mom begged our neighbors, Cecil and Hattie, who owned a boat held together by rust, to put Daddy Gil through Boat School 101. Cecil and Daddy Gil became best friends and the little whaler turned into a ski boat. Then they got into shrimping and crabbing so Daddy Gil bought a huge commercial fishing boat with a boom. During the week, my sister would take the nets down and attach two huge speakers, the big old-fashioned kind with the fuzz on the front, to the stereo and she and her friends would go out on that boat and dance. They'd drop the boom and ski on Lake Pontchartrain. And every so often, she'd let me, her little sister, tag along.

But on weekends, the boat was family time. We'd trawl and catch pounds and pounds of shrimp. We'd ski and swim and laugh our heads off. We had a ball.

Daddy Gil came from a family full of Catholic Democrats, but Mom had always been a Republican. As I got older, she became politically active, helping candidates at the local level and even giving the keynote address at Mrs. Reagan's Just Say No dinner. By the time the '88 Republican National Convention rolled into New Orleans, Mom had "converted" Daddy Gil and enlisted Sophia and me to pass out straw hats while she and Daddy Gil ran a voter registration booth.

I loved the Convention because I loved parties—that's all a Convention is, the party part of a Party. We Sachet women were pros when it came to throwing a great soirée. Mom always hosted a Mardi Gras float and Jazz Festival celebrations, and once Sophia turned eighteen (in NOLA the legal age to drink), our backyard became *the* place to be for her high school sorority keg parties (those sororities being a purely New Orleans phenomenon). I soon followed in my sister's footsteps and became president of my own sorority, inheriting Sophia's backyard keggers.

Mom knew we'd find someplace to drink regardless. She also knew every single one of my friends. Where they lived, where their parents worked, how many siblings they had, and what car they drove. If we were going to make a party, it had to happen where Mom could keep an eye on everyone.

We put kegs in the carport, roasted a pig in the backyard, set up sawhorse tables in the driveway, and charged five bucks for a go cup. Mom and Daddy Gil hosted their own cocktail party upstairs and the adults rotated chaperoning, walking through every twenty minutes. At one o'clock in the morning, Mom cleared everyone out with a forced breath check, a line walk, and if someone was tipsy, a ride home.

For me, drinking wasn't the point. The point was those five-buck go cups. Our little weekend keggers raised enough money so my whole sorority could sneak away to chase boys at Fort Walton Beach in Pensacola, Florida, for a weekend. I have no idea how I talked Mom into that, but I did and we had a ton of fun.

Fun. That was my first impression of the Republican Party. I got caught up in the throngs of people, the fiery speeches, the zany hats, the frenetic flag waving, the confetti, the balloons, the chanting, the outrageous spectacle. When Ronald and Nancy Reagan stepped onto that stage in the Superdome, I swear I felt an electric charge buzz the air.

"Madam Chairman, delegates to the convention, and fellow citizens, thank you for that warm and generous welcome. Nancy and I have been enjoying the finest of Southern hospitality since we arrived here yesterday. And believe me, after that reception I don't think the 'Big Easy' has ever been bigger than it has tonight!"

The roar was deafening. I was an impressionable sixteen-year-old, and the Convention was the biggest party I'd ever seen in my life. Bigger than Mardi Gras. For three days the entire Superdome was an undulating sea of red, white, and blue; an insanely gigantic kegger minus Mom checking people's breath or making them walk the line before they drove home. What a highly unrealistic first impression of the Republican Party.

But it stuck.

I had no clue that hosting parties to raise money was called "fundraising" and I certainly never imagined I could turn partying into an actual career. Parties were my social life. They weren't a job. A job was something that made you miserable, like being an underwriter at Daddy Gil's bank. Or living in St. Louis.

Not to trash St. Louis, but to me, after growing up in New Orleans, spending a year in Italy, and graduating from the University of Florida, St. Louis was a snooze. The city had no pomp, no parades, no lagniappe. What it had was snow and ice and winter. Winter, for heaven's sake! Well, that and my family.

With me away at school in Florida and Sophia shacked up in Austin with a musician, Mom had no excuse to keep her marriage crosscountry. She and Daddy Gil flip-flopped their roles, taking up a more permanent residence in St. Louis with Mom flying back and forth to check on her ever-expanding business. Sachet Connections had grown into a regional company with branches throughout the South, so she kept the house in Metairie. But she just wasn't there enough to warrant my move back to Louisiana. So I moved to St. Louis, rented an apartment near Mom and Daddy Gil, and took a job at the bank just to kill time.

Daddy Gil could tell I was bored out of my mind. Ever the romantic, he began playing matchmaker, connecting me to the offspring of prominent families in the area, saying, "Nothing would make me happier than to walk you and your sister down the aisle."

But the guys he fixed me up with were spoiled old-money brats. Their idea of fun was to boff their way through Europe, essentially buying a different girl in every country, courtesy of their Dad's credit cards. Dating those guys only compounded my fish-out-of-water unease. Until I met Justin.

Every summer, Daddy Gil rented the shelters at Creve Coeur Park and catered a massive barbecue for his employees and their families. Justin and I met when we conked heads reaching into a cooler for a beer. Okay, I admit it, I timed it that way.

He was the first to apologize. "Oh man, are you alright? I'm so sorry."

"It's okay, I'm okay. It wasn't your fault." (It was so totally my preplanned fault. Shhhh.) "I'm Temple."

"Justin." He presented the neck of his beer bottle to me and we clinked glass to glass. "Cheers."

Hoping to keep him nearby, I said, "I've never seen you at the bank." But I caught him mid-swig and had to wait, smiling, before he could answer.

"Uh no, my mom's been a teller there for twenty-some years. I used to visit her there when I was a kid but, you know, work . . . "

"And what do you do?"

"Currency trading." I must have looked confused because he further explained, "I buy and sell foreign money."

Handsome. Tall. Big green eyes. Polite. With a job. So far, this Justin looked good on paper. "So the apple didn't fall too far from the tree, did it?" Justin shot me a quizzical smile. Now it was my turn to explain. "Both you and your mom deal with money all day."

He chuckled. "If I've turned out half as smart and strong as my mom, I'll take that as a compliment." The guy adored his mom? You could have stuck a fork in me right there, I was done.

Justin wasn't kidding about his mom. A single woman, she'd scrimped and saved every dime to put him through college and Justin had done her proud. He finished his MBA in record time and landed his lucrative job, and only after he moved his mom out of her apartment and into a new house did he treat himself to a fully loaded BMW 7 Series. I swear, I think the thing had a refrigerator in the back seat.

We started dating and shortly after, Justin bought a house of his own in a great neighborhood near the river. We picked out wallpaper for his kitchen, furniture for his living room, and by the time the king-size bed arrived I'd moved in, though we kept that a secret from my parents.

Mom wasn't exactly jumping for joy over my new beau. She didn't like that Justin monopolized every free moment of my day. She didn't like that Justin told me how to dress. She didn't like the way he ordered for me at restaurants—or rather, corrected my order when we met Mom and Daddy Gil for dinner.

"You don't like the catfish, have the steak. She'll have the steak, medium rare."

Mom glared at him across the table. Then she smiled her scary smile. "I don't know anyone from New Orleans who doesn't love catfish. Do you, Tee?"

She scared me so bad when she smiled like that, it felt like my spine was coming up out of my throat. A terrified giggle rose in me. I took a quick drink of water just to stuff it back down.

Mom still saw me as that effusively chatty third-grader who'd sit with her sister's black cassette-tape recorder and a hand-held microphone spewing hours and hours of parade commentary. "The krewe of Carolinas are coming down Broad Street. They're turning, they're turning on Chaputules. Now we see the enormous float and the feathers. Ooooh, the colors of the costumes." Stretching the truth made life more entertaining. "The colors, the colors—there are billions of them! They're throwing diamond necklaces from the float!"

Mom did not suffer little white lies. She believed lies were lies, no matter their color. "Temple Leigh Sachet, you know there's no krewe of Carolinas but there is an Argus krewe. There weren't billions of colors but you can say the feathers were a deep ebony. And you know the beads weren't actual diamonds but you can say they sparkled like diamonds."

My embellishments normally drove Mom crazy, but in twenty-two years they'd never disappeared from my repertoire. Until Justin came into my life and they stopped. Completely.

Mom was worried. She felt Justin's hold on me strengthening, and me slipping into timidity. She wanted to summon up the feisty Tee spirit. She wanted to kick-start my joie de vivre. That's when she called in the reinforcements: Brenda Charles. "I know you miss Italy, Tee. Brenda summers there. You'll have lots to talk about."

Brenda Charles was a formidable woman who sat on the board of the Missouri Opera. We met at Kemoll's, a fourth-generation family-owned Italian restaurant with outrageously gorgeous views of the St. Louis Arch. Miss Brenda apparently had a standing reservation. We were quickly ushered to "her" table, where the waiters nearly fell all over themselves to please us. I loved basking in the glow of her importance.

Miss Brenda ordered in fluent Italian, spoke of her summer villa in Florence, and wore colorful silk scarves that seemed to drip like cake frosting off her shoulders. Here was a stylish woman who understood my passion for all things Italian.

"Have you ever noticed, Temple, that Raphael's babies look as if they might be aliens?" Miss Brenda scanned the room, nodding and waving like a queen. "His adult figures are quite angelic but those babies—their eyes are almond shaped, their heads are just the slightest bit too large for their bodies."

Miss Brenda wanted to hear all about my time in Rome. In truth, Sophia had pushed me, kicking and screaming, into a semester abroad. She was determined to transform me from the baby of the family, sheltered and naïve, into a woman of the world. Sophia had said a semester in Italy would change me. And once again, Sophia was right. Italy did change me. It made me brave. Fast.

I shared my memories with Miss Brenda. "My second day in Rome, I was riding the bus back to my dorm when this man jumped in and jerked a woman's purse right off her shoulder! Scared me to death!"

Miss Brenda stopped eating and her eyes widened. "Goodness gracious. What a rude welcoming!"

I continued my tale. "Mom had been so worried about me traveling alone she got me this purse with straps that wrapped around my waist and shoulder. I may as well have tattooed 'tourist' across my forehead, I looked so ridiculous."

Miss Brenda tossed her head back and laughed. "I've seen those purses! Aren't they just dreadful!"

I brightened. Miss Brenda was genuinely interested in me. "If that man had grabbed my purse, I would have ended up a splotch of grease on the side of the road. I thought, 'To heck with this,' and even though I wasn't ready to cut the purse *strings,* I cut those purse *straps* right then and there."

Miss Brenda actually applauded me at the table. "Bravo, bravo! Most girls would have flown straight back to America after a day like that, but you made the choice to stay."

I'd never actually thought of it that way before. Hearing Miss Brenda's praises, I puffed a little with pride. "Yes, ma'am, you're right. In fact, I was so inspired by the beauty of the architecture and the language I added a double major in art history and stayed an extra semester."

Miss Brenda reached across the table and grabbed my hand. "That trip to Italy made you fearless in the face of the unknown."

With Miss Brenda so convinced of my courage, I sensed a faint swirling of bravery through my veins. Which is why I didn't even flinch when she announced, "I have a little project for you."

Miss Brenda wanted to expose younger people to opera. Its blue-haired audiences were beginning to die off, literally, and Miss Brenda knew her organization desperately needed a transfusion of youth.

Mom had offered me up as the voice of the next generation. I just wasn't sure what I was supposed to say. I'd never even seen an opera. But Miss Brenda's enthusiasm was contagious.

"I've already secured the St. Louis Museum of Art for the venue. You can use any of their displays or props." Though I was only two bites into my tiramisu, Miss Brenda motioned for a check. "Once you've created the theme for the evening, we can talk about ticket price." Miss Brenda grabbed my hand and gave it another firm squeeze. "Oh Temple, isn't this going to be a wonderful collaboration?"

My mouth full of espresso-dipped ladyfingers, I nodded enthusiastically. Anything Miss Brenda wanted, Miss Brenda could have.

The opera, the museum, a party, meeting new people . . . I blabbered on and on while Mom listened intently and waited for me to finish. When I'd run out of both breath and story, Mom said the ten words that would continue to follow me through every job I'd take for the next seven years.

"You realize you've signed on to do a fundraiser, right?" A fundraiser? What in the hootie-patootie was a fundraiser?

Mom immediately burst into a Sachet tearstorm and loaded me into the Banana. She hit the gas with a lead foot. "Why would you agree to such a thing? You don't know anything about fundraisers!"

"I'm so sorry, Mom! We were talking and I got caught up!"

By the time Mom dragged me through the front doors of Infinity Hair & Beauty, we were both completely overwhelmed and drowning in prolific tears. Mom's hairdresser, Danny of the Flawless Skin, spotted our dramatic arrival and rushed to our salvation, leaving a wet-headed client dripping in his chair. "Hedy, my love, you're a disaster! What's wrong? What's wrong?"

Mom choked on her alarm, "Tee is [sob] going to [sob] embarrass me [sob] to death!" Danny reassuringly pooh-poohed Mom's concerns until it was revealed my party was on behalf of *the* Brenda Charles, that *all* of St. Louis society would be gathering, and that I'd never even been to an opera. Everyone, except apparently me, knew that Miss Brenda could make Mom's life a living h-e-double-toothpicks. If Mom ever wanted to be able to show her face in public again, I'd have to pull this off. Beautifully. The eternally tanned Danny actually paled before my eyes and I burst into a fresh round of salty wails. "I'm doomed!"

Danny rolled up his sleeves. "Never fear, the queers are here."

Thank God for Danny. He enlisted every community-theater costume builder, set designer, makeup artist, and hairdresser in the state of Missouri to help build sets, dress the wait staff, and turn the stodgy museum into a lavish Tuscan vineyard.

Still, a beautiful venue, fantastic food, and the promise of hobnobbing wouldn't be enough to get thirty-somethings to an opera gala. We were going to have to bribe them with prizes. Good ones. Danny had done everything he could. It was my turn to step up to the plate and beg for donations. This was going to require a new wardrobe.

Mom took me to Units at the mall. Essentially a Garanimals for adults, Units was full of solid-color, modular, one-size-fits-all knit clothing that mixed and matched to create coordinated outfits. I chose jackets, skirts, pants, and blouses in hot pink, sherbet orange, lime green, and lemon yellow. Scarves, I needed scarves; Miss Brenda wore scarves, I absolutely had to have scarves. And highlights, definitely highlights. It didn't matter I was already naturally blonde. I was going begging. I had to make a strong first impression. It was utterly essential to be more blonde.

I arrived for my first donation appointment wearing my new orange suit accented with a jade-green scarf, black hose, pumps, and a matching orange headband that kept my now-platinum blonde hair out of my face, which was, in my convoluted brain, a much more professional hairdo. I'm most certain I resembled a giant, walking jack-o'-lantern.

"Thank you for meeting with me, Mr. Matthews. I've got a proposition for you." It was all Daddy Gil could do to keep a straight face, but I pressed on. "If the bank will sponsor the gala by donating a $10,000 grand prize for our raffle, then people who buy a ticket will have a 1-in-300 chance of winning. That will help us to sell tickets. If you think about it, those are better odds than the lottery!"

My brazen request for ten grand caused Daddy Gil to sit up straight. "That's true, Miss Sachet. But why should the Bank of Central Missouri write a check to the opera? What's in it for us?"

I had learned, while preparing for the Miss Orleans Parish Pageant, that if you are startled by the question you're asked, you should take a big breath, smile, and lie out of your a-double-s.

"I'm glad you ask, Mr. Matthews. Not only will the bank receive top billing in our newspaper ads, which is essentially free advertising for you, but we can also provide you with two free tickets to the gala. The bank can then use those tickets to create their own contest. Like, anyone who opens a new checking account is eligible to win. Plus, with your generous donation we can call the event 'Il Gran Premio,' which in Italian means the Grand Prize, which will draw even more attention to your bank."

I had no idea if there would be newspaper ads, or if I was authorized to hand out free tickets, and had totally pulled the name "Il Gran Premio" out of my Il Gran Butto. Still, it worked. Daddy Gil wrote the check.

Fearless with stupidity and backed now by the bank's financial support, I talked the president of Midwest Air into donating our second prize: two round-trip tickets to Italy. Then I tracked down a distant, distant relative of Luciano Pavarotti and convinced him to donate one of Luciano's scarves, which became our third prize.

The weekend before my big fete, Justin decided we needed to celebrate our six-month anniversary. Two weeks early. In the Bahamas. I stumbled in from another full day of work and party-planning to find my half-packed suitcase waiting on the king-size bed.

Justin picked me up and spun me around. "Surprise, surprise, surprise! Our flight leaves in three hours so finish packing!"

I couldn't leave town. My bash was only eight days away. I still had tons to do. "But Justin, I'm supposed to meet with the florists—"

Justin's tone switched quickly from romantic enthusiasm to an angry ultimatum. "I'm your boyfriend. The one who never sees you. Don't I mean more to you than some stupid party?"

Guilt put me on that plane to the Bahamas, but it was fear that froze me in place when Justin dropped to one knee on the soft, sandy beach of Paradise Island and proposed. "Temple, you're the woman I love. I want to take care of you and build a life together. I want you to be the mother of my children. I want you by my side. Forever."

I seriously couldn't move. Here was this good-looking, determined young man who had a plan for my future, our future as a couple. I didn't want to get married but anything seemed better than ending up a lonely, middle-aged underwriter in Daddy Gil's bank. The word "yes" leaked out of my lips and I returned to St. Louis a woman engaged.

Il Gran Premio sold out. One hundred and fifty of Missouri's most prominent couples arrived, the women waging quiet wars with ball gowns as they attempted to gracefully exit limousines. My simple white eyelet dress paled in comparison but I was so thrilled people were showing up, I couldn't have cared less.

I cued the string quartet to begin playing selections from the opera's upcoming season, then rushed to inspect every corner of the Tuscan vineyard so beautifully constructed by Danny and his army of gay men. The buffet station was absolutely breathtaking. I'd finagled a gondola from the Children's Theatre and Danny had used it as the centerpiece of a massive and extravagant spread of pastas, olives, cheeses, bruschetta, and decadent desserts. The surrounding cocktail tables were draped in green, red, and white silks that shimmered under the twinkling lights woven through garlands of grape leaves that circled the room and climbed the columns. Everything was perfect.

Mayor Gaffney and his wife arrived, instigating ripples of twittering gossip that swelled as the recently divorced governor entered arm-in-arm with his new, much-younger girlfriend. All of Missouri's society air-kissed, shook hands, and patted backs. I spotted Mom and Daddy Gil at the entrance, but thankfully they didn't see me. I quickly spun the diamond of my engagement ring into my palm. I hadn't yet had a chance to tell them about the Bahamas but had forgotten to take off my ring. Justin wasn't around to be offended. He'd stayed home with a sudden, excruciating migraine, which gave me both the freedom to supervise and, for one more night, to lie by omission.

The tide of arrivals subsided and the waitstaff swiftly bobbed and weaved through the labyrinth of revelers. I stole one second alone to admire my success. The food was delicious, the music was beautiful, the mayor and governor had shown. I'd actually pulled it off.

That's when the realization smacked me squarely across the face. The room was filled with silver-haired men and cat-eyed women squinting from one too many face lifts. There may have been a few partygoers pushing late forties, but there were definitely no thirty-somethings and, waiters excluded, I was for sure the only twenty-two-year-old in sight. This was bad news. I'd been given the mandate to attract a younger audience and clearly, I had failed.

I tried to duck behind a large column but Miss Brenda spotted me and rushed over to kiss me once on each cheek. "Temple! Here you are! Don't you look adorable!"

I forced myself to hold back brewing tears. "I'm so sorry, Ms. Charles. There are no young people. I don't know what happened—"

"Don't be ridiculous, sweetheart. You've raised over fifty thousand dollars with this party. I couldn't be happier!"

Fifty thousand dollars! People had given *me* that much money? "Really?"

"You must, must, must meet David Nichols. He's just raving about what you've done. Come with me!"

David Nichols. David Nichols. Why did I know that name? My mind raced but not fast enough to keep up as Miss Brenda whisked me over to meet a distinguished man sporting salt-and-pepper hair.

"David, darling, I must interrupt you. This is the talented young lady responsible for our party, Temple Sachet." I instinctively reached out my hand to shake and nearly lost an arm to his vigorous pumping.

"You must be Hedy and Gil's youngest."

As soon as I heard his voice, I recognized him. David Nichols was the president of Midwest Air, the man who gave me round-trip tickets for my raffle. We'd only spoken by phone; we'd never actually met.

"So nice to meet you, sir. Thank you so much for—"

"Brenda, this is the best party I've been to in years! Your little protégé here has really outdone herself." Miss Brenda and I both flushed with color. I from pride and embarrassment; Miss Brenda was pink with tipsy.

"Taught her everything I know!" she trilled as she sipped air from her empty champagne flute. I quickly snagged a waiter by the elbow, swiped a full flute, and replaced her drink before she could blink. But the waiter had moved on and now I was stuck holding her empty glass.

Emboldened by bourbon, David swept his massive arm, gesturing to the grandness of the venue, and nearly beheaded the governor's girlfriend in the process. Fortunately, she was floppy from booze and bounced back like a child's bop bag.

"This is im-press-ive. How old are you, Temple? Are you still in school?"

"No, sir, I graduated last May."

Out of the corner of my eye, I saw Mom wave in my direction and without thinking, I waved back, left-handed, revealing the blinding gleam of my one-carat indiscretion. The look on her face cinched my stomach closed as if by drawstring. I tried not to projectile vomit.

"I have friends in D.C. who tell me they always need good young people to work as interns. Is that something you would be interested in?"

Mom made a beeline for me. I knew I had only seconds to live. "Yes sir, that sounds fantastic. If you'll excuse me, I need to check on the coffee service."

I made a mad dash for the bathroom, full well knowing Mom would follow. We absolutely could not have a Sachet Scene in the middle of my party. I'd worked so hard. I was not going to let a little thing like an unannounced engagement ruin my big night.

I checked the stalls for feet as Mom locked the bathroom door behind her. "Temple Leigh Sachet, you show me that ring."

I turned the stone and extended my left hand. The sparkle of the diamond dulled under her withering gaze. "I was going to tell you after the party."

Mom released her grip. She wasn't angry. But she stared at me with a sadness I hadn't seen since Papa left.

"When you were twelve years old, you, me, and Sophia were in a dressing room. Do you remember this?"

"I don't know, Mom, we shop all the time."

"There was a woman in the room next to us and she was trying on a dress. And she was so nervous about the price that she kept talking about it. And she hemmed and she hawed and she finally asked the sales lady if she could use the store phone to get permission from her husband before she spent their money. Do you remember now?"

"Yes, ma'am."

"You and your sister were just dying to see the dress that was causing all this commotion. So we all peeked out expecting to see the most beautiful ball gown ever made. And do you remember what she was wearing?"

"A little church dress."

"That's right, a little summer cotton church dress. Probably on sale. You and Sophia thought that was funny. But I grounded you both for laughing."

"Yes, ma'am."

"I told you then and I'll tell you again now. Don't you ever get yourself in a position where you have to ask a man's permission for anything. Don't you ever forget that terrified woman calling her husband for a cotton church dress." Mom unlocked the bathroom door. "It's a beautiful ring, Tee."

I broke up with Justin, two weeks later, over a romantic dinner at Kemoll's. I'd ordered the paglia fieno and he changed it to veal piccata. If there was one thing in the world I knew better than Justin, it was Italian food. I slid the ring across the white linen tablecloth and he didn't say a word.

Our ending turned out to be the start of my whole new life.

{ *Two* }

You Must Believe

*M*r. Nichols did actually nominate me for a Ray of Hope internship. Pepper Channing, the White House intern coordinator, left a message on my answering machine. "Can you make it to D.C. for an official interview?" I thought it was a prank call. Until I called back and suddenly I was on the phone with the *White House*. They wanted *me* to be a Ray of Hope. They wanted *me* to move to Washington.

Daddy Gil thought I was crazy. "You've got a paying job. You could work your way up to being a senior underwriter." I was like phhhhh-hhhht. *This,* this was my life raft! Bye-bye, Justin. Bye-bye, banking. Bye-bye, St. Louis. ARRIVEDERCI!

All I knew about politics was the '88 Convention. I remembered the fun and the frenzy. The frenzy part was still accurate but the fun? Man, was I in for a rude awakening. Fresh off the boat, I showed up and everyone was dressed in black, running like chickens with their heads cut off and soooooooooo serious. All the time.

My fellow interns were uber-achievers, National Merit Scholars, debate champions, kids who'd done Outward Bound or backpacked across Europe by themselves. I hadn't done anything like that. Yeah, I'd been to Italy, but with, you know, the safety net of college classes, a dorm room, and deodorant. I realized I needed to step up my game. Fast. I needed to work harder. And I needed a whole bunch of black suits.

Once the initial shock of my transition subsided, I thrived. New Orleans, St. Louis, they moved too slowly. My life before D.C. seemed lazy. And after meeting my competition, I was deeply afraid of being lazy.

Thankfully, we interns learned to play as hard as we worked. We kept a list of the bars that served free food with happy hour (since none of us were being paid), and at six o'clock every evening we'd swarm like locusts, sucking well drinks dry and ingesting any hors d'oeuvre left unattended. Bottom Line on Monday, Lulu's on Tuesday, Third Edition on Wednesday, Tortilla Coast on Thursday. We could drink. By the end of summer, we all looked like we'd put tire pumps in our mouths.

Fall arrived, bringing with it a whole new crop of wild and terrifying interns, girls who cursed like sailors and danced on the bar at Lulu's. They haunted the Capital Grille, picked up congressmen, and had affairs. Daddy Gil had a name for those kinds of pickup joints—"he-ing and she-ing places"—and trust me, there was beaucoup he-ing and she-ing going on. Their ringleader was an abrasive and skinny Russian named Calina Vyosky who chain-smoked menthols and slept with military officers at the Hotel Washington. Calina scared me so bad I probably should've changed into knee socks and pigtails.

I laid off the bars and started hanging out with Jeanette "Netta" Michon. Delicately featured with thick strawberry-blonde hair she tamed by twisting it into her signature French braid, Netta had jade-green eyes, pale freckles, and an unyielding Texas smile. She was a total Ivory girl and—though at twenty-seven only four years older than me—a "senior intern." Netta had skipped the summer's never-ending bar crawl, preferring instead to spend her hours chatting long-distance with her hometown honey, Zack, who was still back in Texas finishing law school. They were engaged to be married exactly six months after his graduation. Netta had already chosen their future children's names. "We'll have our son first, Zavier with a Z not an X, so he and Zack will be the Zs. Our daughter will be Jasmine, not Jazz, not Minny, just Jasmine, and she and I will be the Js."

Netta was convinced Zack would one day be president and she would be first lady. The internship was simply a stepping stone, the anchoring corner of Netta's amazingly well-planned jigsaw puzzle. Once all the pieces were joined, she and Zack would own the White House. Of this, Netta was certain.

As a junior staffer, Netta had the primo job. She was assigned to handle celebrity visits and once we became friends she "hired" me as her assistant. All the other interns were totally jealous. They were stuck in the "shop" doing FBI background checks on potential Ray of Hope wannabes.

Our biggest responsibility was coordinating Michael Jackson's visit for a Rose Garden ceremony. President Gray was going to honor him with a special commendation for the work he did for (and apparently with) children. The day of, Netta was extremely anxious. She briefed and rebriefed me to make sure Mr. Jackson's sizeable entourage made it quickly past Secret Service.

"Sachet." (When Netta only used my last name, I knew she meant business.) "These are the press kits, Secret Service will give them badges. If they don't wear the badges, Secret Service will moonwalk their asses right out the door, you understand? Make sure they keep them on!"

I nodded vigorously and took off, badges and press kits in hand. Pennsylvania Avenue was lined with screaming fans and paparazzi. Mr. Jackson arrived in a white stretch limo and his fans screamed bloody murder. I thought my eardrums were going to burst. He emerged wearing a black military jacket trimmed with bands of red, secured by silver buckles and an enormous rhinestone pin. His hands were covered by black gloves.

I yelled as loud as I could, "MR. JACKSON, CAN YOU PLEASE COME WITH ME?"

His bodyguards quickly whisked us into the safety of our Secret Service holding area. I performed my duties and leaned in closely to hear his faint, high-pitched "Thank you." Though I couldn't see his eyes—he was wearing sunglasses—I did catch a glimpse of Mr. Jackson's face. His skin was nearly translucent and pieced together like a patchwork quilt. I tried not to stare.

Netta arrived to escort us all to the Rose Garden portico, where every White House employee from secretary to maintenance man had gathered with straining necks and clicking cameras to witness Mr. Jackson chew his hair through the entire ceremony.

Interns were either part of the Hello Team or the Goodbye Team (for when the president was arriving or leaving by helicopter) and Netta and I were Goodbyes. It was our job to run to the velvet ropes, frantically waving the American flags we were handed against the tornado of those whirring helicopter blades and smile for the cameras. I loved being a Goodbye. The sweetness of red roses was so heavy in the swirling air that my heart ecstatically soared. I was high on a potent perfume of patriotism and beauty. I was nobody from nowhere but there I was, on the green South Lawn of the White House, in my ill-fitting black suit, squinting up as Marine One eclipsed the blinding sun. I'd caught Potomac Fever, for which there is only one cure: a nasty-tasting spoonful of disillusionment.

First dose. Netta got fired. She had the bad luck to answer a transferred call from the main White House switchboard. A deejay from Texas was live and on the air asking how to nominate someone for an internship.

"We've got a young man in our studio who would like to become a Ray of Hope. How does he do that?"

Netta was very professional at first, all business. "You can't self-apply. You have to be nominated by someone." Then she realized she was speaking with her hometown shock jock. "Oh my gosh, is this Wildman Dave? From KCRL?"

Netta was not one easily starstruck. She'd barely blinked twice in Michael Jackson's direction and whipped me into shape with a sharp "Shake it off Sachet, shake it off" if I ever got too dreamy-eyed around any of our celeb visitors.

But knowing she was on the radio with all her childhood friends, family, and sweetie listening, Netta lost her head. "This is Jeanette Michon. I grew up listening to you!" Interns quickly gathered to witness the excitement. Netta was on the radio. It was big doings.

"So you're in the actual White House, Jeanette?"

"Yes, sir, I am."

"Have you ever walked into the wrong bathroom and caught the president peeing?"

Netta laughed, caught up in the whirlwind of her instant hometown fame. "No, sir, I've never seen the president but I have been outside when his dog peed and pooped in the bushes. Does that count?"

All of a sudden we heard—clump, clump, clump—the thunderous footsteps of the press secretary marching down the long corridor.

He was a big, scary man. He walked into the room and terror went through the shop. He bellowed, "Put that phone down now!"

Netta drained of all color and hung up. They packed her pencils and escorted her out right then and there. I didn't even get to hug her goodbye. And I was really good at goodbyes. I'd had all that practice.

That's when I realized how much access and power I had, even as an intern, just by being in the White House. It never occurred to me that an intern could take down the president, but losing Netta to a random phone call made it clear. Everything I did or said had to be taken seriously. No more "I'm leaving for lunch" notes on White House stationery.

Shamed and jobless, Netta moved back to Texas. I was on my own. Mom had put me in a high-rise on the Hill that was safe, clean, and full of little old widows. All the other interns, because they were still in college, were living in dorms at Catholic University. Plus, I had no desire to join Calina and her clique of tramps dancing their way through Georgetown. But sitting at home alone . . . that stunk.

It only took two boring and lonely weeks before the true love of my life came scampering. Her name was Goldie. An adorable five-year-old Yorkshire terrier with black ears, round eyes, and a puffy golden-brown muzzle, Goldie belonged to the elderly woman who lived down the hall. The frail lady had recently taken a bad spill and her middle-aged sons were moving her to a nursing home. They were struggling under the weight of a large china cabinet when Goldie broke free and made a mad dash for the open door of my apartment. She zipped behind my couch and refused to budge. No amount of coaxing or crawling would move that little girl. And when the sons informed me she would be dropped at the pound once we did get her out, I became the proud mama of the newest member of the Sachet clan. Since she was already called Goldie, I followed tradition and gave her a proper middle name: Hawn.

Goldie became my constant companion. She'd climb into my purse and off we'd go to the museums. We'd sit for hours in front of paintings. I'd sketch or daydream about Italy and Goldie would nap, patiently, in the contours of my purse, occasionally waking to lovingly lick my hand. We became inseparable.

November rolled in and President Gray lost the election. Within days, the Ray of Hope office began to empty as one by one the interns sent out résumés, applied to law schools, took new jobs, or headed home. It was an ugly lesson in loyalty. Rats off a sinking ship. By the time the presidential Christmas party rolled around, it was just me and my boss, Pepper Channing, left to attend. Pepper took the festivities to new heights, sneaking off with her ultra-dorky beau to have sex in the West Wing, the East Wing, and the OEOB. She returned to the party, glowing as brightly as the lights on the Christmas tree. She winked, "Let's see if the next administration can top that!"

With nothing to keep me in D.C., Goldie and I begrudgingly returned to St. Louis. The thought of reclaiming the underwriter job at Daddy Gil's bank or running into Justin put me in a funk of massive proportions. It was as if D.C. had just been a dream.

Then Mom heard that Mayor Gaffney was hiring for his new Take Back Your Neighborhood program. Take Back would use volunteers to help rebuild and beautify the parks, streets, and sidewalks in low-income and long-neglected neighborhoods. They just needed someone to recruit and organize the volunteers. That sounded a heck of a lot more interesting than underwriting and even though I was wildly under-qualified, I landed the job.

Out from under the oppressive fashion restrictions of D.C., I vetoed all things gray, black, or navy. On the days I needed to look "professional," I was back in hot-pink, neon-orange, and sunny-yellow suits, though mostly I could be found covered in mud, planting trees along the river with inner-city kids and sweet old ladies from the Forest Park Garden Conservatory. Goldie loved our new outdoor lifestyle and supervised from a shady patch of grass.

It was all working beautifully until the beavers started eating my trees. I couldn't have kids and old ladies cutting chicken wire—the city was too worried about liability and insurance. We needed men. So every Tuesday morning, Goldie and I bought boxed lunches from Safeway, then loaded onto a school bus headed for jail. I'd pick up the sheriff and twelve trustees, my own personal chain gang minus the chains, and the whole lot of us would work by the river, building beaver fences.

I had big, burly inmates chasing off beavers to the left of me, white-haired ladies-who-lunch planting petunias on my right, and behind me a gaggle of underprivileged preteens painting park benches. We'd all sit down for lunch together and Goldie would make the rounds, begging bites from all who adored her. Which was everyone. Daddy Gil was convinced I'd lost my mind. I'd chosen juvies and jailbirds over a "cushy" indoor job with his bank. But once he saw us in action, cleaning and building and planting, Daddy Gil became my biggest cheerleader. He made sure our efforts were profiled in the local newspapers and even had the bank sponsor our Earth Day celebration. Take Back grew and grew, and Mayor Gaffney was thrilled with my work. I loved my job and two years flew quickly by. I would have happily battled those beavers forever if the mayor's office hadn't suddenly been tossed into chaos.

Mayor Gaffney was voted in on a promise to revitalize the downtown shopping district. But on his watch, a major developer reneged on building the mall that was supposed to be the backbone of new development. Worse, they left a huge, unsightly pit in the center of the city. If Gaffney ever wanted to be mayor again, he'd have to find some way to fill that gaping hole.

He flew to Japan and secured foreign investors, which set off a firestorm of negative national publicity. Things looked bleak until the mayor squashed his critics by securing all American retailers for the stores once they were built. His local victory became a national story, which in turn became a spontaneous, crazy-fast run for governor.

The mayor called me to his office and I arrived, caked head to toe in mud. He'd seen me in worse condition. "Beavers?"

I took off my work gloves. "Groundhogs." The mayor motioned for me to sit, but I took one look at his upholstered chairs and said, "I better stand."

"Now Temple, I know you love your job, but this gubernatorial campaign I've gotten myself into, well, Election Day's just over a year away. I've got a ton of hands to shake and money to raise and I need to do it quick." I had no idea where this was going so I just nodded and listened as he continued, "I remember that party you threw for the opera. What was that called?"

I beamed with pride. "Oh! You mean the Il Gran Premio party."

"Yes, yes, the Il Gran . . . , so I was thinking that you should be my event coordinator, which essentially means you'd be in charge of all my fundraising parties. Would you, could you do that for me?"

I couldn't believe my ears. My first real election campaign had just dropped into my lap. It wasn't Washington but it was politics. I'd take it. "Yes sir, Mayor. When do I start?"

"Today."

The mayor teamed me with his finance director, Elma Harmond. Elma was the walking definition of a "tough old broad," with her disaster hair, Ann Taylor suits, and pantyhose sagging around her ankles. She absolutely could not tolerate my overly polite Southernisms and made it her personal (but futile) mission to rid me of my cheery "fantastic" and "yes, sir" and "no, ma'am," and to "toughen up my thin skin." I loved that she was scrappy; Elma could haggle the pants off the devil himself.

Elma handled the politics and I handled the logistics, but we ran everything we did by each other. We'd leave the mayor's office, head for a bar, buy a bottle of champagne, and start brainstorming.

"We want to go west. We want to go west." The governor's mansion was in Jefferson City west of St. Louis and we wanted in that mansion badly. One bottle into a brainstorming session, I started skipping like a broken record. "West, west, west."

Elma tipped her napkin as if it were a cowboy hat. "We need a whole rodeo theme."

"Rodeo? In St. Louis?" I simultaneously hiccupped and giggled. "Everyone will think we're nuts."

Elma threw her arms in the air, revealing the pale-yellow circular stains that consistently marked the end of our day. "Because we are, girlie, we absolutely are!"

We might have been crazy but we were also really good. The rodeo was a gigantic hit. We followed it with an outrageously decadent Evening on the Orient Express party, and by the time all was said and done, we'd raised $10 million.

Suddenly, our congressman's office was in touch, happily supportive and genuinely interested in everything from our party invitations to my personal life. Excited to hear from them and flattered they would copy our ideas for a federal campaign, I gave Elma the good news during another one of our champagne sessions.

"Congressman May's chief of staff wants to copy our rodeo idea! Isn't that fantastic?"

Elma's normally unflappable demeanor shifted and she eyed me warily. I knew my constant superlative "fantastic" drove her crazy so I quickly corrected myself. "I mean, isn't it wonderful?"

But Elma had something else on her mind. "Did he offer you a job?"

Her question felt like an accusation. Without pause, I burst into tears. "I love the mayor, Elma, I would never—" I wiped at my cheeks with a sandpapery napkin.

Elma relaxed at the sight of my upset. "A funny thing happens when a candidate raises a ton of cash. Other candidates poach their fundraisers."

I was confused and defensive. "Mayor Gaffney is going somewhere. He's stimulating and fantastic and mesmerizing. That doesn't have anything to do with us."

Elma clucked her tongue three times fast. "Girlie, all they see is an endless river of checks flooding our office. And me and you sitting there opening them."

Champagne wasn't going to cut it. I needed a drink drink. I flagged down the waiter and ordered a whiskey sour, two cherries. Elma joined me.

"I don't know which of 'em is worse, the fortune-tellers or the, pardon your dainty ears, girlie, star-fuckers."

I was mortified. "Do Congressman May's people think I'm a star-you-know-what-er?"

Elma was a sucker not a sipper. She'd already downed the hooch and was munching ice cubes. "They think you're a fortune-teller. They think you have a magic crystal ball." Elma theatrically rubbed her dewy glass as if having a vision. "I see parasites in your future. Hangers-on in thousand-dollar suits." I couldn't tell if Elma was joking. "They come knocking, Temple, and they don't care if you believe." Elma bit and tugged at the stem of her cherry, popping the fruit off against the back of her teeth. "But you *must* believe. Believe or die. Those are your choices."

I nodded as if I understood. "So what do I do, Elma? Not return his phone calls?"

"Let's show 'em how to really star-fuck." She swallowed the cherry whole. "If we can get a Barrymore endorsement . . . " She didn't need to finish the thought, I got it.

U.S. Senator Phil Barrymore was Missouri's golden boy, a self-made billionaire whose name graced many a building in the city. A year ago, he'd entered the Republican primary, shocking everyone with his meteoric rise in national popularity. He didn't win the nomination but rumor had it he was planning to run again. Barrymore was a big, big fish in our little local pond. We needed him on our line.

Actually, what we really needed was his list.

Just like clicks are donor crack, donor lists are fundraiser crack. Fundraisers swap them, rent them, buy them, and yes, steal them from each other. The hotter the candidate, the more desirable and expensive the list becomes, ranging anywhere from ten grand to hundreds of thousands of dollars. The most highly coveted lists are those owned by the Republican fundraising trinity: the Presidential Committee, the Senate Committee, and the House Committee. But those lists are totally off-limits. The closest we could get to a big-money list was Phil Barrymore.

Problem was the senator was based in D.C. and rarely visited St. Louis. Elma's repetitive calls to his office made it abundantly clear Barrymore wasn't endorsing at the city or state level. It was looking more and more likely we'd have to make friendly with Congressman May's manipulative, scheming staffers.

Then, we caught a lucky break. Elma was in the northern part of the state, wooing two new potential donors, so I was running campaign headquarters. Mayor Gaffney was at an intimate donor-sponsored breakfast where Senator Barrymore unexpectedly showed up. The men sat beside each other and apparently, the mayor talked nonstop about the success of Take Back.

"Barrymore feels Take Back could serve as a model to privatize city services nationally." Mayor Gaffney was a smiley man with ears just the slightest bit too big for his head. He'd returned to our offices after the breakfast, grinning from one oversized ear to the other. "He was very impressed. In fact, he said if we could hold a press conference today, he'd endorse me before he flew back to D.C."

I couldn't believe our luck. "Wait, what? He said those exact words, that he'd 'endorse you'?"

The mayor nodded. "I thanked him but I told him we couldn't possibly throw it together this last-minute."

I absolutely went bonkos. "Mayor, don't be ridiculous! You're looking a gift horse in the mouth! And you're turning your back on it! He wants to do more for you! Use your head! You just have to ask him to come back!"

I could tell from the shock on our staff's faces that I'd pushed it a bit too far. They were all policy wonks blinded by Gaffney-itis. They walked around him like little yes drones. "Whatever you say, Mayor," "That's brilliant, Mayor." They just wanted to touch him.

I'd just chewed out their hero and they weren't happy with me. Neither was the mayor. He furrowed his brow and spoke slowly. I was very close to being in big trouble. "They are on their way to his plane right now. Let it go."

I just couldn't. We were going to get that Barrymore endorsement, even if it killed me. I crept into Elma's office and surreptitiously called the senator's office in D.C. Nine months as a Ray of Hope had trained me well. I'd seen many a panicked intern save a last-minute situation using the I'm-about-to-lose-my-job approach. I turned on my best terrified and ditzy voice and blurted out, "This is Mayor Gaffney's office in St. Louis and the mayor is supposed to be meeting Senator Barrymore at the airport and I didn't write down which airport on his schedule and now the mayor's in a car and he's calling me and—"

"Slow down, slow down. I've got it right here." The secretary had clearly dealt with her fair share of incompetents. "St. Louis Downtown Airport. They're scheduled for departure in thirty minutes. I hope your mayor's got a fast driver."

If that lady only knew, my right foot was made of lead. I owned a little white Volkswagen so I jumped in and drove like a lunatic, trying to catch Barrymore's private jet before it took off. The airport was itty-bitty, only used for non-commercial flights. I could see Barrymore and his flashy, well-heeled entourage beginning to board. There was no time to park. I hit the gas and drove right up onto the tarmac, squealing to a terrifying stop.

I jumped out of the car and charged them, wearing my hot-pink suit, dangling earrings, flying blonde curls, and a big Cheshire cat grin, trying to look sane and failing miserably. I could barely breathe I was so winded but I managed to blurt out, "Mr. Barrymore, sir, my name is Temple Sachet and I work for Mayor Gaffney and it would be fantastic, sir, if you would consider coming back here to be our guest of honor at an event."

Mr. Barrymore was simultaneously startled and amused. He wasn't sure whether to have me arrested or hand me a medal. Realizing I was harmless but serious as a heart attack, he said, "Why don't you give Prudence your number and we'll see if we can find a date that works." And then, he called over the most put-together, professionally attired woman I'd ever met. Her name was Prudence Whipley.

Ms. Whipley was DKNY head to Ferragamo toe in monochromatic shades of gray. Thin, tall, and imposing, she wore her golden-blonde hair in shiny, sleek long sheets that hung past her shoulders. Slashed across her forehead were severe bangs that hovered just above her rectangular eyeglasses. She was a striking woman, a little bit scary in her black patent-leather pumps. This was a woman who didn't down bottles of champagne or chase candidates onto tarmacs. Even her perfume reeked of money. She was the fundraiser I wished I could be.

Ms. Whipley shook my hand and with a cool, detached, and intimidating gaze, she gave me a once-over I could literally feel. All she said was, "Chutzpah."

But I got him.

Ms. Whipley gave me six hours of Barrymore's time, three weeks later. Determined to make a better second impression on both Mr. Barrymore and Ms. Whipley, I stepped up my game. I straightened my unruly curls, invested in what would be the first of my many sexy black YSL power suits, toned down my makeup to neutrals, and skipped the hoop earrings. The Gaffney–Barrymore fundraising tour had to be a Washington-caliber event.

Our first stop was a 5 p.m. cocktail party hosted by the Grande Dame of St. Charles. From there, we attended a 6 p.m. cocktail party with the board of the Children's Hospital, then at 7 p.m. scurried over to Washington University for a five-hundred-person dinner, for which everyone had paid a thousand bucks a ticket and where Barrymore officially announced his endorsement of Mayor Gaffney for governor. After dinner, the university's president hosted cigars and brandy in his office for six men who'd written $100,000 checks. And by 11 p.m., I had Mr. Barrymore and Ms. Whipley back on that infamous tarmac, their plane fueled and ready for takeoff. The evening had been flawless.

This time, before Mr. Barrymore boarded, he grabbed my hand and said, "If you ever need a job, you give me a call," and my arms filled with goose bumps. A job with Barrymore was the real deal. A presidential campaign would take me back to D.C., maybe even back to the White House.

Ms. Whipley took one look at my shivering skin and shaking hands and almost smiled. That half smile. It was hard to read. Did she see in me a younger version of herself? A prodigy? A protégé?

I know I saw in her a woman of style, power, and prestige. I loved working with Elma, I did, and I admired her immensely. But I was awed by Prudence Whipley. She'd worked for the IRI, the International Republican Institute, and with Ronald Reagan; her first husband had been on the board of the *Washington Post*. She was connected. She knew people. She was remarkable and I wanted to be remarkable. Not in ten years. Not in twenty years. I wanted a remarkable life right now.

Clearly, patience was not my virtue. I wanted to close my eyes, click my heels three times, and have it instantly be Election Day. I knew Mayor Gaffney was a charismatic man with a loyal following. I knew the governor's mansion would soon be ours. We just had to get through six more months of hard campaigning, then we were going to get in that mansion and fix the whole state. This, this was exactly what I wanted to do with my life. This was the best job ever. I'd found my calling.

And then he lost.

Mayor Gaffney lost.

It seemed impossible. I could not wrap my brain around it. We were, at that moment, the most highly funded gubernatorial campaign in the history of the United States. We'd raised over $15 million. We'd gotten the Barrymore endorsement. We'd done everything right. And still, he lost.

I crawled into my closet and curled up, fetal position, with Goldie in my arms. I bawled like no other Sachet woman before me had ever bawled. I cried myself hoarse. When the tears finally dried and I realized the rest of the world had not come to a screeching stop, I returned to help Elma clean up the fallout. Gaffney still had a tremendous amount of money left in his coffers. He felt we needed to mail each of our donors a partial refund. (Now, what politician does that? Nobody does that! No wonder I stumbled wide-eyed into Washington—I thought politicians gave back the money if they lost!) We mailed out refund letters and people actually sent us more money, so that didn't work. But Gaffney was done with politics. He wanted time with his wife and kids. He wanted his life back.

I resolved to call Ms. Whipley. If Barrymore was going to run for president, I wanted in. I didn't know if, at twenty-seven, I had enough experience to be taken seriously, but I knew I had to try. I found Ms. Whipley's business card and picked up the phone.

I wasn't even sure she'd remember me.

{ *Three* }

Losers Still Work

"*O*f course I remember you and please, please call me Prudence." Prudence seemed genuinely thrilled to hear my voice. And now, we were on a first-name basis! "We're so sad about Mayor Gaffney. What are you doing now?"

My heart was racing. "Actually, that's why I was calling. Mr. Barrymore mentioned maybe there would be something for me?" I squenched my eyes closed and braced for the worst. Laughter, silence, a condescending snort?

With barely a breath, Prudence replied, "Are you kidding? Absolutely!"

My spirit leapt until I heard her say, "We'd love to have you start organizing volunteers and identifying donors in the Midwest."

The Midwest? I'd been in St. Louis for over three years. I wanted a life in D.C. I tried to mask my disappointment with forced enthusiasm. "If there's something I can do nationally, I'm a fantastic learner."

"This will give you the federal experience you need if you want to continue on this path."

Federal experience? I was so doop-de-doop-de-doop. I didn't realize a federal campaign was different. "I definitely know I want to continue on this path."

"Well, right now the Midwest is where we need you."

I was bummed but agreed to become their "Midwest person." Wow, what a wake-up. I thought I could just call my top twenty donors from Gaffney's campaign and ask for $100,000 checks. I thought I'd impress Prudence and jumpstart my involvement with a $2 million afternoon. I had no idea it was illegal to ask for contributions larger than $2,000 in a federal campaign. I was so naïve it was amazing I wasn't walking into walls.

Over the next year, Prudence and I coordinated volunteers, donor meetings, and small parties throughout Missouri, Kansas, Oklahoma, Indiana, and Illinois. During Mayor Gaffney's campaign, Elma and I talked about an event for three hours and then we'd do it. Working with Prudence was a whole different level. We were on the phone for hours and hours, discussing minutiae from which donors should be seated together to what I should wear. I'd call from a hotel room, unable to pick between a red suit and a blue dress. She didn't know whether or not I looked like a buffoon but she'd counsel me. "Blue, definitely blue. Red's too flashy."

We spoke every single day for a year. Even on the exceedingly rare occasions when there were no work details to hammer out, we'd call to chat about any and everything; from my near-miss engagement and lack of current dating prospects to her argumentative boyfriend and a breast cancer scare that, thankfully, turned out to be a benign cyst. We never missed our daily phone call even though our travel schedules kept us too busy to actually see one another.

"Phil says you have a guy in Muncie who can do, what did he call it, 'digital' photography? He said the guy printed pictures at the actual event?"

Prudence had called to discuss the details of her upcoming fundraiser at the Waldorf Astoria in Manhattan but her voice sounded strange. Sluggish and sad. "I do. But they're fifty bucks a piece." Prudence always spoke with such confidence. It worried me. "Are you okay?"

She paused, then stated painfully, "Carl and I broke up."

I cooed my sympathy, "Oh dear, that's terrible." But I didn't really think it was. From the stories Prudence had shared about the man, he sounded like a pompous jerk. Good riddance to bad rubbish.

Prudence continued, "Plus I'm turning forty on Saturday."

Now *that* shocked me. I didn't realize Prudence was twelve years older than me. I thought maybe she was making thirty-two or -three, but not forty. I kept my surprise to myself. "We need a girly weekend. I'll meet you in New York and we'll do massages, manicures, cocktails. My treat, for your birthday."

I could hear the relief in her voice. "That sounds, as you would say, fantastic!"

I flew to New York for the Barrymore fundraiser, where I was met at the door by Prudence's assistant, Kendra, a girl not much younger than me, with a quick step and a pointy nose. "Ms. Whipley asked me to bring you to the green room."

I scurried to keep up with my speedy guide. "I hope we recognize each other. We haven't actually been in the same room since I worked for Mayor Gaffney. And that was almost two years ago."

That stopped Kendra dead in her tracks. She stared at me with eyes wide as saucers. "Two years? Ms. Whipley talks about you all the time. I thought you were best friends."

"Because we are." I recognized Prudence's voice immediately and burst into a sunny smile. I ran over and gave her a big hug. Seeing Prudence felt like a reunion.

The next day we went to the Chinese back-walkers and had lunch at Pastis, where I presented her with birthday gifts. Prudence was much more traditional than me and I'd made the mistake of mentioning, during one of our daily phone calls, that I thought pot should be legalized. She just about had a heart attack, so for her gag gift I bought her a hemp belt with a giant gold pot leaf for the buckle.

Prudence couldn't stop laughing. "Tee, I swear, you're a closet libertarian."

I then gave her a real present, a sterling silver cable bracelet capped with blue topaz stones. I made her wear both that night when we went out dancing and took a million pictures of my ultra-conservative, new best friend flashing her marijuana belt buckle and the peace sign.

I yelled over the music, "If you're ever mean to me, I've got blackmail!"

It was back to the salt mines for us both. This time, I was shipped to the small city of Davenport, Iowa, to get the ball rolling and set up Barrymore headquarters for the summer's straw poll. Best known for frequent flooding, Davenport was a Democratic stronghold and located within Scott County, which had just been declared the poorest county in the nation. People were actually living in cardboard boxes and it was my job to convince them that my billionaire senator was the right guy to represent their concerns in Washington.

The word "frigid" doesn't even come close to describing the day I arrived in Davenport. I'd borrowed Daddy Gil's old shearling coat, which was huge and made me look like a polar bear. I only owned one pair of boots, Chanel ski boots, which were flashy with their interlocking Cs, but also triple-quilted and warm. Poor three-pound Goldie couldn't stop shivering even with her booties and matching coat.

Despite Barrymore's deep pockets, we were trying to keep costs down. Prudence had booked me, sight unseen, in an inexpensive motel that turned out to be a glorified truck stop. The tub was the yellow of a smoker's tooth and browned by rusty water dripping from the pipes. I opted not to unpack for fear of what might be in the drawers.

I put poor shivering Goldie in the car and set out. The roads were covered with ice and snow and the neighborhoods just kept getting worse. I could not for the life of me find the address Prudence gave me. I had to stop at a gas station and they directed me to a parking lot right beside a liquor store. I pulled into the lot and there it was: a trailer jacked up on cinderblocks, maybe thirty feet away from the railroad tracks. Spray-painted across the trailer was a huge red CONDEMNED. Still, my key worked in the lock; it had to be the right place. I set Goldie down and she pooped in the middle of the floor. That's when I knew it was really bad.

Prudence trusted me to handle Iowa on my own, but the situation was dire. I called her, sobbing, "It's not a building, it's a trailer [heave]. There are rats, I can hear them in the wall [sob] and there are droppings all over the floors. Two of the windows [gasp, sob] have been shot out. It's condemned for demolition. There's no phone service [sob]. There's a toilet on a concrete platform and it's black with gunk. There's not even a door [heave] or partition [sob] to hide it. There's no heat but apparently [and this is where my voice rose to an octave heard only by dogs and small children] the winos *love* this place because there are bottles of Mad Dog in every corner."

Prudence instructed me to breathe deeply. "Tee, calm down, calm down." She waited until I stopped bawling before she broke the bad news. "The problem is we rented that space from a major donor. He said it was a commercially viable rental. If I call him to complain, I'll offend him and we could lose him."

I pulled myself together, tightening my internal corset. "If this is what we have, then I will make it work." That night I lay, fully dressed, on top of the filthy bedspread and cried myself to sleep, but the next day I wiped my eyes and undertook my own personal Extreme Makeover: Trailer Edition.

First, I took pictures of the entire place, inside and out, prescrubdown, in all of its filthy, repulsive glory. Then I hit the Kmart. I bought heavy-duty garbage bags, punched holes to create sleeves, and wore them like ponchos. I covered my flashy boots and frozen legs with bags duct-taped around each knee, and bought elbow-length rubber gloves. The side benefit of being covered in plastic was that I was stifling despite the lack of heat.

Every forty minutes past the hour, like clockwork, a train would pass by, wooo-wooo-wooo, and the whole foundation of the trailer would bounce up and down. The first time it happened, I grabbed Goldie and ran outside only to realize if the trailer hadn't yet capsized, it probably wouldn't. I kept an eye on my watch and at forty past grabbed for something solid and held on for the ride.

I yanked up the urine-soaked carpets and bleached down the floors, walls, and that unbearable toilet. I strategically placed rat traps and, for good measure, poison. The first night's kill: fourteen rats. The second night: seven more. That went on for three more days, for a grand total of forty-three rats. I bought six-foot tables and some chairs, and convinced the phone company to install phone lines. I hunted down the gas company and got the heat turned back on. The serviceman thought I'd gone loony. "You want heat in here? You don't even have windows."

He had a point. I went to Sears and had them cut plywood to cover the windows, and I hung a shower curtain around the toilet. Finally, I spray-painted white over the red CONDEMNED and decorated the entire building, inside and out, with Barrymore for President signs. I won't say the place sparkled, but Goldie stopped pooping on the floor.

I took another round of pictures and mailed the before and afters to Prudence. She called me immediately. "You should've gotten on a plane and come home!"

"No, this is what Barrymore paid for and it wasn't his fault. We would've had to rent something else."

Prudence was racked with guilt. "What can I do to make this up to you?"

"How about a hotel with a clean bed, and an assistant?"

"You have someone in mind?"

I did. Jeanette Michon from my Ray of Hope internship. We'd stayed in touch since her premature exit from the White House, and I was one of her bridesmaids when she married Zack, exactly as planned, six months after he graduated. Zack had landed a prestigious clerkship with the Supreme Court and they'd moved to D.C., where Netta ended up in my same line of work, fundraising for a Texas congressman. When the congressman lost his seat, they launched Phase Two of Netta's master plan: baby-making. Unfortunately, neither Zavier nor Jasmine were cooperating. Netta was halfway into her second year of trying, with no luck. I figured she might like a break from tracking ovulation to jump back into national politics. She was a hard worker, a real lemons-into-lemonade kind of girl. It was an easy sell to Prudence. Netta joined me in Iowa and Prudence upgraded us from the truck-stop motel to the Radisson, where we had clean beds, a pool, and a gym.

Netta and I drove around Davenport with Goldie, enlisting the locals to volunteer for Barrymore. It didn't hurt that both of us were skinny little blonde things with huge boobs. You'd better believe men would come and talk to us when we handed out flyers. Friday nights, our headquarters was a singles scene, all the men wanting to help Miss Jeanette and Tee. We had fourteen "regulars"—No Teeth Larry, Tattoo Dave, and Dan the Man who always smelled a little like bourbon—men who showed up every evening for the free pizza, cookies, coffee, and root beer. I wasn't quite sure if we were running a volunteer recruitment center or a homeless shelter.

The men handed out flyers in the town while Netta and I called donors. We started with people we knew would be supportive. I was on the phone with Mr. Corman, a bajillionaire who owned the largest highway contracts in Iowa: "I know it's very early to be thinking about our next president, but I'd like for you to meet Mr. Barrymore personally."

I hadn't looked at my watch and all of a sudden, wooo-wooo-woooo, the train was coming. The tables started bouncing, the walls started shaking, the phones plugged into the walls broke in and out of static because the foundation was rocking. I could hear Mr. Corman screaming, "Temple, Temple, are you okay?"

I yelled back, "Sir, the train is coming. The train—" and we got disconnected. When everything stopped swaying, I called Mr. Corman back.

He was terrified. "What happened? Did the roof fall in? Are you okay?"

I tried to downplay the situation. "No sir, there's a train and when the train comes by—"

"A train causes all that commotion in the building?"

"Oh no, sir, I'm in a trailer."

"Oh my God, darling, how much do you need me to raise? We've gotta get you out of there." Mr. Corman got so upset he raised one third of my budget. I started calling all my other donors at train time.

Six months later, Barrymore landed a distant second-place straw poll finish, which meant he was now the only challenge to Senator Gray for the presidency, which meant Prudence needed more help. Goldie and I, we were finally headed back to Washington.

It took almost two years of Prudence's Fundraiser Finishing School, i.e., paying my dues in tiny towns, but now my prodigal return to the White House was underway. Only now, I'd arrive not as an overworked intern but as a primary player in a presidential campaign. This was the real deal.

Things moved so fast I didn't have time to find a real place to live. Prudence moved me into the Embassy Suites despite my protests. We were working sixteen-hour days. Every meal was take-out. I didn't need a hotel suite with a kitchenette. I just needed a place to sleep. "No, no, no. Those suites are hundreds of dollars. Phil doesn't need to spend that on me. I can stay in the Southeast Holiday Inn. It's only thirty-five dollars a night and they allow dogs." Clearly, I was still living in ice-cream land. Southeast D.C. was murder central. Prudence said, "Over my dead body," and Embassy Suites it was.

Operating out of Prudence's house was not glamorous. It was illegal to run a presidential campaign out of the senator's office, so Prudence converted her upstairs bedrooms into campaign headquarters. She and Kendra, the swift assistant, had somehow managed to cram a dining room table into the smallest bedroom for use as a shared desk. The closet had been stripped of its doors and turned into a makeshift copy/fax area with wires strewn all over the floor.

The second bedroom was only slightly larger and equally cramped. It functioned as home base for Goldie, me, and Netta, whom Prudence hired full-time (at my urging) after our success in Iowa meant we needed more staff.

Much to our horror, Prudence had also quickly contracted a freelancer off a recommendation without knowing much about her. Walking in, the three of us, Goldie included, were absolutely mortified to discover we'd be working side-by-side with the bar-dancing, chain-smoking Russian, Calina Vyosky, from our Ray of Hope days.

Calina was just as I remembered her: aggressive and brusque with a raspy voice that verged on perpetual bronchitis. The six years since our internship had not been kind to her. Girl looked like she'd been rode hard and put up wet. I did my best to keep my distance but quarters were cramped, there was no privacy, and it quickly became obvious we each had our own personal fundraising style.

Netta was making money hand over fist. She was a natural shark. A woman who set seemingly unreachable goals, conquered them, then set even more outrageous new ones. Out of sight of donors, she spoke about people as if they were checkbooks. Every donor had a dollar value. "He's a bundler." Or "They're a maxed-out couple."

Prudence was the consummate professional. Calm, collected, and always on top of her game, she had a core of thirty powerful donors that had tremendous respect for her. She was serious about the issues and talked policy like a pundit. Her donor relationships were based on strong intellectual connections that paid off in big ways.

Calina was a "Crash & Burner." She'd crash through a list of six hundred people in an afternoon, yelling, "Five dollars, five dollars, five dollars, five dollars," and then that list would have to be burned. She'd hound donors until they wrote her a check just to get her to leave them alone. If she found a well, she'd dip and dip and dip.

Calina made me bristle. Her suits always reeked of smoke and she nervously chewed the caps on all our pens. We were oil and water, extreme points on the same spectrum. I had to have an emotional connection with a donor before I'd ask for a dime. I wanted to know about their families, who was sick, who was getting married, where their kids were going to college. And I certainly never called the same person more than once. It was impolite. My approach made me an anomaly but my donors were "bundlers" collecting checks from their own connections. They handed me envelopes bursting with checks so no one ever complained.

Prudence kept us insanely busy; it left me very little time to find my own apartment and living at the hotel felt too temporary, too tenuous. I wanted this move to Washington to be permanent. I needed help, so I asked Mom to come up and look at apartments with me.

Of course, the week she visited, the halls filled with kids on spring break. We didn't get one solid night of sleep. Goldie and I took Mom to the apartments I'd picked out, tiny boxes in frat-boy neighborhoods with smelly halls and loud neighbors. Mom was so distraught by my choices that she announced, "Tee, I'm taking over," and ushered me into the closest restaurant, a local hangout for Georgetown coeds. Mom pushed me past the long oak bar and vintage railroad posters to find the pay phones in the back. The whole place reeked of stale beer. I kept Goldie in my purse for fear she'd pull an Iowa and poop on the floor.

Mom picked up the first phone and the receiver fell apart in her hands. She took out her hanky and wiped down the second phone before punching at the sticky numbers. As she waited for an answer, she scanned our surroundings. "You are a grown-up and I know I can be overpowering, but the fact that you would even consider any of those apartments makes me worry for your sanity."

"Mom, we've been so—" I was interrupted as Mom spoke into the hanky-wrapped phone.

"Oh, thank God you're home. Tee is here, as you know, and Eunice, she absolutely cannot live anywhere we've looked."

Mom motioned for me to find paper and a pen and I nearly terrorized poor Goldie as I tore through my purse. A pen was recovered and I gingerly uncrumpled a napkin from a nearby table. Mom scribbled down a name and a number. "Thank you, we'll call her right now."

Mom handed me the napkin. "Eunice said Delores Simms helped Jack find his apartment when he first moved here."

"My God, how old is she?"

Mom had no patience for me. "You call Ms. Simms and you beg, from the tips of your toes to the ends of your hair, for her to help us."

Ms. Simms agreed to meet us in Georgetown on Olive Street. She was exactly two thousand years old but absolutely determined to guide Mom, Goldie, and I through every nook and cranny of the apartment. "It has phenomenal closet space, two bathrooms, and a nice kitchen."

Through the living room windows, I could see an enchanted garden. "Ms. Simms, how do you get out there?"

But Ms. Simms was hard of hearing and couldn't be distracted from her presentation. "You could use the second room as an office or a den."

Mom raised her voice and gestured vigorously toward the windows. "How do you get out there?" Louder. "HOW DO YOU GET OUT THERE?"

Ms. Simms squinted to see. "Oh, that? That comes with the apartment. You go through the patio."

Sold.

Goldie and I moved in immediately, sleeping on an aero-bed as painters covered the living and dining room walls with a bright Chinese red. My office/den was painted a cheery sunflower yellow, and my bedroom glowed apple green. Once the painters cleared out, Sophia flew in town and took over with the decorating. I didn't have time to furniture shop and I trusted and loved her flamboyant style. Just because I had to wear black suits every day didn't mean my house had to look like a mausoleum. Sophia threw down leopard-skin rugs, filled the rooms with black-and-white-checked club chairs, and found a bamboo headboard with hand-painted flowers for the bedroom. Finally, I had the perfect place in the perfect city with the perfect job.

The job got even more perfect because Calina moved away. She abandoned us for a nationally watched Senate race between two super-star candidates, the War Hero and the Witch. The War Hero decided Calina had one of those "magic crystal balls" Elma had warned me about. He hired her, put her in a hotel, gave her a car and driver, and offered her a contract where she earned 25 percent of the money raised. Her windfall was the subject of much discussion.

Prudence was particularly ticked by the news. "The industry standard is virtually non-negotiable: ten percent of what you raise, you keep. Maybe, *maybe* if you're a big name in the business, like my friend Dominica, you take fifteen. But Calina at twenty-five? That's absurd."

Netta tallied the cut in her head. "She's going to walk away with millions."

Netta wasn't exaggerating. The War Hero was running against the most hated woman in America. Donors who were Republican and Christian absolutely did not want to see that woman win. Plus the War Hero was infamous for drunk-dialing donors. All Calina had to do was hand him a drink, a donor list, and the phone. He'd slobber all over the mouthpiece, yelling, "I don't have time to talk to you right now so just write me a check. I need you to write me a check. I told you, I don't have time to talk to you right now. I don't need to hear any of this. Get your fucking pen out of your desk or wherever you keep it and write me a check. Do I hear a pen on paper? Do I hear a pen on paper? Do I hear a pen on paper?" That was his technique. It was essentially extortion and apparently very effective. A fundraiser didn't have to be a rocket scientist to make money on that campaign. Checks were rolling in.

But Calina was a greedy, greedy woman and she wanted more. She wanted direct mail, which is fundraiser speak for solicitation letters that arrive in mailboxes asking for $5, $50, $500. They're usually signed by a hometown senator and they encourage people to donate $100 to become a privileged member of the War Hero's Eternal Flame Club or some other silliness. Direct mail is all about gimmicks.

Trust me. There is no secret "Founders Wall" with your name on a plaque. There is no "Eternal Flame" burning in your honor. There are absolutely no special member groups for anyone donating 50 bucks here and 75 dollars there. Until you've written a check for two grand, you're not a Major Donor, so forget it. No parties or plaques for you.

And here's the secret *nobody* wants you to know: Every single one of those letters is coded so fundraisers can take their percentage off the top. Let's say you get a letter from your hometown senator asking you to donate $100 to the War Hero. You send back $100 because you trust your senator and you want to make a difference. Of that $100 donated, the first $10 to $15 goes to your hometown senator's fundraiser, someone like me, who will spend her money on a house overlooking the Potomac or a condo in Boca Raton. (Well, not exactly like me. You wouldn't catch me dead by the pool in a condo complex in Boca Raton.)

Then the direct mail house contracted for the mailings takes their cut, which can be humongous, up to 50 percent, so they grab their $50 and line their coffers. And by now, your $100 contribution is worth $35. All of which will be spent on advertising and polling and parties for people who write bigger checks than you. And it's worse if you donate by phone. Telemarketing companies take 90 cents on the dollar. That's right. You give a dollar and the War Hero gets a dime.

But Calina wanted those dollars and dimes. She hired her husband to run direct mail, which meant he was the one "caging" all the checks. He changed the codes on all the returned letters so Calina made an additional $2 million *on top of* the 25 percent she was already taking. Their reprehensible behavior continued to be the hot topic at our headquarters.

Prudence had ears in offices all over Washington. "All the mom-and-pop places they used for support services, they're stiffing them. They haven't paid the bus drivers or the caterers or the florists. One bus driver had to default on his mortgage. He lost his house."

"That driver should move in with Calina since her hubby left her." Netta always had the most scandalous tidbits. "He's living in a condo down in Boca Raton. With a stripper. That he got pregnant!"

Prudence and I actually both screeched at the same time. "WHAT!?"

But Netta was dead-on. There was a huge lawsuit. By the time the trial started, Calina and her hubby were bitter enemies. She sold him down the river big-time: She denied knowing he changed the codes and because all the documentation had only his name and signature on it, he went to jail. Calina moved on to her next super-star candidate. She can still be found, sitting beside senators, yelling into phones for donors to send her "five dollars, five dollars, five dollars."

Barrymore was Senator Gray's only competition for the Republican nomination. Although Gray was the nephew of a former president and the clear leader, by a wide margin, Barrymore still had the ability to give him a run for his money. Literally. Barrymore had deep pockets and friends with big bank accounts. Election Day was over a year away and Gray was already having cash flow problems. Our nagging presence was forcing Gray into markets he wanted to ignore. He was spending money he didn't want to spend, money he'd need to fend off a Democratic nominee if he made it to the general. Which is why Gray showed up at Prudence's front door.

We were all yapping into our phones when we heard Kendra racing up the wooden stairs with an urgency that meant trouble. Everyone gathered on the second-floor landing to hear Kendra whisper, "Gray is in the living room. Alone."

After much hullabaloo, Senator Barrymore was summoned and the two men sat down to discuss the future. We women retreated up the stairs, slipped off our heels, and knelt on the landing, straining to catch their conversation. If only Goldie could have whispered what her tiny ears heard.

Netta whispered, "Will he ask him to VP?"

Prudence touched a slim finger to her lips to shush Netta as we all leaned forward, hoping for any overheard snippet. I could feel my pulse throbbing in my ears. A Gray–Barrymore ticket would be unbeatable. The White House was within our grasp.

We heard Barrymore and Gray say their goodbyes and as the front door closed, we all dashed into our offices and threw on our pumps.

Barrymore ascended the stairs and everyone gathered in Prudence's tiny office. "He's promised me secretary of commerce once he's elected. Let's call a press conference in the morning."

Barrymore headed back down the stairs as we all stared at one another, bewildered. Kendra gave voice to our confusion, "Is it over?"

Prudence sighed. "It's over."

My second failed campaign. I thought I was finished. I thought my life in Washington was over before it'd begun. I didn't get that fundraisers jumped from candidate to candidate like fleas skipping from dog to dog. I had no idea there would be job offers. I didn't understand that I had value beyond the candidate I served. I didn't understand that losers still work. I thought I was toast.

Worse, I was convinced I'd just lost my big sisters. Prudence, Netta, and I had become inseparable in our cramped quarters. Barrymore jokingly referred to us as his secret weapon, his Blonde Bombshells. I dreaded not spending each day in their company. We set a standing weekly "Bombshell" dinner date and promised to stick to it.

Netta returned to tracking her monthly cycle. Prudence joined forces with her friend Dominica to open their own consulting business, and I was invited to breakfast by Senator Ivy's chief of staff, Jameel Howrani.

You know that saying, breakfast is the most important meal of the day? That particular breakfast turned out to be the most important of my career.

{ *Four* }

Go Gay or Go Grey

*J*ameel, or "Jamie" as he preferred, asked if we could meet at Teaism at Dupont Circle. Though it was a Sunday morning before noon, I assumed our "tea" was actually a job interview and dressed accordingly. A three-button YSL suit in cherry bomb red since it was the weekend and I could go a little wild with color.

I clipped past the teak-and-iron benches of Teaism's front garden, nervous I might not recognize him among the sloppy-eyed morning lovers and sickeningly healthy joggers skipping Starbucks for oolong. Not to fear, Jamie was a daisy in a patch of wheat. He was meticulously groomed, impeccably dressed in his conservative navy suit, darkly Lebanese, and clearly gay.

My heart sunk just a tad with that realization. Every meeting, I hoped against hope I might meet a straight man under the age of three thousand. Dating in D.C. was either pineapples or prune juice. Gay or grey. I hadn't sowed an oat for ages. I certainly couldn't date a donor, lobbyists creeped me out, and I knew from my Ray of Hope year that congressmen preferred interns.

But there were only two types of fundraisers in the Republican Party: overachieving former sorority sisters (such as myself) and Type-A selectively closeted gay men. Depending on the gender of the person I was meeting I could safely assume:

1. They had competed in local beauty pageants (female) or run for student body president (male).
2. They had a minimum of one purebred dog.
3. They were single (female) or gay (male).

Within five minutes of our handshake, Jamie laughingly referenced his time as the president of Yale's Young Republicans and whipped out professionally shot wallet-sized photos of his three chocolate Labs: Simon, Newton, and Oscar. I thought it safe to assume he played for the pink team and I knew immediately we would be great friends.

I had, however, wrongly presumed our meeting was an interview. Jamie had just contracted Prudence and Dominica as consultants to help launch Senator Ivy's new international AIDS charity, Operation Shine. He'd mentioned to Prudence, in passing, that the director of Ivy's Political Action Committee had just quit. Prudence gave him my name and though I knew not one iota about how to run a PAC, I was well prepared for the "tell me about yourself" conversation.

Anyone who works inside the Beltway knows the phrase "tell me about yourself" is code for, "Give me your career starting at the top and listing the most impressive people . . . fast." I was ready to wow Jamie with my whole spiel. He never even looked at my résumé.

"Everybody we work with wants to work with you." Jamie hovered over his bento box, blazingly adept with chopsticks. He'd opted for the cold veggie bento while I'd gone with the more traditional breakfast of French toast. Which I slathered with butter. "I have to admit, Jamie, I've never worked with lobbyists."

Jamie was undeterred by my revelation. "What it comes down to is this. Every major corporation has a lobbyist. Their job is to make deals for dollars. Every senator has a PAC so they can take those dollars. Your job is to plan the parties, set up meetings, and collect the checks. Lobbyists max out their contributions like they're paying membership fees. You don't even have to call them, they call you."

I nearly choked on my Mutan White tea. "That sounds a little ... ," I searched for the proper word, " ... blatant?"

Jamie pecked at his lips with a napkin. "I think you mean icky and shameless."

I laughed, relieved I hadn't offended. He continued, "Look, all senators, on both sides of the aisle, take from pharmaceuticals with their left hand and General Dynamics with their right. They've got drugs healing people and guns killing people." Jamie spoke candidly and without the slightest trace of cynicism. His tone was matter of fact, efficient, and nonjudgmental, even though the practices he described seemed inexcusable. "It doesn't matter how civilized the comped lunch at Signature's may be, you're still having legislation as your entree. It's unavoidable." Jamie added a bit more sugar to his chai. "But Senator Ivy's a good man. I've been with him for twelve years. He's smart, fair, a true leader. A visionary. Someday, he'll be president."

Jamie spent the next hour telling stories. How Ivy recruited him straight out of college, about the struggles they'd had during the last campaign cycle. Then we finished our meal, shook hands, and parted ways. I wasn't sure, but I thought maybe I'd just been given the job.

In times of doubt, I call home.

I knew Mom and Daddy Gil were in Metairie, packing shut the lake house in preparation for their annual Sail-to-Somewhere. Mom was first to pick up.

"This is Hedy Sachet speaking."

"Mom, *c'est moi*." I quickly pulled my cell away, knowing Mom's "GIL! GET ON THE PHONE! IT'S TEE!" would render me deaf in one ear if I moved too slowly.

"Gil's out there piddling around with this flash cooker contraption when he should be packing."

"What d'you mean, flash cooker?"

"We went to dinner with Cecil and Hattie, and your dad saw one of those flash fry things they use. Next thing I know, he's talked some yahoo into welding a skillet on top of a butane tank and now he's got three of them out there on the porch!"

"Mom! That has to be the most dangerous thing ever made in this world."

"I know! But he's convinced he can put them in a catalog. Gil and his constant hobbies. One day there's going to be a big yellow flame ball where our house used to be and you'll know what happened."

The thunderous fumbling of their upstairs office phone alerted us both that Daddy Gil was now on the line. "Hey, how's my girl? What's your day been like so far? What's new? What's on the agenda?"

"Well, I think I just got offered a job with Senator Ivy running his PAC."

Mom piped in. "Now, what's a PAC exactly?"

"From what I can tell, it's basically a separate bank account so senators can take funds from lobbyists."

Mom always had plenty of questions. "For themselves personally?"

"No, for their campaigns and so they can back other candidates they want to put in office."

"So you'd be working directly with the senator?"

"It sounded like mostly I'd be throwing parties for lobbyists. But I guess I'd see the senator too."

"Ivy, hmmmm, I don't know much about him." That was typical Daddy Gil, ever the skeptic. "Where's he stand on things?"

Candidly, I couldn't answer the question. I had no idea who Ivy was as a politician or a person. From seeing him on the news, I knew he was a tall man with sloped shoulders who kept his hair in a tight crew cut. From Jamie, I'd learned that he was married, had three daughters, and spoke fluent French but other than that, I knew zippo. Worse, I'd forgotten everything I knew and learned about the Senate in middle school civics class. All I knew for sure was that I needed a job. "I met with his chief of staff. He adores the man."

Mom was as confused as I. "Did he offer you the job or not?"

"Honestly, I couldn't tell."

"Did he talk money?"

"No."

"Did he ask about a start date?"

"No."

"And you haven't met the senator yet?"

"No."

"Now, what makes you think you have a job?"

"This guy was giving me his résumé as if he wanted *me* to like *him*."

"Hmmmmmm . . . says here Ivy was a pharmacist." I could hear Daddy Gil tapping on his computer. "From Minnesota. Hasn't been a senator very long—that's a good sign."

"Are you going to take it? If they offer?"

Mom's question signaled she was worried about Italy. Sophia, now a professional groupie, was already in Rome, shacked up with either the drummer or the guitarist of Goo Goo or Foo Foo Something-or-Other. I could never keep the bands straight. Mom and Daddy Gil would be there in late September. Goldie and I were joining them shortly after. We were already booked on a flight out of Dulles.

Mom knew it would be hard for me to walk away from D.C. She'd raised Sophia and me to be hard workers, to achieve. My sister was following her wanderlust but I, not wanting to end up a casualty of privilege, leaned more towards Prudence's workaholism. To Mom, my calling to announce a new, more impressive job with more oppressive responsibilities sounded like I was bailing on the family vacation.

"Don't worry, Mom. Even if they offer, I'll be on the boat. Goldie is so excited, she's probably home right now trying on her bikini and flip flops."

The tea had been a job offer, subtle but real. I started my first day as Senator Ivy's PAC director with the phone ringing off the hook. Everyone wanted a lunch date and silly me, I thought, "Fantastic! All these new people want to break bread."

Well, of course they did! I was the one standing between them and an appointment on Senator Ivy's calendar. I'd mistakenly assumed Jamie had grossly inflated the sleaziness of lobbying to, I don't know, make for interesting small talk. Uh, no. Unbelievably, he'd *understated* the truth. The lobbyists calling me were in no way, shape, or form savvy or shrewd. They were outright pushy. They'd come right out and say, "No meeting, no money," and sure enough, since we needed their checks they got their meetings.

Barely two weeks in, I felt the blinders had been ripped from my eyes. Some of the Big Guys lived like CEOs with their exorbitant salaries, compensation packages, private jets, and all the perks. They had so much control over legislation on the Senate floor it was horrifying, and the vast majority slept on both sides of the bed, promising twelve different things to nineteen different people, just to hedge their bets.

And then there were the thousands and thousands of Little Guys, for groups I'd never heard of like the Association of Privately Owned Public Golf Courses or the Indoor Tanning Association. It was simply endless.

I'd Marmaduked my way into the position—dum de dum de dum—and I was in over my head. A fact that was perfectly clear to my new assistant, a petite, raven-haired snob-in-a-bob named Alicia. Alicia hated me. Though she was five years my junior, she was deeply insulted she'd been passed over for promotion.

Alicia came equipped with the world-weary attitude of a woman twice her age. She loved to use any question I asked to "school" me with a condescending lecture. I'd ask a simple, "Are these guys listed in the phone book or what?" and Alicia would sigh with exasperation, pull out two giant yellow tomes, and drop them on my desk with a booming thud.

"These are called Reps Books," she'd explain slowly, as if I took the short bus to work. "They come in two parts. This one is for lobbyists that represent associations and this one is for the lobbyists that represent corporations. You know the difference, right?"

Her venom was hard for me to stomach. I'd never had a job that made someone dislike me. I'd never been on the receiving end of jealousy. It completely freaked me out. I had no idea how to handle the situation. Daddy Gil suggested I "kill her with kindness." Prudence advised me, as Elma had before, to toughen up.

"At this level, if this is your first big career enemy you must be made of Teflon. It's not normal to move through this world without enemies."

I was mortified. "There'll be more?"

"People aren't scared of you, Temple. You're too nice all the time. You need a good public firing."

"Why would I do that?"

"Because you can."

I wasn't going to fire Alicia. She knew the job inside and out. Plus, I needed her to help run the Carver Classic. The Carver Classic was one of two major senator–lobbyist golf trips that happen every year. People don't realize how often the Senate is on break. Typically, senators are only in session about 130 days a year. The other 235 days, they're attending parties, raising funds for their next run, stopping by their home states to kiss babies, or more likely than not, they're golfing with lobbyists.

The Ian Hart Open was held every July at the Greenbrier Resort in West Virginia, while the fall Carver Classic traveled to various resort locations. Senator Ivy was this year's chair and my first trip as his PAC director was scheduled for Arizona.

Technically, it wasn't *my* trip. Alicia had handled the logistics long before I was hired. Still, I wanted to make a good first impression with the senators and since I'd be shuttling several of them from the airport, I splurged and rented a red convertible.

My first passenger was Senator Brogan. Only in her late forties, Brogan was a rowdy teenager by Senate standards. I liked her immediately. She wasn't afraid of color. She arrived at the airport wearing a bold violet pantsuit topped off with her signature diamond stud earrings and her heavily lacquered, wavy brown hair. It hadn't even crossed my mind that senators might not appreciate a windblown ride.

"I can put the top up, Senator."

"Absolutely not! This is the closest I get to a vacation; let's go for the whole enchilada."

We made quite the pair in my fire engine-red Mustang—I in my pink plaid golf pants and she borrowing the yellow scarf I had tucked in my purse to protect her perfectly coiffed hairdo. I loved having a partner in "flashy" crime. By the time we got to the hotel, Senator Brogan's hair was standing on end like the Bride of Frankenstein. She laughed it off and gave me a joyous hug.

"I'd forgotten how much fun it is to ride in a convertible!" As she released me from her friendly embrace, she tried to hand back my scarf.

I protested, "Keep it and we'll go for another ride later!"

Unfortunately, we never got the chance. Everything in the Frank Lloyd Wright–designed hotel was beautiful but falling apart. New management had just started renovations, which explained the outrageously cheap rates Alicia had negotiated. The disasters were biblical in their proportions, with days of drought, famine, and fire.

Drought came when poor Senator Brogan suffered quietly with no running water for two nights; she finally asked for another room when a gas leak made it impossible for her to breathe. Famine took over as the hotel wait staff walked out in solidarity with a fired chef. Our entire gathering had to be bussed to an off-site conference center for meals. The fire ignited as Senator Ivy made his speech at a morning session. A projector in the rafters overheated and began spitting flames and sparks onto the audience. Senator Ivy ran to help but the stage was built on risers that weren't level. He fell, hit his face, and cut his lip open. I had a bleeding senator, fire raining from the ceiling, and Alicia avoiding me like the plague.

The day of the Carver Classic, Jamie begged me to borrow the convertible so he could take Majority Whip Harrington and Franklin Cirlot to lunch. I'd not yet met Franklin but had already been warned about him. Franklin Cirlot was Senator Griswold's infamously high-maintenance chief of staff. Rumors abounded that he handed staffers a college textbook on American history which they were required to memorize. And that he'd actually spring pop quizzes like a nasty schoolmarm. He was also Jamie's best friend and, I presumed, beau.

I'd quickly adopted Jamie as *my* gay beau. Since my hiring, we'd become inseparable at the office and our evenings were filled with business dinners that dissolved into D-and-D: drinking and dishing. Jamie promised to return my car right after he and his pals had a burger at In & Out.

Seriously, they went to In & Out.

Six hours later, there was a three-way tie for third place and my car was still missing. I had thirty minutes to buy two extra golf clubs as prizes but there were no taxis and I couldn't find anyone with a car. I commandeered a golf cart and took off for the Sport Chalet. Six miles away. My top speed: 25 mph. On a major highway through the middle of Phoenix.

Motorists were not happy with me. They zoomed past, honking and screaming out their windows, "Get off the road!—" I won't repeat the rest. I had my pedal to the metal but that buggy just wouldn't chug any faster. And the sun, Lord have mercy, the sun. Arizona was in the throes of a heat wave. It'd been over 115 degrees for three days in a row. My thighs were stuck to the vinyl seat, my makeup was melting off my face, and I was drenched in sweat. I looked like I'd entered a wet T-shirt contest and lost. As I putt-putt-putted along, I cursed their names: Jerky Jamie! Horrible Harrington! Flipping Franklin!

I didn't even know this Franklin and already I hated him. These trips were for lobbyists; senatorial staff weren't even supposed to attend unless they were working. But Jamie had insisted Franklin accompany Senator Griswold.

Months later, it would all make sense. Franklin's guy, Senator Griswold, was Chair of the RSCC, the Republican Senate Campaign Committee, which doled out dollars to senators for their campaigns. Jamie wanted the full resources of the Committee to help *his* guy, Senator Ivy, in the upcoming election. He also needed Majority Whip Harrington to drum up consensus behind Ivy's pharmaceutical tax breaks. Jamie knew Harrington was worse than Wimpy when it came to burgers. He knew Franklin would never turn down face time with the Majority Whip. Jamie loaded Franklin and Harrington into that convertible and fed them more than beef and buns for lunch.

Driving in that God-forsaken golf cart, I didn't know what was happening. I was convinced this Franklin character had led my kind and considerate Jamie astray. He'd probably checked them into a hotel and they would be gone the rest of the night. What a mudbug.

I managed to make it to Sport Chalet and back to the awards ceremony in time, sweating like a stuck pig, but safe and in one piece. That's when the boys waltzed in, their cheeks all shiny. They'd been hiking.

And there, in all his glory, was their ringleader, Franklin, with his well-groomed eyebrows. Despite his casual khakis, tucked-in, sky-blue button-down and loafers, I could tell the man was wound like a top. But he was Mr. Popularity with Jamie and Senator Harrington so I forced myself to smile as he boasted and bragged about their wonderful jaunt. "It was a hot one but we made it to the top. That's determination!"

"But Jamie," I squeezed through gritted teeth, choosing to ignore Franklin entirely, "you had my car for hours."

"I know, darling, but you were here on the golf course all day."

"No, *darling,* we ran out of prizes and I had to drive a golf cart to the Sport Chalet."

Franklin overheard my complaint and found it hysterical. "Are you serious? You had to drive a golf cart? That's hilarious! Senator Harrington, did you hear this? Temple, tell him the story."

For their amusement, I played the good sport and described my impromptu, comedic quest, but Jamie could tell I was furious.

That night, during the dinner and dancing, Jamie and Franklin were all over each other, sharing a drink. I was still ticked at Franklin, who hadn't apologized about the car. Rude.

Jamie knew the way back into my heart was through laughter. He convinced Senator Olin to pull me out on the dance floor. Now, Senator Olin was just the most ridiculous dancer. He was no Pat "Cut-a-Rug" Roberts, let me tell you. Senator Olin danced like a jack-in-the-box, popping up and down off-beat and I couldn't stay angry. Jamie I forgave. But the polling numbers on Franklin were very, very low.

It felt good to blow off steam. I refused to drink in the presence of politicians or donors. Dancing was a surrogate release. But Alicia reminded me I was staffing the hot-air-balloon ride at 5:30 a.m. so I called it a night and went to bed.

At 4:30 sharp, my alarm went off. I fumbled in the pitch black, my hand wildly flailing to stop the blaring buzzer. I pulled myself out of bed and into the shower, hoping it would bring me to life.

Half-awake, I headed downstairs, where fourteen hungover people were waiting for the bus. After half an hour, there was no bus and in fact, no signs of life in the entire hotel. Everyone started glaring at me, gnashing their teeth, demanding to know when the bus would show.

I was livid. My rock-solid reputation was dissolving into mud, through no fault of my own, and I just couldn't handle one more failure. I called the hotel's director of transportation and berated the man. "This bus is forty minutes late!" Then I called the director of security for the hotel to see if we could get another bus. Then, finally, the assistant general manager came down to see me. He was polite but aggravated. "Ma'am, your bus isn't scheduled to arrive until 7:30. The hot-air-balloon ride is only fifteen minutes away and it doesn't start until sunrise, which is at 8:15 a.m."

I was flabbergasted. "Are you kidding me?"

He handed me the forms to prove it—all signed by Alicia. I went from livid to enraged. I apologized, profusely, to everyone—management and ticked-off donors alike—then bounded up four flights of stairs to confront Alicia in person.

Thump, thump, thump, thump, thump—I pounded, unconcerned about people sleeping in neighboring rooms. Alicia had barely cracked her door when I barreled in, guns blazing. "You realize the bus isn't coming for another hour?"

Alicia struggled to wake. "I was afraid people might oversleep so I put it on the schedule at 5:30."

I was yelling now. And I'm not a yeller. Cryer, yes. Yeller, no. "It's not your job to police people. If they miss the bus then they miss the bus. You lied to fourteen donors and senators and you lied right to my face."

She tugged at her hotel robe, cinching it tighter around her tiny waist. "I needed you there on time."

"I don't work for you, Alicia. You work for me."

Alicia rolled her eyes. "Yeah, don't remind me."

"Look, I get it. You hate me. But that doesn't give you the right to keep people sitting around for hours." I could feel my heart pounding against my ribcage. "What if they'd given up and gone back to bed? If I hadn't been running around like an idiot calling people, giving them a show, they would have left. And now I have to apologize to the whole hotel because you lied!"

Alicia's lackadaisical demeanor was infuriating. "What do you want me to do about it, Temple?"

"It's Miss Sachet, and what you're going to do is pack your bags and go back to Nashville."

"Why would I go to Nashville?"

"Because you no longer have a job in Washington and your parents need to teach you some manners."

I hated being the Wicked Witch of the West, I did. But Prudence was right. A good public firing did the trick. Everyone took me more seriously and my PAC staff started working their hind-ends off to keep me happy. It may have taken me a month to get my act together but now, the job was mine.

Thank God for Italy. I'd been working nonstop since Gaffney's gubernatorial run and the Arizona fiasco completely wore me out. I needed a vacation, desperately. I was meeting my family in Monte Carlo, where we would attend the Seakeepers Ball hosted by Prince Rainier. Then it would be just the five of us (including Goldie), plus the crewmembers, cruising the Italian Riviera.

Packing Goldie into her Louis Vuitton Sac Chien, I told her all about our trip. "We'll get out on the water with your Aunt Sophia and Mamaw Sachet and Grandpa Gil and everything will be calm and relaxing. Your mommy will finally be able to sit still because the boat's moving and that means she doesn't have to."

Goldie and I uneventfully made it to Monte Carlo and joined our family aboard SS *Gil & His Girls*. I was eager to relax, forget D.C., and cleanse myself of the Alicia firing with a dip in the Mediterranean. Unfortunately, all Sophia wanted to talk about was my new job. Actually, the new men at my new job.

"So . . . any hot senators?" Sophia twisted her coal-black hair into a loose loop and secured it with a quick lean against her chaise. We both got Mom's boobs but Sophia had also been blessed with her luxurious curls, height, and olive undertones.

"None for me, thanks. But may I recommend House members. No broken hips. No wives. Up past ten." I sipped from my cool glass of limoncello. "Plus they're easy to find. Just try the bar at the Hotel George. You'll have to fight the interns and staffers over the straight ones."

"*Mais* no, I'm more of a Senate slut, I think." Sophia slicked her skin with oil guaranteed to register less than 8 SPF. I held out my hand for a dose. We were Southern women, after all. You go on vacation; you'd best come home with a tan.

"That, my dear, is taking on the floozies and the femi-men." I gestured to her all-over appearance. "You'd have to rein in all your hot babeness."

"Yeah, I've been to Mazza Gallerie. I had no idea Jimmy Choo made a Naturalizer." I hooted with laughter and tried not to choke on the lemon rind. "Apparently, Dior has a Matronly Collection, because it's hanging in that mall."

I teased my sister. "You've got to learn to embrace the matron within you. Like this lobbyist, Lila Weinstock. Jamie said she used to show up in skin-tight leather pants and see-through blouses, stare down Senator Nayland, and rub her breasts right in front of his wife." I stood and repositioned my chaise, playing catch-up with the sun. "Oh, but now she's all St. John's suits and slicked-back hair because she caught her man." I fully reclined the back rest and settled in on my tummy. "The guy was a preacher until he dumped his wife and bought Lila a ring from Zales. Don't even get me started that she lobbies for liquor."

Sophia laughed. "So a preacher senator cheats on his wife and then marries a lobbyist whose job it is to hawk liquor."

I propped my chin on the back of my hands. "You can't make this stuff up."

Sophia's laughter subsided. "Wait, is that even legal?"

"It's . . . inappropriate." We quieted for a moment and that moment stretched into the beginnings of a nap. I was calmed by the lapping waves, the hum of the yacht's engine. Until I realized the hum was Sophia. I looked up to find her deep in meditation. "Oooooooooom-mmmmmmmmm."

"What are you doing?"

She opened one eye and smirked. "Channeling my inner matron."

One week into our excursion, we found ourselves stuck in Riva Ligure with an Italian captain refusing to take us out to sea because he'd fallen in love with a local waitress. Riva Ligure was a sleepy little village with nothing to do. Our crew was twiddling their thumbs and Daddy Gil was stressed by making arrangements to fly a new captain in from the States.

Sophia and I decided we all needed a shopping day to take our mind off the current hiccup, but Daddy Gil couldn't keep up with us. He was winded and couldn't catch his breath. He was so tired Mom took him back to the boat. By the time Sophia and I returned, loaded with bags from our spree, Daddy Gil couldn't get out of bed.

Now, we all knew that Daddy Gil had type 2 diabetes but he never took it seriously. He'd say, "I'm borderline," but come on, borderline, what does that mean? It means stop eating the candy bar. And he'd have numbness in his feet or his arms but he'd pooh-pooh it.

But this, this was something different. And it was really scary. Mom called for an ambulance and Daddy Gil was transported to Guardia Medica Centro. None of the doctors spoke English and my Italian was conversational, not medical. I translated what I could. "I think they're saying that his heart is not getting blood. I don't know these words, Mom."

It was a horrible, horrible feeling—utter powerlessness. Mom called his doctors in the States. They wanted to bring Daddy Gil home but the Italian doctors didn't think he could make the trip. With translators at every end, we finally learned Daddy Gil had a blockage near his heart and was in worse shape than the Italian doctors were even able to diagnose. The decision was made to sedate Daddy Gil, put him on a ventilator, and air-ambulance him back to St. Louis.

It's amazing what an American Express card will do. In less than twelve hours, we had an air ambulance landing on top of the hospital. The pilot showed up with a bucket of ice and a bottle of scotch and handed it to Mom for the trip. We needed it. The last forty-eight hours had been a nightmare of crisis management. All three of us had pushed down the tears and the fright to just take things moment by moment. There were international phone calls, hospitals, boat captains, insurance companies, family, and friends to handle. But once that air ambulance lifted off and we were on our way back to America, the three of us dissolved. I was crying so hard, I couldn't see. All I could feel was my Mom's hand in mine as we held on to each other and prayed for strength.

In Missouri, the doctors performed an emergency bypass but Daddy Gil had been down too long. He was alive but devastatingly weakened. The doctors felt it safest to keep him sedated and on a ventilator for the time being. His cardiologist also wanted him moved to the Mayo Clinic in Minnesota. But if you're from out of state, getting into the Mayo is a political process. Mayo beds are filled with kings and queens, quite literally. Daddy Gil was a pillar of St. Louis society, but that wouldn't be enough.

His cardiologist took me aside. "Why don't you have Senator Ivy call?"

I said, "I barely know him. I've only been around him like three times. I don't think I can bother him with this."

The doctor looked at me strangely. "Your father is sick. When exactly would you bother someone?"

I instantly felt terrible; the doctor was right. Not only was Ivy the senator from Minnesota, he'd been a pharmacist there for years. He probably knew the Mayo doctors personally, or knew someone who did. I rushed out to the parking lot to call Jamie. I didn't want Mom or Sophia to hear me. I didn't want to raise their hopes.

"Jamie?" I swallowed back sobs, warbling like a pigeon. "Would it be appropriate for you to give me Senator Ivy's cell phone number? Or could you find a time when I can speak to him?"

"Are you okay? What's going on?"

I barely managed to croak, "My dad. He's in intensive care."

"Hold on. I'm putting you through right now."

Within the week, Daddy Gil had been moved to the Mayo and was sleeping comfortably in a bed Senator Ivy secured for his care. And from that point on, I would have stepped in front of a speeding train for Senator Ivy.

I just wasn't sure I should leave my family. Daddy Gil's recovery was going to be a long-term process. There would be no miracle cure. Mom decided to rent a furnished apartment near the hospital rather than stay in the hotel we'd been using as home base. Sophia was staying but Mom insisted I return to work. Saying our goodbyes as we checked out of the hotel, I was racked with guilt.

Mom hugged me tightly and rubbed my back, soothing her own pain as much as mine. "What are you going to do, Tee, sit here all day?"

My voice was weak. "I want to help."

"Honey, because of you, your Daddy has the best doctors in the world."

I flew back to Washington and made an appointment to see Senator Ivy immediately. I wanted to thank him, in person, for everything he'd done for my family. I had no intention of having a complete emotional breakdown in the senator's office but that's what happened. With a face streaked by running mascara, I resigned from my new job.

"Sir, I don't know if my dad will ever get to go home. It's important I spend as much time with him as possible. I have to resign."

The senator came equipped with a long face, thin lips, and droopy eyes that already held melancholy. My heartbreak caused him to rise from his wingback chair and sit by me on the antique loveseat. Even in my agony, I could tell his wife had decorated the office. The senator had a calming presence. "Is there anything I can do to keep you?"

And that's when I remembered how Daddy Gil used to work in St. Louis from Monday to Thursday then fly to New Orleans to be with us for the weekend. Suddenly, everything felt so much better. I could make that work.

"Actually, sir, maybe there is."

Senator Ivy happily agreed to my Daddy Gil–style work week. For the next two months, I worked my PAC director tail off schmoozing lobbyists four days a week, but every Friday through Sunday I was at the hospital, where I belonged, visiting Daddy Gil. His recovery was slight and slow but he was speaking again and able to do some limited physical therapy. We were all of us thrilled.

And that's where I was, at the Mayo Clinic, watching CNN and holding Daddy Gil's hand, when Majority Leader Haught apparently skipped his morning "hair of the dog" and shot off his racist mouth on national television. I paraphrase, but the general gist was "blacks are a problem," an inflammatory and idiotic remark that was, no duh, picked up by every major and minor news outlet in the known world and perhaps beyond.

Even by D.C. standards, the Haught debacle registered a big old ten on the Richter scale. Haught's pasty white jowls jiggled in profile on every television, in every paper, on the cover of every magazine. It was worse than Dean's primal scream in terms of its catastrophic career consequences. Haught's five apologies were rendered impotent by NPR, Internet bloggers, and plotting insiders who just wouldn't let that lying dog sleep. The buzz at every table, in every restaurant, was that Haught would face censure. Then the Dems came right out and called for the majority leader's resignation. It was bad news for the Party but really, really good news for Senator Ivy.

{ *Five* }

Beware Sudden Intimacy

*S*enator Ivy officially announced his run for majority leader, turning our offices into chaos central with incessantly ringing phones. My poor new assistant froze in her seat, her mouth bobbing silently as if she were a guppy swirling water as air.

I breezed past her desk with a "Just let them ring until we've been briefed," shut my door, and flopped onto my big, lovable couch. Goldie shimmied out of my Louis Vuitton and trotted across the floor towards my desk, her usual perch. She wanted up but, now that she was pushing ten years old, didn't have the oomph to jump. I was out of oomph myself, too tired to cross the room to help her. Running back and forth to Minnesota every week was grinding me down to bone. I just needed some peace. How in the world was I going to face even more insanity?

A tap, tap, tap at my opening door put Goldie into hysterics. She just adored Jamie and waggled like a honey bee, circling in and out between his freshly polished oxfords. He greeted her with his standard "Oh, Goldie! How many Goldies does it take to run the Iditarod!"

and smothered her with kisses. "You're back. How'd your dad do this weekend?"

"Better, actually. I thought you said this job would be a breeze."

"I guess I meant hurricane. Briefing in ten."

"I didn't sign up for this."

"I know. Hey listen, I want you to come with me this weekend to New York. Franklin bought a table for Eartha Kitt at the Carlyle. It will be amazing."

Bleck, Franklin. "I don't know, Jamie. I think I'd better fly back."

"Don't you think your parents would like some alone time?" Goldie was resting comfortably on Jamie's knee. He bounced her gently up and down, quietly humming "C'est Si Bon."

I contemplated my choices: a private audience with Eartha or another weekend of beeping machines, hospital smell, and IV tubes. I could tolerate Franklin for a weekend. I was desperate for an ounce of fun. Mom had urged me to stop flying back every weekend. "Alright, sign me up."

Had I not been completely drained, I would have stopped to ask the obvious questions: Why invite me along on this little foray? Wouldn't *Jamie and Franklin* like to have some time alone? Why was Jamie leaving town in the middle of Ivy's power grab?

We were supposed to take the shuttle to New York but a horrible snowstorm blew in. We opted instead for a cushy drive. Yes, in a limo paid for by PAC dollars. It was that or fly through a blizzard, so I picked guilt over death. The icy highways turned our four-hour drive into a seven-hour crawl but it wasn't the roads that were dangerous. Jamie and Franklin had me right where they wanted, a captive to their plans. Jamie peppered me with questions while Franklin plucked at his BlackBerry. "You're not going to leave us, are you?"

"Daddy Gil wants me to look after his bank. I should go back to St. Louis and run things until he's better."

"So you're going to leave your friends *and* your family to be in St. Louis by yourself? That's a bad, bad idea."

In all truth, I had no desire to be the "She's Running Our Bank Because Her Dad Is the President" girl. Everybody hates that girl. "What do you think I should do?"

Jamie's response was jarringly interrupted by Franklin's howling laughter. A picture on his BlackBerry put them both in stitches. "Temple, you know my husband, right?"

Franklin leaned forward to show me the screen. There, in all his pixels, was Evan Vaughn blowing Franklin digital kisses. Evan Vaughn. The guy who ran one of the most lucrative and influential lobbying firms in the Capitol. Evan Vaughn was gay?

"Wait, what? I thought you two—" I gestured from Jamie to Franklin and back. They howled in response.

"Oh God, no, no, no! We'd kill each other." Jamie patted Franklin's knee but Franklin was completely absorbed, instant messaging with Evan. "Evan and Frankie are married now, what, eleven years?"

"Don't call me Frankie."

"Yes, yes. And I've been with my man, Denver, for five this past January."

"Off and on." Franklin shot me a smile. "They have drama."

"Not now. We're good now. Denver's a chiropractor. We just bought a new house near Lake Harriet. It's beautiful, you'll have to visit."

"A house?" I couldn't stop myself. They were telling, so I was asking. "But I've been to your apartment. You mean you don't actually live in D.C.?"

"Does it look like I live there?"

"Actually no, I remember thinking, 'There's not a picture in this place!'"

"You think I'm bad, Franklin keeps a suite at the Hotel George."

Franklin smirked. "If it was up to Evan, we'd send out Christmas cards of us in matching sweaters."

My head was spinning. Not only had Jamie and Franklin willingly outed themselves, they weren't a couple *and* they had completely secret lives with houses, husbands, and apparently, matching holiday apparel.

How in the world were they able to juggle two separate worlds for so long? I could barely manage to deal with the one I had. And somehow, in a city fueled by gossip, they'd succeeded in keeping their personal lives entirely private. Yes, we women assumed they were gay. But I'd never heard so much as a peep about Evan and Franklin. And once a story is out there, everyone knows.

The boys were smiling at me oddly. I could tell by the look on their faces they were gauging my reaction to this new level of intimacy and trust.

"I adore Evan. He's a sweetheart. I'm so glad you both have found someone you love. I can't wait to meet Denver."

Jamie and Franklin nodded like two parents proudly praising one another for their child's report card. Jamie grabbed my hand and gave it a gentle squeeze. "Now, about that move to St. Louis . . . "

The boys wanted me named finance director of the RSCC, but I couldn't take that job. "No, no, absolutely not." I shook my head vigorously while the boys pleaded for my consideration. "First and foremost, Daddy Gil. I have to have the freedom to travel back and forth to check on him."

Franklin clapped his hands as if finishing a great meal. "Done and done. You can keep your Monday to Thursday work week. Plus you'll have a much bigger staff to help do the job."

"A bigger staff *is* the job! There are what, fifty people in that office?"

Franklin did some quick arithmetic. "No, just forty-seven."

"Just forty-seven!" Oh, these boys trapping me in this car. Strike two for Franklin. And I mean *big* strike two. "I don't even know how to do that job! Why in the world would anyone let me run the Committee? A third of the seats are up for grabs! I could completely blow it!"

Now it was Jamie's turn to talk me off the ledge. "It's a presidential year. The money's gonna flow like water."

"Mr. Jameel Howrani sir, you are full of pure bull hockey!"

Franklin took up the argument. "Traditionally, giving doubles in the presidential cycle. We've seen what you've done with the PAC. You raised $6 million in less than three months."

I protested. "It's not the same thing. Those guys write checks in their sleep."

Jamie jumped in. "You doubled our house file. That's unheard of, Temple."

Franklin leaned forward to make his point. "Once Ivy's in as majority leader, all we need is you."

Flattery, heavens, I'm such a sucker, but I was determined to wiggle out of this. "You both know Prudence is my best friend." Prudence had been acting as a temporary consultant to the RSCC since their finance director had his heart attack. "Taking the job is the equivalent of stealing a client."

Jamie whispered his delicious secret. "Prudence is the one who recommended you."

Lord, those boys knew how to play me like a fiddle. They knew if Prudence recommended me for the job, I'd find it nearly impossible to say no. Still, I did my best to ward them off in the back of that limo sliding towards Manhattan. I should never have said, "Maybe, maybe. I'll talk with Prudence about it." With just those words, I sealed my fate.

The boys became a plotting escalation machine. Jamie initiated a wild series of phone calls with senators, encouraging them to recommend me to Senator Griswold and Franklin. Franklin was, of course, secretly already on "my side" and working behind the scenes snuffing out snafus that might interfere with my approval process. I, the Marmaduke of Money, had no idea my name was being bandied about like a badminton birdie. For two weeks after New York, the boys didn't mention the job again and I didn't ask. I was too busy handling the massive influx of new lobbyists writing checks now that Senator Ivy was Majority Leader Ivy.

It was Prudence who told me the boys were still scheming. Our standing weekly Bombshell dinners at Café Milano were my best source for insider information. Netta's baby plans had sadly been postponed by a second early-term miscarriage. She and Zack had submitted to fertility testing and were now researching their options with in vitro fertilization. Though she wasn't back in the fray full-time, Netta was helping Prudence with clients just to keep her mind off her troubles. Between the three of us, somebody always had good gossip.

Netta started with our usual appetizer: Abramoff. "Guess who just bought a $4 million office building? On the Hill."

Prudence shook her head. "He can't be that stupid."

"No, but his little protégé is." Netta sipped gingerly at her red wine, her tolerance compromised by months of hopeful maternal sobriety. "And we know that kid didn't inherit it."

"Jack never shows at our events. He never even calls. I mean, why bother calling me when he can just call Ivy directly?" I offered. "But Jamie just pulled him off the Greenbrier golf tournament invite list."

Prudence furrowed her brow in response. "I smell indictment."

"You think?" Netta ran the palm of her hand over her hair, smoothing the strays that had wiggled out of her braid.

Prudence continued, "Jack just hired Calina at two hundred grand a year. She's one of fifteen and they don't have a client list. Something's going on."

"Calina!" I nearly spit her name. "What a cockroach. She'll outlive us all."

"And what about you, Temple?" Prudence distractedly tugged at the bread. "Are you going to take the Senate Committee job?"

It took me a second to remember what she meant. "Oh, that? No, no. That's your client."

Prudence dipped her chunk in a little olive oil but didn't take a bite. "It's an election cycle, they need someone full-time. Permanent. I've got other clients."

Netta chimed in. "God, that would be amazing, Temple! A job like that is history."

Prudence nodded her support. "It's a remarkable opportunity."

Remarkable. Prudence had said the magic word. So many years ago, as I ran out onto the tarmac to stop Mr. Barrymore, Prudence had emerged from the plane and I'd been awed by her. Everything about her had seemed . . . well, remarkable. I'd wanted to be that woman, I'd wanted to be Prudence, and here was my opportunity to finally emerge out from under her shadow to become her equal. This was what I'd been working to achieve. This was the dream, all wrapped up in a big red bow and handed to me. With just one catch: Daddy Gil's health.

The thought of taking responsibility for the entire Republican Senate while trying to be a good daughter made me lose my appetite. I tossed my menu back onto the table.

"Maybe just a salad."

Nana Sachet often spent long stretches of days cross-stitching by Daddy Gil's bedside. Mom eventually joined in, replacing her incessant pacing with the busywork of needle to cloth. With her hands occupied, Mom could now sit for hours by Daddy Gil's bedside and worry less. It was a coping mechanism. Nana had finished a Spirit of Christmas tree skirt and needed a new kit.

I was pushing a stubborn cart through the needlepoint supplies aisle in a Wal-Mart in Minnesota when the boys called to tell me the job was a done deal. I was now the finance director for the RSCC.

"Nope, nope, nope!" I tried hard not to yell but my frustration was palpable. Being back at the Mayo had made it perfectly clear: I wasn't tall enough to ride this coaster, the soaring heights of mania in D.C. then the terrifying dips into depression in Minnesota. I didn't have it in me.

Jamie chimed in, "You said you would take it. You can't leave us hanging with the senators."

"I said maybe, *maybe*. I never said I'd actually do it."

"Think long-term, Temple. My guy's going to run the following cycle and he's going to win." Franklin's confidence rubbed at me, arrogant sandpaper up my spine. Couldn't he just take no for an answer?

"I'm standing here trying to buy pioneer patterns for my sweet little mamaw and you two are harassing me!"

Jamie wouldn't let it go. "Senator Ivy will be so disappointed."

Shame on Jamie, he knew how indebted I felt to the senator. "I'm hanging up now and I don't want to hear another word about it." Twenty seconds later, my BlackBerry rang again. "Boys, I warned you—"

"Is this Temple Sachet?"

I recognized Senator Griswold's labored breathing instantly and quickly swallowed my rage. "Yes sir, senator, this is."

"Wonderful, wonderful. [Huff] I was just speaking with my chief of staff, Franklin Cirlot, here. [Wheeze] He thinks you and I need a sit down to talk about how we're going structure the Senate Committee. [Gasp] Tuesday morning good for you?"

Over and over, rolling through my brain, the mantra: I hate you boys. I absolutely hate you boys. "Yes sir, that would be fine."

"Wonderful, wonderful. [Wheeze] We'll see you at 9 a.m. sharp."

That Tuesday, at the somehow-still-gullible age of twenty-nine, I officially became the youngest finance director in the history of the RSCC. It took two gays and a bigot to put me there but apparently in the Republican Party, two parts homo-nepotism with just a splash of racist scandal equals a powerful new job.

There I was, at the top of the food chain. The second most powerful fundraiser in the Republican Party. Just one rung under the President's guy. Without even trying. Without even knowing where to start.

And now, I had to raise $95 million.

Here's the sign that you've taken the wrong job: You have to buy a sleeping bag to keep at the office.

The RSCC was a behemoth monster that swallowed my life, spit me up, and gnawed on my soul just for fun. Franklin and Jamie neglected to mention that the three major job duties were:

Never leave your desk.
Don't eat.
Don't breathe fresh air.

They also failed to mention that the last three finance directors had suffered major health traumas. I knew my predecessor had a heart attack but I didn't know that the lady before him had a minor stroke at forty-two, that the guy before her had a full-blown heart attack, and that Franklin himself was so stressed from overseeing the hiring for the Committee that he'd developed a heart murmur.

My job, which began at 7:00 each morning and lasted until well past midnight, was to play den mother to all the fresh out of college staffers I dubbed "the young ones;" enlist senators to call donors by baking their favorite cookies or bribing them with candy (you think I'm kidding); oversee the minutiae of massive monthly dinners, parties, and the Convention; and oh yeah, while I was at it, make sure the Republican Senate retained the majority in the next election. Add flying to Minnesota every weekend to visit Daddy Gil and you get . . . the office sleeping bag.

The Committee's finance department was divided into two large divisions: Direct Mail and Major Donors. Direct Mail was headed up by Acton Farley, a legendary old-timer whose mailings were so inflammatory everyone called him "Blaze" and forced him to run things by legal. Blaze was a right-wing guy who walked a fine line between story and slander. I knew better than to talk politics with Blaze. He would have been appalled by my "live and let live" attitude.

Blaze oversaw a database of six hundred thousand people who responded to his letters like clockwork. His FEC reports were pages and pages of Americans who earned their money by working for it, like the custodian at TJ Maxx who'd been giving five dollars a month every month for the last ten years. His donors were unceremoniously referred to as the House File and over the course of an election cycle he could wrangle $8 million out of them. Though technically Blaze reported to me, I trusted him to run his shop the way he wanted. As long as he was on schedule and avoiding legal trouble, there was no need for me to micromanage. My focus shifted to Major Donors.

Major Donors was divided into four programs: Team Victory, Force GOP, the Patriots, and the Upper House. Each level had its own particular brand of fanaticism, which ran the gamut from the uber-rich and ultra-eccentric demanding legislation for checks to the straight-out senseless who charged their memberships on credit cards just for a whiff of status and power.

It all started at the bottom with what my young ones called the "Nut House"—a nickname I despised. The Upper House members were our bread and butter; I would not tolerate the staff making fun of them. Any time I heard a junior staffer use the phrase "Nut House," I'd give them a little lecture. "Those donors keep our doors open. They pay your salary. You should thank each one of them personally."

And then, I attended my first Nut, excuse me, Upper House annual meeting. Within three seconds of stepping into the opening-night reception, I knew I was in trouble. The ballroom was a three-ring circus.

Starring in Ring One were the Hapless and the Helpless. Like Mrs. Houghton, an overweight, older woman who'd get smashed and pass out on tables in her sunglasses. Or the lady who always wore a white bed sheet as a ball gown. Or Brookie Judge, a close-talker who insisted I take one of her personalized pens that said "Brookie Judge, Happy Republican." I smiled politely and slid her pen into my jacket pocket. By the end of the night, my shirt and jacket were covered in ink.

In Ring Two were the Asians with Agendas. Dr. Yang and Dr. Chung weren't actual doctors but they claimed to be billionaire real estate developers in Asia. They traveled with a huge entourage of people nicknamed the Asian Mafia and demanded private meetings with senators. They came with lists of things they needed to get done. None of which got done.

Featured in Ring Three were the Women You Don't Want to Meet in a Dark Alley. The Baroness of Brazil made her own makeup and seemed to wear all of it at one time. She tried to sell her beauty products to my staff and when that didn't work, she started giving them away. (I forced them to throw the jars in the trash for fear it might burn their faces off.) She was outdone only by the Granny Stalker, a seventy-year-old mamaw in a micro-miniskirt and a Farrah Fawcett sausage-roll hairdo who stalked all the single senators, trying to sleep with them. Apparently, it worked: She had sex in the back of a cab with a greasy one-term senator who will here go unnamed.

I quickly made the executive decision to put the young ones on Normal Patrol. "If you see a first-timer who looks like they might be normal, take them under your wing quickly and get them upgraded fast."

Somewhere, amidst the circus, were nice people who maybe owned a small but very successful business in their hometown and had gotten a certificate in the mail saying, "You have been selected by Senator Griswold to become part of the Upper House," and they'd framed the thing and sent in their $2,000 check and made the trip to

D.C., only to be bombarded by leaking pens, a sex-starved mamaw, and Asian con artists. We had to find the nice people and get them out of that pool of peculiars before they hightailed it home.

I was ready to run home myself.

Upgrading from Nut, excuse me, Upper House to Patriot meant a donor had to pony up $5K a person or $7.5K per couple. Most of the Patriots were yuppies looking to dip a toe into the waters of politics. They were our most ripe candidates to upgrade because their income was also moving upwards. They were excitable and wanted the maximum for their dollar. They had two conferences a year but they wanted forty senators mingling around the room. They wanted to feel they had a personal relationship with the senator who repped their home state. But it was tough to get senators to a Patriot event. They'd make up excuses: "There are too many donors in the room," "It's difficult for me to drive across town to get to the hotel." I had to *beg* senators, "Please Senator, Occasions is catering. I'll have them make your favorite. Sweet and sour meatballs!"

Of course, I had no trouble at all getting senators to attend Team Victory events or Force GOP trips. Force GOP donors gave $15K every year and tended to be New York's prominent couples, former ambassadors, and those who had buildings or streets named after them. It was the oldest individual donor program within the Senate Committee and for a long time, it was also the most prestigious. Once Team Victory came into play Force GOP got pushed to the side.

The Force donors were outrageous in an old-money way. Most of them were used to being the center of attention and refused to be ignored. They wanted pampering and special privileges. They wanted the respect that a family name used to buy. They were the last gasps of a bygone generation.

There was one old man named Mr. Kendt whose kids were dividing what was left of his estate as if he were already dead. He hadn't paid his membership dues in years but he still wobbled into every party on his cane and lined up for a click with the President.

Force GOP had meetings once every three months across the country, from Washington to Naples to Beverly Hills to Vegas. In Vegas, they were always hosted by a donor secretly referred to as Fake Elvis. Fake Elvis had made his fortune selling insurance door-to-door eventually buying the company. He lived in a replica of Graceland, where he housed his seemingly infinite collection of Elvis memorabilia. Walking into his home, a visitor was greeted by a life-size wax figurine of the King himself decked out in a full white-leather jumpsuit studded in a Thunderbird pattern. The living room was an exact reproduction of Elvis's, with the fifteen-foot white couch and stained-glass peacocks. In the dining room hung a large oil portrait of Fake Elvis, with his dyed black pompadour, posing with his wife . . . both of them naked. All eighty-six pounds of him, wearing nothing but his gold watch, gold chains, and his big gold rings. One on every finger. His parties were full of B-list stars and Vegas personalities schmoozing with lobbyists, donors, and senators. Bo Derek chatting up General Schwarzkopf.

I actually adored Fake Elvis because I love the American rags-to-riches story. I'm a total sucker for it. I'm a good capitalist, I am. I spend. I earn. I love meeting people who came from nothing and now own half a city. I love hearing their personal stories. I love that they are eccentric and needy and deeply human. I love watching their faces light up as they get to the good part, the part where everything looked dire and bleak and then a miracle happened. The business sold, the idea took off, the loan was approved.

Maybe it's because I remembered life before Daddy Gil, when Mom quit working at the hospital and took a risk with her own business. Whatever the reason, I loved being out on the road and meeting people from all over the country who built America. As zany as they were, they were responsible for creating communities and providing jobs. They kept me inspired.

Team Victorys were my biggest donors. They were people who wrote $25,000 checks and in exchange received a lapel pin full of cubic zirconias and invitations to ultra-exclusive events like the President's Dinner, the Senate Celebration, the Leadership Luncheon, and frankly, anything else they wanted to attend. Team Victory donors were predominantly captains of industry. They handed over donations because they believed in the Republican platform, but their calendars were full. They rarely showed up.

Heading up Team Victory was a prestigious job within the Committee. I needed someone polished who could sit at a table with Lee Iacocca and be savvy enough not to show that she didn't understand a word he was saying. Which is why I hired Netta. I needed someone I trusted. Team Victorys didn't want to be asked directly for money. They couldn't be hounded. They wanted to feel invited and included but never burdened. Netta was the perfect handler and she needed the distraction. All the baby-making was driving Zack insane.

Some of her donors were just evil. Like this man I'll simply refer to as Gordon Gekko since it's apt. Gekko would demand a meeting with Senator Griswold and since he was a Team Victory member, Netta'd make the appointment. He owned everything from media companies to military weaponry manufacturers, so a meeting with him was usually all over the map. He'd come out and tell Senator Griswold, "I'm not going to write any checks unless I can get this bill passed. Where are you on this legislation? Where is senator so and so? I hate that son of a bitch. Where is he?"

So Senator Griswold would task us to e-mail our research guy, whose *actual* name was Abe Lincoln, to look up the legislation that affected Gekko's pending billion-dollar business deal . . . while Senator Griswold was sitting across from him in the office. It was absolutely illegal but when those two got together, the product for sale was legislation.

A donor database is a living organism. There's always attrition at the top. Donors who give more expect more. They become disgusted and they walk, or they're old and they die off, or they're Enron and things get ugly. If we weren't continually feeding the organism from the bottom, it would have withered and died. We had to keep scraping the bottom of the barrel while continuing to feed it. It's called prospecting. Like Okies mining for gold, the young ones would sit in their cubicles, shake their BlackBerrys back and forth, pan the contact entries, and go blind peering for shiny nuggets. It was my job to examine each and every rock they overturned. I was overwhelmed and exhausted.

To make matters worse, I'd jumped in without doing my home-work on Senator Griswold. Griswold was what we in New Orleans called a grand bedee, a big old clumsy oaf, though he fancied himself a modern-day toupee-wearing Roy Rogers, complete with cowboy boots, ten-gallon hats, and plaid shirts. If the Senate Face Book would have allowed it (and the horse could have taken his weight), Griswold would have been photographed in full rancher regalia sitting on top of his steed, his shellacked rug blowing in the breeze. Never mind that he was a lawyer from Greenwich, Connecticut, Ivy-league educated and morbidly obese, and owned no horses. He had a "salt of the earth" image to maintain.

And Lord, was Franklin a handful. He needed to see, hear, touch, approve, and sign off on anything related to Griswold. At first, I took his micro-managing invasions personally. I thought Frank-lin considered me an idiot. Then I realized the level of Griswold's incompetence. Franklin wasn't worried about me. He controlled Griswold's every interaction so the senator couldn't sabotage his own career.

Senator Griswold wouldn't fundraise to save his life. The only meetings he'd take were those with Team Victorys. I'd make call sheets—lists of donors for him to phone—and he'd just sit around talking to me about branding steers. If I actually got him to look at a call sheet he'd say, "Has this guy ever given to MacLeish?"

Though MacLeish was a Republican, Griswold hated him. The two had gone head to head for years, their rivalry binding them like spiteful brothers. But Griswold avoiding donor calls wasn't about his jealousy of MacLeish. It was about laziness.

"I don't know, Senator."

"Well, pull his contributions and let's see if he's ever given to that son of a bitch."

Why did it matter? A donor has to be called, and he or she expects that call to come from the chair of the Senate Committee, not me. But Senator Griswold would stall and stall. I had to get creative.

The only way I could get Senator Griswold excited about raising funds was to launch the Senator Griswold Cowboy Club. The club was open only to elite-level lobbyists who pledged to raise $100,000 in new dollars from their execs and membership. In exchange they would be invited to private, exclusive events with Senator Griswold, and if they fulfilled their financial commitment they would receive a classic black Stetson and a bear-claw belt buckle or, for the women (though very few were invited), a pair of rattlesnake cowboy boots. Of course, Senator Griswold demanded his own hat, buckle, and boots as well.

Word of our elite club spread like wildfire among upper-echelon lobbyists when a Big Guy called the program Red Door/Green Door. Meaning the door to our ultra-exclusive club was red for the Little Guys and green for the Big Guys. That's how the lobbyists liked to play. Like bratty elementary school kids with a sing-songy "Nah-nah-nah-nah-nah-nah, you can't come in and weeeeee can." Senator Griswold loved it as well. All he had to do was show up at free meals, eat, eat, eat, and talk cowboy for an hour.

Regional swings were impossible. I could not get the man to travel. I had Netta organize a trip for him to Texas, where I thought we would do very well. There were beaucoup ranchers who liked Griswold and his parents had retired to Dallas, so Netta even booked family time into the trip. Of course, at the last minute he cancelled.

Even through the phone I could tell Griswold was moping. "I don't want to go and I'm not gonna go."

"But Senator, the whole trip is already planned. We've built fundraisers around you. You can't not show."

"I'll tell Senator Brogan to go instead. She wants my job so bad. She can go and see how grueling this is, that'll teach her."

Grueling? The man spent half his morning lying on the couch watching TV. The other half was spent eating. He had a calendar full of white blocks and free meals and was seriously considering himself presidential material. Presidents don't have white-block days. Well, most don't. I wasn't going to let this one go without a fight. "What's your excuse going to be when Brogan asks you why you're not going yourself?"

"It's too far to travel and we have votes."

"So you're going to tell her that even though it's too far to travel and we have votes and you are the chair of the Committee that she should go instead."

"I'll think of something!" And he hung up on me. So I went down the hallway and got Netta. She was totally freaking out. "These are my personal contacts! People who could be helpful if he runs for president. Why is he doing this to me?"

Drastic situations call for drastic measures. I quickly grabbed some rubber bands, copy paper, markers, scissors, and tape off Netta's desk. "What are you doing, Sachet?"

"Come with me, you'll see."

I called ahead to make sure old Blubberboy was in his office (probably asleep) and that Franklin was nowhere to be found. All clear. I grabbed an intern and made him drive as Netta, under my strict instructions, frantically cut stars out of copy paper. I did my best to mimic the shape of a six-shooter but the paper pistols looked more like boomerangs. They would have to do.

As the completely befuddled intern pulled up in front of the Capitol, I instructed him to pull into the senators' parking lot and wait. "If we don't come out in an hour, we've been arrested and you should probably just go back to work."

Netta and I jumped out of the car, hiked up our skirts, taped the stars to our tushies and our bodacious ta-tas, and used rubber bands to put our hair in pigtails. We each grabbed two of our paper boomerang pistols and ran into Griswold's office.

We sang at the top of our lungs, "The stars at night are big and bright!" Our hands full of flimsy paper, we couldn't clap so we stomped four times fast. "Deep in the heart of Texas!" We then orchestrated an impromptu dance, all the while screaming, "The cowgirls say you have to go to Texas, pardner! The cowgirls won't take no for an answer, pardner!" After a few revealing high kicks, a lot of attempted holstering of and feigned dueling with our paper six-shooters, and a bad rendition of the bump, Senator Griswold heartily applauded our performance. It was hard to tell if his laughter or his weight had him sucking for air.

Whatever, he agreed to go.

Franklin forced all female staffers to stay in a hotel a minimum of twenty miles away from the senator and his wife—another one of his ridiculous, incomprehensible control tics—and we'd overestimated the time it would take to drive to collect him. Our early arrival instigated one of Mrs. Griswold's well-known tirades. The senator's wife referred to her staff as "the little people" and this morning her ire was raised against Carrie, a mousy girl sucking back tears and shaking.

The woman was evil and just as fat as her husband. She'd crowned herself queen of the Country Club, a malicious clique of senators' wives who acted as the Old Guard. They didn't like the wives who had their own careers, they didn't like second wives, and they absolutely had a stroke when Senator Row married a B-list actress from that Sodom, Hollywood. It didn't help matters that the new Mrs. Row wore sexy dresses to political events and shot a provocative calendar of herself in swimsuits and slinky evening wear. *The Hill* went berserk over that one: HOLLYWOOD HOTTIE FROM THE COLD DAKOTAS. Lord, what a brouhaha over nothing. The Senate wives just about clucked their tongues off.

Mrs. Griswold was only half dressed when we walked in, her bra straining to contain rolls of flesh as her love handles dripped over the sides of a bold black-and-white diamond-patterned Carlisle skirt stretched taut across her sizeable thighs. A Carlisle Consultant, Mrs. Griswold held private showings of their new collections twice a year. Because she was the wife of the Senate Committee's chair (the man in charge of their husband's campaign funds), all the Senate wives felt obligated not only to attend these private functions but to also buy the clothes.

Buying Carlisle clothing is not like buying Tupperware. You can't just throw the girl a bone and then stash the stuff on your top shelf. I mean, those clothes are expensive—like $4,000 for a coat. But twice a year, Mrs. Griswold would huff and puff and peddle her wares and the Senate wives had no choice but to buy. They all showed up at events wearing the same things.

"I just can't handle these mistakes anymore, Carrie, things need to function properly. If I need to be dressed at a certain time then I need the proper amount of time allotted in my schedule." It wasn't Carrie's fault. We were the ones who arrived early, but our apologies did nothing to temper Mrs. Griswold's continuing attack. "You should wake up knowing every day is *my* wedding day and you are just here to be one of my bridesmaids. If you ever get married, you will understand."

Carrie ran from the room crying as Mrs. Griswold shot us a creepy, practiced smile. "I'll send the senator down. When he's ready."

The rest of our Texas trip was equally disastrous. In San Antonio, Netta had identified a potential new donor: a tiny, rude man recently profiled in several magazines for his heralded collection of Imperial Chinese artifacts. His collection spanned nearly four thousand years and included priceless paintings, jades, bronzes, ceramics, textiles, and lacquerware—all of which seemed to be displayed in his cramped office.

Right out of the gate, Senator Griswold takes his big old foot and crosses his flabby leg and kicks across the man's desk, hitting an irreplaceable vase that goes crashing towards the floor. I'd never seen a person move so fast in my life. The hoped-for donor threw himself to the ground and magically managed to grab the vase just before it shattered into a million little pieces. This won't come as a surprise: no check that day.

Houston brought no relief. I'd scheduled a stopover with a sure thing, Avram Glassberg, who was always good for a check as long as you'd listen to him talk. He owned a TV station. He owned a bank. He got into real estate. His résumé was long and illustrious and all Senator Griswold had to do was keep his mouth shut. I prepped him as we made the drive to Avram's penthouse.

"Don't talk hobbies. Don't talk about religion and don't talk about your wife, because he couldn't care less."

Griswold snorted his contempt. "What I'm supposed to talk to him about?"

"Nothing. He's going to talk nonstop the whole time and that's how we're going to do this. You won't have to say a word."

So we get in the meeting and it's like a buzzer went off, Avram talks and he talks and he talks and he talks. Senator Griswold half winks at me and I shake my head because I don't want him to draw too much attention. Everything's going well until Avram's receptionist brings in some sodas. Senator Griswold vigorously pops open his Coke which, of course, causes the whole thing to start dripping. The receptionist scurries to get him a napkin and to my and Netta's absolute horror, Senator Griswold says, "That's okay, I've got it," and with his big old camel tongue he slurps up the side of this filthy, dirty Coke can and licks the drippings away. I truly thought Avram was going to eject us through the window.

Griswold had to be handled like a child. If he was scheduled for a donor appointment, he'd show up with coffee stains on his shirt, or his tie on backwards. "What's going on there with your tie?"

He'd look down. "I flipped it over, see, because it has food on the other side."

This was a constant occurrence. Netta finally bought two full shopping bags of socks and ties, two extra suits, and four white shirts to keep in her office to ensure the senator didn't embarrass the Committee. The last thing we needed was for Griswold to cross his legs in front of a Team Victory donor and reveal holes around his ankles. And this was a grown man who was one of the most highly respected senators in the country.

The Texas trip had been a complete bust and we were now millions of dollars behind our projected schedule. Something had to be done. Crying, I rushed over to Jamie's office and was grateful to find Prudence there. They would know what to do. Jamie took immediate control. "You need to focus on the things you do well. Everything else will fall in place."

"Focus? I spend my whole day putting out his fires; there's no time to plan upcoming events. If we don't meet any of our numbers, I'll be the one blamed. He knows he's putting me in a bad situation and he just doesn't give a hoot."

Prudence listened attentively but Jamie, thank God, had a plan. "You're going to ask Senator Ivy to host a party."

"Griswold will feel overshadowed," Prudence volunteered.

"Exactly; he'll be so jealous he might actually do his job." Jamie knew just which buttons to push to get senators to run like children after chocolate.

"Franklin's not going to be happy," Prudence warned.

"I'll take care of Franklin." Jamie poked at his BlackBerry until he found the number. "But you, my darling"—Jamie gazed directly into my eyes—"You're going to have to talk Senator Ivy into this one yourself."

{ *Interlude* }

Favor Means You Owe

*A*ha! That! That was how I ended up locked in a closet with Gray Two, having a completely internalized four-minute nervous breakdown! Senator Ivy had said yes to my desperate plea for a party. No, Senator Griswold was an idiot making my life miserable. No, Jamie and Franklin had tricked me into a job I didn't want. No, no, no, no, no! None of that was it. None of it.

Standing, pressed breasts against POTUS, I could see with such clarity and disgust. There was no end product. I was raising all this money, but what was the point? To fund advertising? To make polling companies wealthy? To support this utter hypocrisy?

Ninety-five million dollars. I could have been eradicating poverty in Appalachia. I could have been funding a whole new inner-city school system in the Bronx. I could have been chasing away beavers in a park!

What happened to that young, spunky girl who'd shared her love of Italy so an opera house might thrive? What happened to the girl who convinced a mayor to let prisoners plant flowers alongside little old ladies in Queeny Park? The girl who'd brought a rodeo to

St. Louis, who overhauled a condemned trailer for a candidate she believed in—a candidate she adored. That girl had, in her own small ways, made the world a more beautiful place.

Elma had warned that girl! Crazy, wonderful, drunk, and possibly psychic Elma had looked into the bottom of her shot glass and seen her—seen me—surrounded by expensive suits, parasites, the unbelievers. The unbelievers! She'd warned me. She'd said "believe or die," and I didn't understand she meant it literally.

And now, here I was in neck-deep, supporting a Republican platform of "family" when most of the senators were divorced (one on his eighth wife!), having affairs, or otherwise living by a different set of rules than those they espoused. The senators were so hateful about homosexuality and yet their own offices were entirely staffed by gay men. Even Senator Ivy, whom I adored personally, was beating the homo-bashing drum. He knew Jamie was gay. Senator Griswold knew Franklin was gay. They trusted these men to run their lives and their careers, and still they traded in hatred for votes. For heaven's sake, rumors abounded about several of their own Senate colleagues. Everyone knew Senator Yust greeted his new interns by answering his front door naked. People were whispering that Senator Ogburn had a penchant for public bathrooms.

My involvement wasn't making things better. I was part of the problem! I was stealing money from plumbers, tellers, and teachers. I was stealing money from that custodian at TJ Maxx in five-dollar increments per month. It wasn't some distant machine, not some conspiracy theory, not a theory at all. It was me. Me!

Everything had to stop right now. It all had to stop.

I summoned the courage to tell President Shorty just what I actually thought of him and his Party. What I thought about him promising to appoint Barrymore as Secretary of Commerce then reneging on the promise. I wasn't going to smile anymore when I felt like screaming. I wasn't going to nod reassuringly so everyone could feel okay about themselves. I had been a true believer and I still was, I still was!

My mind raced. Should I confront him with a "If people want to get stoned in the privacy of their own house and pay some tranny to come over and shake his/her shama-lama-ding-dong in their face, how is that any of your business?" Or should I go right for the jugular with a "If men want to wear matching holiday sweaters and pay taxes as a couple, why is the government complaining?"

Before I could choose my weapon, the pocket doors slid violently open and President Gray was whisked so quickly away that it was as if he'd never been there. I blinked hard against the bright lights of the room, a deer blinded by the headlights of an oncoming existential crisis.

"What happened to you?" That was Genevieve, anxiety just under the surface of her photo smile.

With a quick glance around, I saw eager eyes upon me. My young staffers, donors I now considered friends, friends I now considered family. Prudence, Jamie, Netta, even prickly Franklin. They were all staring at me, slightly shocked and wowed by my private closet session with Gray Two.

What was I supposed to do? Announce my newfound and highly shaky enlightenment aloud? Make a scene in the majority leader's library? Storm out in a fit of straight-girl indignation on behalf of my log-cabin friends who weren't fighting for themselves?

I pulled myself together and quickly rejoined Senator Ivy and Genevieve in the click box. "Advance closed the door on me, I'm sorry. Did anyone pass you didn't recognize?"

"We were lucky that time," she reached for my arm. "Step up here closer, Temple, we don't want to lose you again."

Three never-ending hours, two long-winded speeches, and a four-course meal later, the crowd finally cleared so Netta and I could walk our final survey of the home, eyeballing every antique, every chair, every book in the library. Leave no trace.

"Temple, before you go—" Senator Ivy motioned for me to join him on the terrace. Netta nodded her goodbye and I stepped out into the chilly night air, my whole body immediately rippling with goose bumps. It was good I had this moment alone with the senator. After all he'd done for Daddy Gil, it was only right to resign in person.

"My father always said a brisk night would kill you or cure you." The senator inhaled deeply and swallowed as if drinking from the sky. "He wasn't much on medicine, or politicians for that matter. I probably disappointed him twice."

"I truly doubt that, sir."

"Your father sure is proud of you, brags on you every time we speak. He always asks if I'm happy with your work."

I hung my head, unable to look Senator Ivy in the eye. This man had saved Daddy Gil's life. For the last four months, he'd made daily calls ensuring Daddy Gil was treated like royalty at the hospital. He was helping our family through our darkest hour. I owed this man everything and I was contemplating betrayal.

"I am, Temple, I'm so happy you're part of our team. I know what you're up against with Senator Griswold. We all do. I sleep better at night knowing you're there. Your efforts don't go unnoticed."

"Thank you, sir."

"This election we're facing, we need the Senate majority. And we need you to stay."

My goose bumps instantly internalized, spreading cold chills of terror through my heart. Had I been rude, transparent, distant? Had I accidentally spoken my thoughts aloud? Was Senator Ivy psychic? I croaked my questioning, "Stay?"

"There's talk the president's people want you. I'm afraid tonight's haul will have them foaming at the mouth. It's a great opportunity for you and I promise, after this election, I'll be the first one on the phone singing your praises. It's just we're so close, Temple, I can see it." Senator Ivy reached for my hands and gave them the same gentle squeeze Daddy Gil used when he wanted me to listen. "You're the one I trust. I need you to stay with us."

Instinctively, my head nodded in reassurance, the job so in me that nodding precluded all other responses. "Senator, I work for you."

"Thank you, Temple."

I left him on the terrace, still smiling and nodding. I walked out into that brisk night not knowing whether it had killed or cured me.

Part Two

CHANGE

{ *Six* }

There Are No Secrets

"*Y*ou've got vacation days and assistants, that's what they're for."
Mom was on the other end of my phone. I spared her the details of my existential closet crisis. With Daddy Gil still at the Mayo, she didn't need more on her mind. I only called to hear her voice and had to blame my obvious weeping on the usual daily ailments: exhaustion and Griswold.

"Just take a week and get some sun. What, Gil?" Now that Daddy Gil was feeling better, he often demanded the phone. "Your dad wants to say something, hold on."

Mom handed off the phone, then I heard Daddy Gil's "Hey, Tee."

"Hey Dad, how you feeling?"

"I'd be better if you'd do me a favor."

"Name it."

"I need you girls to escort your mom for Mardi Gras. She's going to be Empress of Argus!"

I was tucked under my comforter as Goldie snoozed on the opposite pillow. Daddy Gil's request caused me to sit up and Goldie to stir. "Wait, what?"

Daddy Gil couldn't answer immediately. He and Mom were arguing on the other end. I heard her vehement "I'm not leaving you for some party!" before he returned. "Tee, you still there?"

"Yes, now what's going on?"

"You know I was asked to be king this year, but the doctors won't let me out of here." Daddy Gil actually sounded . . . hopeful. "I want your mom to be empress in my place."

Not wanting to rain on his literal parade, I hesitated then asked, "How's that even possible? There's a king and a queen, but the queen's always a college girl. I've never heard about an empress."

"Aha! See, this is where it gets interesting." Daddy Gil's voice trembled with excitement. "Did you know that, originally, Argus used to crown an empress instead of a king?" I heard my Mom's muffled "Here he goes again" in the background, but Daddy Gil continued. "That's how it was originally done. The things you learn when you lay in bed all day."

I was still confused. "So they're making Mom the empress to stand in for you as king?"

"Yes, exactly, I talked them into it. But now, your hard-headed mom's refusing to leave my bedside." I heard Mom's continuing muffled protests in the background. I wasn't sure if Daddy Gil was speaking to me or to her but heard him say, "My three girls need to spend time together somewhere other than this godforsaken hospital. You need to stop worrying about me, I'm fine." His voice was suddenly more clear. "I'd be a lot happier if you could get your mom to have some fun." Okay, yeah, that last part, he was definitely talking to me.

"Put her on."

I heard more muffled arguing before Mom got back on the phone. "Don't you start with me, Tee."

I spoke gently, not wanting the import of my words lost to emotion. "Mom, I haven't heard him sound this happy since before Italy."

All her defenses fell away. Though I couldn't see her, I knew Mom's famous sparkling tears would be flowing. "He's more like himself every day."

"He wants to give you this gift. You have to go."

"Fine, I'll go." Mom announced her defeat to Daddy Gil, not me. "But I won't have any fun at all!" I could hear them both laughing and laughing. It was a most joyous sound.

Prudence declined my invitation to Mardi Gras. Hedonism wasn't her style. Netta felt it unsafe to leave Griswold unsupervised with Major Donors, so only Jamie joined me for the trip down South, bringing along his man, Denver. It was a big deal. Jamie never allowed his Minnesota life to overlap with Washington. It was a whole new level of friendship for us.

Mom with her Mardi Gras mini-convention package was undeniable proof I came by my party-planning skills honestly. She'd scheduled five days of nonstop festivities that started as soon as we jumped on the Happy Bus, a stretch Hummer with a full bar that shuttled her ninety-person entourage from the airport to the hotel. The party began on Thursday night but Jamie, Denver, and I arrived with the rest of the late-comers on Friday afternoon. We hugged Mom hello, and slid down the long leather seats to make room for the twenty other colorful and eclectic revelers, most of them gay men and stiff Midwestern conservatives who'd learned that while in the presence of one Hedy Lamarr Sachet, it was best to loosen up and *laissez les bons temps rouler*. Cocktails began immediately. I grabbed Denver's and Jamie's hands in both of mine. "I'm so honored you both are here. We're going to have a fantastic time."

And that's when our BlackBerrys started ringing. Though Mom was hosting at the far end of the Hummer, she shot me a look that meant big trouble. She'd grown to despise my BlackBerry. "Tee, those things are an invasion!"

"Don't get exorcised, Mom." I took the call full well knowing I'd hear about it later. On the line, Netta was furious. Senator Griswold had cancelled yet another trip. "Look, Netta, just continue planning like he's going, because he's going."

Prudence was calling Jamie, wanting him back in town for an Operation Shine charity dinner. Jamie was a fixer, not a fighter. He folded under Prudence's demands. "I have to go back Monday. She needs me to confirm attendees."

Denver was devastated. "But we'll miss the float."

"My eye!" I absolutely wouldn't allow this trip to be ruined. I needed to laugh and drink and party and have a good time. "They're all sponsors. They have to show up anyway."

Jamie wasn't budging. "She needs my help."

Denver resorted to pouting like a good little wife. "She's just jealous you have a life."

"Is there a problem up there, Tee?" Mom's assertive tone caused the revelers to turn as if summoned to the throne.

Jamie swallowed hard. "There's an emergency at work."

Everyone on the Happy Bus booed to show their disdain for work. Mom smoothed over the bad news with her gracious, "That's a shame, but you'll stay for the weekend, won't you?"

"Of course."

"Good, good. Now everyone, I need to have our driver make one quick stop. Does anyone need a topper?" Bottles passed and the party resumed as Mom picked up the limo phone and spoke with the driver.

Denver's pouting darkened into full-scale sulking. Jamie patted his knee. "You can stay and ride the float."

"I'm not going to ride without you, Jamie."

I tried my best to give them space but the Hummer was chocka-block with people and Denver's hurt was palpable. I was relieved when we came to a stop.

Mom clapped her hands and shooed everyone out. We unloaded in front of the Argus warehouse. "I've already been to the China Man and bought our stock throws. There are doubloons and medallions with the Argus Krewe logo for sale inside." Mom handed each of her guests a hundred-dollar bill. "Use this is for specialized throws like stuffed animals or long beads. Everything for sale matches our 'Egyptian Rulers' theme so go wild! While we're here, try on your costumes. If you have any fit issues, let me know and we'll get them back to the seamstress. We'll meet back at the Happy Bus in an hour!"

As Mom offered hundreds to Jamie and Denver, they protested. "We won't be staying."

She pressed the bills into their palms. "Just in case."

The minute we entered the seventeen-thousand-square-foot warehouse, the energy of the entire group skyrocketed from off-the-plane fatigue to childish giddiness. Stalactites of blue, gold, black, and white beads dripped down every square inch of wall surrounding the stunningly beautiful and massive float: an elaborately bejeweled 110-foot-tall replica of the Great Sphinx of Giza. In every corner, people tried on their poly-satin blend togas and personalized them with blue sequined masks, gold beaded collars, white feathered headpieces, and shimmering black Cleopatra wigs. The room was electric with glee.

Mom modeled her outrageous feathered headpiece and twirled me into a black boa. Jamie snapped a photo "for Daddy Gil" as Denver stared, agape, at the spectacle that is a krewe warehouse four days before Mardi Gras. "It's like I've died and gone to drag-queen heaven. *I love it down here!*"

Denver was beaming. His smile was so infectious, Jamie laughed out loud, "Screw Prudence. I can't miss this." And there, in the middle of a million beads and a Hummer full of Republicans, Jamie kissed Denver. A big juicy kiss right on the mouth.

I squealed with delight. Jamie was so relaxed, so free! Mom gave them both big hugs and pecks on their cheeks. "I'm thrilled you're staying!" She shot me a quick wink and disappeared among the frenzy.

Jamie and I made a pact right then and there to turn off our Black-Berrys until Wednesday morning. For just five days, we would be normal people, civilians. No black suits. No ties. No buttoned-up, pressed shirts. No constant demands from needy senators. No call lists, click lines, upset donors, or catering contracts. The only business that needed deciding was which throws would garner us the three Bs of Mardi Gras: Boobs, Butts, and Booze.

The parade was five hours of nonstop dancing, drinking, and bead-throwing. The closest a no-name nobody can come to being an adored rock star. We were lucky enough to have the St. Augustine High School Marching Band leading our forty-float parade and they rocked it. Literally. The Great Sphinx swayed back and forth like a ship lost at sea, everyone too trashed to care. Mom's history-making turn as Empress of Argus was featured in the *Times-Picayune,* but more important, I MET A STRAIGHT GUY!!!!

His name was Kelley and he was abso-flipping-adorable. Sophia, Denver, Jamie, and I had disembarked and were walking Houma

Boulevard with our go cups when Denver decided he needed to be stoned. He kept walking up to random strangers asking for pot. Kelley was one of those strangers.

He was very sexy and I was very tipsy. I reached out and fingered his long brown hair. I died for long hair on guys. D.C.'s men wore nothing but shaved necks and close crops. Queers with ears. I tried, in vain, to speak without slurring. "I-shlove-yuh-hair."

He shot me a smile that could cause a girl's toes to melt. "I'm growing it out for Locks of Love."

My sister, three sheets to the wind, yelled, "It's all over for you, sis!"

Lord, she was right. Not only was the boy hot as heck and growing his hair out to help kids with cancer, he also lived in Mexico, was a certified scuba instructor, and had just won the title of World Masters Surf Champion. He'd even rescued a mutt from the pound.

He ducked his head sheepishly as he recounted, "After I adopted him, this James Taylor song came on the radio, 'You've Got a Friend,' and I know it's so gay but I decided to name him Taylor." Kelley had no political interests or aspirations, no purebred dog, and he willingly used the word "gay" to describe his actions without checking for reporters first. The boy was straight, straight, straight! Maybe I could *finally* sow an oat.

No such luck. Kelley was sharing a hotel room with a huge group of guys and I was rooming with Mom and Sophia. We had to settle for a heavy-duty make-out session in my hotel lobby. So yummy. His hair smelled like spring rain. The desk manager finally told us to get a room. I felt like a troubled teenager.

I slept alone that night (fitfully), but the next morning Kelley joined the Sachet entourage for our Ash Wednesday breakfast. It could have been a total disaster, kicking a brand-new love interest out of the skillet and into the fire, but Kelley was completely unfazed. Everything about him seemed solid, pure, and honest. Denver and Jamie adored him. Mom called him a "really good guy" and Sophia pulled me aside to voice her astonishment. "What did you do to him? He's totally infatuated with you already!"

I couldn't stop smiling. It was a strange new feeling. A *genuine* smile. "I know!"

Kelley had to fly back to Mexico that afternoon. He wrapped his strong hands around my hips and pulled me closer. "When are you coming to see me?"

"Let me look at my calendar." I surreptitiously turned on my BlackBerry, not wanting Jamie to catch me cheating. As the screen flickered white, I skipped the dozens of pending e-mail messages and scrolled through dates. "Not this weekend or the next, but the one after?"

Kelley whispered in my ear, "It's a date," then nipped at my neck. We kissed goodbye and I watched him walk away, imagining the blue-green waters of the gulf gliding over his shoulder blades. Oh, in three little weeks I was going to eat that boy alive.

I tried my best, I did, but I couldn't resist the temptation of a quick voice mail check. Thank God I did. There were dozens of frantic calls from Netta and Prudence. Franklin and Jamie had been dubbed the first recipients of a blogger's "Roy Cohn Award" for outstanding achievement against the gay community. I ducked into the hotel lobby to call Prudence for details. "I don't get it. A blogger is suddenly a credible threat?"

Prudence was frustrated I hadn't called sooner. Her voice was a bit testy. "It's not just the blog. He's on *O'Reilly* tonight."

"Have you talked to Franklin?"

"Franklin's not answering his phones. Has Jamie heard yet?"

"No." I was completely sick to my stomach. These past few days with Jamie, I'd seen his loving, affectionate, playful spirit and now, with this news, I knew he'd hide himself away. "I'll tell him."

I didn't have to. He and Denver had opted not to fly back to D.C. that night and were already barricaded in their suite, Jamie incessantly reading aloud the online fallout.

I did my best to calm him down. "Senator Ivy's a loyal man; he won't let this affect your relationship."

But Denver was rubbing salt in open wounds. "Senator Ivy will toe the party line. If they tell him to bash us, he'll bash us." Denver directed the full force of his anger directly at Jamie. "And you still raise money for those people!"

Jamie stopped reading and fought back. "I've worked for Ivy longer than I've known you. He has to do whatever it takes to stay in office. The guys that want him out, Denver, they're worse."

Denver wouldn't let it go. "I'm just saying, there are consequences to your actions. National consequences."

"Ivy's been more of a father to me than my own. And you know that. If he needs me to step down, I'll step down. But I won't ever abandon him."

"It's idol worship!"

"Stop, Denver, okay, enough." Jamie locked himself in the bathroom as Denver took over with the laptop. He yelled through the closet door. "Listen to this one. *How can a gay man work to elect those that would ensure his own second-class citizenship?* It's a good question, Jamie, how are you going to answer that one?"

Jamie yelled back, "Enough!"

Denver continued clicking through sites, his mania fueled not by fear or panic but by joy.

"Denver," I whispered so Jamie couldn't hear my horrible question. "Are you happy about this?"

Denver looked me straight in the eyes. "I don't live in D.C., Temple. I live in Minnesota. Jamie's work makes life harder for me."

"He could lose everything he's worked to accomplish."

"Maybe then I'd see him more than twice a month and we could have an actual life."

It was clearly an ongoing and endless argument between the two. I knocked on the bathroom door to let Jamie know I was leaving. "I love you, darling, this will all blow over and you'll be fine."

Denver stood to see me out. "You should stop enabling his hypocrisy."

I hugged Denver. "I'm his friend. It's my job to love him unconditionally. Let the rest of the world judge him. They already do."

That night, I holed up with Mom and Sophia to watch O'Reilly chastise the blogger while managing to out a state supreme court judge himself. Jamie was never mentioned by name but as O'Reilly's obnoxious in-your-face style turned the interview into a yelling match, Franklin was identified outright.

Jamie survived the fallout. Senator Ivy was, in spite of his public facade, privately loyal to Jamie. He allowed the storm to blow over. Franklin wasn't as lucky. Senator Griswold's Kitchen Cabinet had presidential plans. They didn't want a gay man running his upcoming campaign. Never mind that Franklin had spent his last thirteen years successfully turning an obese hick into a congressman into the chair of the Senate Committee. Senator Griswold asked Franklin to join him for a walk (which, given Griswold's girth, should have been the warning sign), and on the sidewalk outside the Capitol, fired him.

Goldie and I did make that promised trip to Mexico. We stepped off the plane in Cancun, the gulf breeze blowing Kelley's sexy hair into his eyes. Kelley lived half an hour south, near Puerto Morelos, and drove an old yellow Scout with a hula dancer shimmying on the dashboard. Goldie and Taylor cozied up in the back seat. Taylor was a border collie mix, easily three times Goldie's size. She loved him instantly and wiggled her tiny tail to please him. He reciprocated with a nose nudge to share his Frisbee.

We went kayaking and it was clear that, after years spent pecking at BlackBerrys and nibbling from buffet tables, I had absolutely no upper-body strength. "Can't we just get to the beer?"

Kelley thought I was joking. He was an active, outdoorsy type who loved everybody and everything. Kelley was cool with the world. He just wasn't cool with us sowing an oat so early in the relationship.

"I like you, Temple, a lot. I want to give us time to be a couple before we, you know, *couple.*" I'm quite certain my jaw dropped out of my kayak and sank to the bottom of the coral reef. Somehow, amongst the Mardi Gras debauchery, I'd met a man who wanted a girlfriend. So much for just sowing an oat. Kelley wanted to fall in love.

I was game. Kelley was amazing. He challenged me physically with the kayaking, the snorkeling, the hiking. He was an extreme-sports guy. He'd been bungee jumping and skydiving, and he'd backpacked through Costa Rica and New Zealand. Everything that scared me to death but sounded like fun, Kelley had already done.

We'd been so busy kayaking, hiking, and surfing (well, he surfed with his buddy Shade, and I lay on the beach eyeing the waves for shark fins) we hadn't really had a chance to *talk* talk. I wasn't sure what Kelley thought about . . . well, anything. Watching him rise from the surf, slinging his wet hair out of his face, his smooth chest speckled with sand, I decided to pull a Scarlett O'Hara and think about it tomorrow.

Franklin was thinking about his tomorrows as well. Before the blog-ger blow-up, he had surrendered to Evan's wishes and they'd pur-chased a brand-new house together. The mortgage payments were already stacking up and Franklin was panicked. So panicked, in fact, that while I was in Mexico he called three times to set up a lunch. We weren't exactly best friends, but I did respect his work ethic and I cer-tainly didn't want him to lose his house. I agreed to meet for lunch.

To the untrained eye, Franklin appeared "fine," but this was a man who had office furniture custom built around the art hung on his walls. A man who never allowed a speck of dust to alight on any surface associated with his being. For him to arrive with his tie slightly askew, no matching kerchief in his breast pocket, and a tiny spot of ink on his right sleeve was beyond disconcerting. It was notice of the pending apocalypse.

His voice held steady but his confidence was shattered. "If you ever want to find out who your true friends are, get yourself fired. My circle gets smaller and smaller."

Franklin needed a strong shot of optimism to lift him out of his rut. I put on my best hopeful smile. "We just have to build you a new circle."

Franklin wasn't biting. "Who's going to take my calls?"

"Lobbyists, darling, lobbyists!" Despite my strong misgivings about lobbyists, I knew Franklin's senatorial relationships would make him a prized possession. I also knew his lobbyist hubby, Evan, could find him a job in a heartbeat. But Franklin would *never* allow Evan to pick up the phone on his behalf. Though he'd been "outed," his relationship was still a closely guarded secret. Franklin was going to have to start from scratch.

"You need to take the guys from Akin Gump to breakfast at La Colline. You need to take the Food Marketers Association to dinner at the Capital Grille. You need to grab a group from Preston Gates, from Hogan & Hartson. You'll turn those meals into relationships."

Franklin's entire spirit brightened at the suggestion. "Maybe I should have an open house? Meet all of them at once instead?"

"Yes, yes, let's make a party! I'll do the calls."

Franklin did throw an open house. Evan and Jamie repainted their brand-new dining room, Franklin rented a huge tent, and Occasions catered. I called the 450 lobbyists I had as personal contacts then played the little wife, picking out linens and the menu. Netta was assigned to greet partygoers while Evan discreetly disappeared for the weekend, removing all trace of his existence.

Though Prudence wasn't able to help with our preparations, she brought Senator Olin, the jack-in-the-box dancer, as her escort to the open house. They were now "officially" attending events as a couple.

Prudence had tried, unsuccessfully, to keep Senator Olin at arm's length. They'd met twenty years earlier, when he was a young superstar congressman and considered a bit of a wild card. He was a big-game hunter, a gambler, and a ladies' man, and his libido received more coverage than his legislation. Prudence knew better than to get involved, though they stayed in friendly contact.

Years passed and Congressman Olin became Senator Olin. He mellowed and gave up skirt-chasing and gambling for a short marriage that ended in a nasty divorce and two even nastier kids. Senator Olin was now a part-time father and looking for his second marriage. Prudence still would not date him.

Having come from the House, Senator Olin was considered B Team. He hadn't come from the private sector, where most senators made their magnanimous fortunes. He wasn't the son or the grandson of an American institution like a Rockefeller. He hadn't been a governor, which is like being a king; he'd come from the Second District of Idaho as a congressman. And the embedded senators, the old guys, the A Team, didn't like it one bit.

Senator Olin's existence gave the lifers an excuse to puff out their chests and feel the weight of their own mystique. They didn't like that Senator Olin moved from junior varsity to varsity. They didn't want to see him out of his old basement office and in the senatorial dining room; they wanted to kick him out of his new, carpeted digs and send him back to the House mess hall where he belonged.

With all that said, in twenty years, his affection for Prudence had never wavered. He was persistent, if not effective. Prudence finally allowed their friendship to blossom into full-fledged romance after a Senator Raines fundraiser in Baltimore.

Now, I had no interest in attending a fundraiser for Raines, despite his overwhelming popularity, his suspected eventual run for the presidency, and the fact that, technically, I worked for each and every senator, including him. Raines was one of those "lifers," a four-time senator and a mean son-of-a-gun who had been known to physically bully other senators if he didn't like the way they voted. He surrounded himself with even nastier people. His chief strategist was a sneaky dirt-digger who viewed elections as warfare. He'd destroy a candidate's family life if he felt it'd make a good sound bite.

Raines had more enemies in his own Party than he had across the aisle, but his popularity among Americans made him untouchable. This meant we all had to smile and make nice with his despicable entourage. The meanest of them all was Dominica Alfaro, Prudence's business partner and Raines's fundraiser.

Dominica stood all of 5'2" but she was slippery as a snake. Originally from Puerto Rico, she could have been forty-five or sixty-five, her skin aged by the sun and pure orneriness. She was what I'd call a Queen Bee fundraiser, the kind that expects donors to ingratiate themselves for access. For Dominica, it was just as much about her as it was about the candidate. She saw herself not as a caretaker of donors but instead a gatekeeper of power. She placed donors in a position of subservience. It was an approach that only worked if a Queen Bee attached herself to a candidate with extreme popularity, which was exactly what Dominica had done. For the last ten years she'd been "all things Raines," making her extremely valuable to Prudence's company.

Jamie and Franklin hated her. They didn't trust her one bit. The boys subscribed to a philosophy of "felt but not seen." They believed the cause should be the headline. If you were truly doing your job, nobody should have known who you were. If you were into self-promotion, you were to be kept at arm's length. But Prudence clearly trusted Dominica enough to start a business with her, so I figured the boys were wrong.

Prudence invited me to the Raines fundraiser because it was held on the *Pride of Baltimore II*, a reproduction Baltimore Clipper that normally sailed the seas as a Goodwill Ambassador from the State of Maryland. The topsail schooner had returned home to her berth in the Inner Harbor and Prudence thought that, given my love of boating, I'd want to join the party.

Cruising Chesapeake Bay in that majestic vessel was truly a once-in-a-lifetime experience. Funny, it wasn't the only one I had that night. I witnessed the normally stoic Prudence spontaneously combust into tears.

Senator Olin was also on board, regaling donors with stupid jokes. "Moshe Katsav, Osama bin Laden, and Uncle Sam find a genie in a bottle. The genie says, 'I'll grant you each one wish.' Katsav says,

'I want a cease-fire between Israel and Pakistan.' The genie nods his head and POOF! There's a cease-fire. Bin Laden is amazed so he says, 'I want a wall around Afghanistan so no Jews or Americans can come in.' The genie nods and POOF! A huge wall rises up around Afghanistan. Uncle Sam is impressed. He says, 'That's some wall.' The genie is flattered and brags, 'It's fifteen thousand feet high, five hundred feet thick, and completely surrounds the country; nothing can get in or out—it's impenetrable.' Uncle Sam says, 'I'd like my wish now. Fill Afghanistan with water.'"

The donors standing near Senator Olin smiled politely but they were clearly uncomfortable. Later that night, Dominica badmouthed Olin, knowing full well Prudence had feelings for the man. "He's an idiot. I don't know why you fool with him. He's an embarrassment."

Prudence didn't say anything at the time, but once we were safely in her car, driving back to D.C., she lost it. She was heaving and sobbing so hard, I made her pull over so we wouldn't crash.

In the stark white glow of a gas station's fluorescent lights, Prudence leaned against her steering wheel and bawled. "People think he's ridiculous."

In the four years we'd been friends, I'd never seen Prudence so completely unhinged. But everyone has their own alpha and Dominica was Prudence's. And that night, she'd hit a nerve. I had to talk Prudence down.

I unhooked my seat belt and shifted in my seat so I could face her directly. "Dominica is just jealous that someone loves you. Her husband dumped her and stole her two kids! She wants you to stay single and miserable."

Prudence dug in her purse for tissues. "Why can't he see how other people see him?"

"Who cares what other people think! If you like him, give him a chance, because he's absolutely crazy about you." In typical Sachet fashion, I got emotional too. My eyes welled with tears. "Trust me, not a one of those gossipers gives a hoot about your happiness. Not even Dominica."

"You're right. You're right." Prudence shook off her upset and unhooked her own seat belt. "I think you'd better drive."

Prudence took my advice to heart and Senator Olin gladly became a more permanent fixture in her life. She could not have kept him away from Franklin's open house if she'd tried.

He pumped Franklin's entire arm with his firm handshake. "Young man, looks to me like you've landed on both feet." Senator Olin gestured to the crush of politicos and players in the tent. Netta had collected nearly five hundred business cards at the door. Senators, including those running on pro-family platforms, hobnobbed with lobbyists, all brandishing skewers of steak kebabs. Even Senator Sears, the most vocally homophobic of the bunch, had shown up, giving Franklin a hug and saying, "We're all behind you."

"Sometimes that thing around your neck isn't a tie, it's an albatross," Olin whispered, referring to Senator Griswold, who'd just arrived with his vicious wife. Their presence signaled to all that Franklin could be hired without political repercussions.

Jamie had even less patience for Senator Griswold than I did. "Oh, *now* he does the right thing."

Franklin wisely kept his mouth shut and excused himself to greet his former boss. The rest of us watched as they shook hands, smiled, and played the game.

Senator Olin wrapped an arm around Prudence's shoulder. He joked, "You'd better snatch Franklin up before you end up competitors."

Prudence stiffened under his touch, not one for public displays of affection. "He doesn't need me. Temple's handed him every lobbyist in town!"

I laughed off my influence but it was true—the vast majority of the revelers were my contacts. It was also true Franklin no longer needed our help. Post-party, he landed a cushy million-dollar position with PhRMA, the Pharmaceutical Researchers and Manufacturers of America. Franklin was now in the lobbying biz, representing the country's biggest pharmaceutical and biotech companies. The blogger had been but a blip. Franklin's world wide web of influence had actually expanded.

Still, his untimely departure left me in a terrible position to handle the upcoming Senate Celebration, an annual formal cocktail reception for our top one thousand donors. Mrs. Griswold had used the Franklin outing as an opportunity to hetero-fy Griswold's entire staff. She fired the gay scheduler, the gay policy director, the gay assistants, even the gay driver. Lost without Franklin's guidance, Griswold was in a state of chaos. Unable to remember appointments or dress himself and afraid to speak with the press, Griswold opted out entirely. He began taking long naps, using his Committee office in our building as a hideout from his dictator wife. The Senate Celebration was our next big fundraiser and we could not fall behind. But Griswold was beyond useless.

It was ridiculous to keep running home every morning when I had a private shower attached to my office. I surrendered to my reality and moved a week's worth of suits, toiletries, shoes, bras, and undies into the office. I even bought a new pillow for my sleeping bag. Sadly, it felt like I was "treating" myself.

I spent the entire lonely weekend creating a PowerPoint slide show in order to convince Senator MacLeish to chair the Senate

Celebration. I knew MacLeish was Senator Griswold's arch enemy, but I didn't care. Griswold had shown his true colors by firing Franklin. I still worked for the man but I didn't have to like him.

Senator MacLeish agreed to chair the Senate Celebration. In fact, he was so enthusiastic he tasked Bob Welby to help. Now, every woman on the Hill knew Bob Welby, aka "Slick." Meticulously dressed in custom-made suits and handmade loafers, he was a seventy-year-old pervert trying his darnedest to look like a twenty-four-year-old stud. His wife had had so many facelifts that her forehead started behind her ears.

Slick was an old-school sexist pig. Female fundraisers tolerated him only because he had the Midas touch in Nevada and more money than God. If your guy was running for office west of the Mississippi and you needed a war chest, Slick was who you called. He was a one-man phenomenon responsible for establishing the highest-level donor programs in the Republican Party. He was also an a-double-s. But beggars can't be choosers and I needed all the help I could get.

For the next four weeks, Senator MacLeish and I ironed out every detail of the Celebration, from ticketing to centerpieces. And every time that phone rang with Griswold on the other line I could happily announce, "I'm sorry, Senator MacLeish is on his way over for a meeting so I can't help you right now." I could hear his blood boiling.

He brought it on himself. While Griswold was sleeping, Slick and MacLeish not only saved the Senate Celebration, they saved our entire finance department. Our goal was $5 million and they raised nine. We were now $1 million ahead and Good Old Blubberboy was taking all the credit. I caught two minutes of him huffing and puffing on *Meet the Press* telling Tim Russert, "We'll win in November because Americans believe in the Republican Party. They trust us and they support us. We'll win it for the American people."

The night before the Celebration, Slick asked to meet for "a quick drink to discuss tomorrow's final details." Late for our meeting, I was trying to force my bulging logistics binder closed when the pit of my stomach rolled with a creepy unease. I walked down the hall and knocked on Netta's door.

"Hey, listen, I'm meeting Bob Welby at Charlie Palmer's then I'm heading home. I'll have my phone."

Netta stopped her work and looked me over. "Button up one." I was wearing a brown Valentino shirtdress with the top two buttons undone. "You'll give the perv a heart attack."

I rolled my eyes at Netta but followed her advice and buttoned up. "Funny girl. See you in the morning."

I spotted Slick tucked into a deep cushioned banquette near a fireplace as I made my way past the glass-encased wine cellar suspended over a shallow pool of water. I'd been here a million times and still this oppressive "water feature" struck me odd. Slick stood at my arrival, but not because he was a gentleman, no. He wanted to make sure I saw tonight's custom-made ensemble: his navy pinstriped suit, brushed-silk dress shirt, and matching loafers. Yeah, I get it, Slick, you've got money.

I ordered the Shiraz and hauled the Celebration binder, stuffed with seating arrangements, dietary restrictions, floor plan, and minute-by-minute cue sheet, onto the table with a thud.

"I know you're meeting MacLeish for dinner so I'll keep this brief."

Slick reached across the table and grabbed my hand.

"It's such a shame I made plans or we could go back to my hotel."

I pulled my hand away. My lungs constricted with shock. "Excuse me?"

"I'm staying at the St. Regis. We could meet after—"

I stood so violently, the Shiraz reddened the white linen table-cloth and spilled like blood down the front of my dress.

"I have to get back to the office."

I rushed out to Constitution Avenue and prayed for the miracle of a quick cab. No such luck. Slick spotted me on the corner.

"Temple, wait!"

As I watched the old man's feeble attempt to run toward me, I convinced myself to accept his apology with grace. We had the Celebration to suffer through tomorrow. I just had to deal with him for one more day.

But Slick didn't apologize. He grabbed my breasts. "You have the most beautiful, firm tits!"

I tried to scream but he stuck his creepy grandpa tongue down my throat; it was like being French-kissed by an iguana. I pushed Slick off and immediately burst into tears. A cab screeched to a stop beside me and I jumped into the back seat. The Pakistani driver was already screaming through the passenger-side window. "What you do to this woman! I see you! I see you!"

I sucked in sharp sips of air, trying to breathe.

"He attack you! Are you okay?"

"No, yes, no, please—" I couldn't make a sentence. "Just drive." My office. I needed to get to my office. I'd get there and I'd calm down and I'd be okay. But as soon as I got upstairs, my crying morphed into howling. Netta heard my moans and rushed in. From the look on my face, she instinctively knew.

"That son of a bitch!"

Within twenty minutes, Netta had rallied the troops. Jamie, Franklin, and Prudence arrived as if miraculously transported by tractor beam. Jamie was beside himself, infuriated. "Where'd he go?"

"He was meeting MacLeish at 701."

Before we could protest, Jamie ran from the room with an "I'm going to kill him!" that actually frightened Prudence.

"You don't think he'll do anything, do you?"

"I'm on it." Franklin was already on his BlackBerry.

"Shake it off, Sachet, shake it off." Netta offered me a coffee mug filled with water. I held the cool ceramic in my hands as she rubbed my back to ease me down. She offered proudly, "You know, I'm the one who turfed his lawn."

My whimpers instantly ceased and Franklin's eyes bugged out of his head. Many a fundraiser had speculated over the gal who'd so publicly shamed Slick and all this time, the hero had silently walked among us.

I was stunned. "Get out of town!"

"I went to his house; he told me his wife would be there, and we were supposed to be reviewing donor lists. He comes out in this short silk robe with his balls hanging out." We all winced from the image— yuck—as she continued. "He's got two glasses of some kind of liquor like this is going to be our romantic interlude! Well, I just grabbed one of those glasses and I threw it in his face." We burst into spontaneous applause. "Wait, it gets better. I run to my car and I can't see because my hair came loose and my heels were sticking in his yard."

The thought of Netta running in high heels with her braid unraveling was too much for us all. Anger melted into hysterical laughter. "That's when I realized the grass was wet so I drove donuts all over his front yard. I wonder how he explained that to his wife!"

Even the normally reserved Prudence was laughing out loud. She said, "Temple, remember that young guy, Mark, was that his name, that Barrymore donor in Kansas City?"

"Oh, Marcus. He knocks on our hotel door and invites us to have a drink in the bar. So Prudence lets him in then goes downstairs to get her luggage. I go into the bathroom to freshen up and when I come out, he's got the radio playing some sappy Barry Manilow song and he's opened up the champagne from the minibar and he says, 'Why don't we ask Prudence to get another room?'"

Franklin was so weakened by laughter that the couch seemed to be swallowing him whole. He squeaked out, "Did he think Manilow turned you on?"

"I know! I yelled at him, 'Are you crazy? What should we do, call your wife?,' and I threw him out. Not only was he a jerk, but I had to pay for that champagne!"

Prudence teased me, "You were angrier about the champagne than the come-on."

"Hotels charge a fortune for the minibar!"

"I can top you all," bragged Franklin. "Senator Enslet asked me to pee for him."

"What!" Prudence covered her mouth in horror.

Netta screeched like a needle across the face of an album. "He wanted you to pee on him?!"

"No, he wanted to watch me pee."

Netta shook her hands as if flinging disgust out of her body through her fingertips. "Where did he want you to do this?"

"I don't know, Netta. I didn't stick around for the details!"

"Oh my God! Oh my God!"

I threw up my hands in defeat. "It's official. Franklin, you win. A pee request trumps a boob grab any day."

Finally our laughter subsided and dinner was ordered via Netta's husband, Zack, who was loudly heralded as our "savior" when he arrived with three large pies and a case of cold Sam Adams. As heels came off and ties loosened, Prudence talked out my future dealings with Slick.

"We all have to eat a little crow with him because we need him for campaigns." I was quite touched by Prudence's indignation on my behalf. She was fired up. "But really, he needs you more now than you need him. You could blackball him from all Senate events. You could turn MacLeish against him."

"Oh my God, we forgot about Jamie!" That was Franklin tossing down his slice and grabbing his BlackBerry. Netta was already dialing from my desk phone.

Prudence wasn't finished with me. "You should cause him some problems."

"Jamie! Jamie! Where are you?" Netta had Jamie on speakerphone.

"I'm outshide sheven-oh-one in my truck. I'm gonna be' him up."

Netta yelled into the speaker, "Are you drunk, Jamie?"

"Jus' a little. Jus' needed a drink 'fore I kill 'im. Gotta bottle of Stoli Razberi wi' me righ' here."

Franklin headed for the door. Zack joined him.

"Listen to me, Jamie. Franklin and Zack are on the way. I want you to put that bottle under your seat and take your keys out of the ignition. The last thing we need is your mug shot on the front page of tomorrow's *Post*." I could see the headline already: MAJORITY LEADER CHIEF OF STAFF—DRUNK AND READY TO KILL.

Franklin and Zack got to Jamie before he did something stupid. And I went home to crawl into bed before tomorrow's big event. Prudence's words kept running through my mind. She was never a woman to advocate revenge. She'd been in the business so long she embodied the political. She was always even-tempered, always weighed each word carefully before opening her mouth. For her to suggest I had power to wield and that I should do so filled me with strength and courage. I knew what had to be done.

At 7:00 the next morning I called Slick on his cell. He was in his car and made the mistake of putting me on speaker.

"Bob, this is Temple. I need you to come into the office ASAP."

From the pregnant pause on the other end of the line, I could tell Slick was terrified of what I might broadcast through the interior of his Mercedes.

"I'm driving *my wife* to the airport. Is this something we can handle now?"

"No, we need to speak in person."

"Oh, uh, well, I've got *my wife* here in the car with me so—"

"I'll be in my office until noon but I'd like to meet with you sooner."

"Yes, okay, but *my wife* is here with me."

"Do you think you can be here by 9:30?"

"Uh, well, yes, I just need to drop off *my wife*—"

He must have mentioned his wife five more times before we hung up. Either the woman suspected her husband was up to no good or her facelifts had pulled her ears so tight that she could no long hear.

At 9:30 precisely, Slick strutted in and I directed him to sit in a chair by my fireplace. I sat opposite and took a deep, cleansing breath to contain my anger. It was important to remain professional and civilized. I wasn't going to give him the ability to dismiss my words as an "emotional outburst" from a "hysterical" woman.

"You have embarrassed yourself and you have betrayed me. Senator MacLeish trusted that you would be a responsible, productive, and upstanding part of what he's trying to accomplish. You've shown yourself to be completely morally reprehensible. If I find that you have been in a situation with any of the young girls on my staff without supervision by me or Jeanette, I will tell the senator, I will tell his chief of staff, I will tell *The Hill,* and I will destroy you." The anger had subsided and I was warmed by an inner calm. "Make sure you completely understand. You took control of me for five minutes but I have the control back now and you will never, while I'm in this position, do that to any other woman again. Because I will always be watching you. You can leave now."

When Slick stood, I didn't even recognize him. His Botoxed face had somehow aged and wrinkled. His back slumped. The arrogance had gone out of his eyes. He seemed to me a broken man. He squeaked out a "Yes, Miss Sachet" and shuffled to the escalator. I forced myself to ignore a sinking feeling of pity and reminded myself he was beyond lecherous; he was dangerous. I turned to find Netta standing behind me.

"You did the right thing."

The Celebration still had to go on. In thirty years, it'd never been cancelled and I certainly wasn't going to be known as the finance director who dropped the ball because some perv grabbed my boob. Twelve hundred people were attending and more important, I'd invited Kelley to come for the party and the weekend. I wanted him to meet Prudence and Netta. I wanted the Celebration to go off without a hitch.

For the main reception, I'd asked the caterer to design interactive stations that turned food into spectacle. We had an omelette station where they served tasty bite-size quiches and freshly prepared frittatas, a fantasy dessert station, and a sushi station with a master chef rolling sushi, which was clearly Kelley's favorite. You could take the boy out of the ocean but you couldn't take the ocean out of the boy.

I appreciated that Kelley bought a suit and tie just for the occasion. Visibly, he stuck out like a sore thumb with his hair in a ponytail and his sunny glow. But Kelley had the remarkable ability to be comfortable, to be content, no matter the situation. He watched me flit about the room with pride and love in his eyes. Every time I looked over, I caught him smiling back. He and Prudence had been talking for twenty minutes and I was glad to see them hitting it off. It seemed the rest of the night would fly blissfully by, uneventful.

Until Griswold opened his brainless mouth. We'd moved the senators and Major Donors, those who'd raised more than $100,000, upstairs to a private dinner in a beautiful room dramatically lit by huge candelabras. Senator MacLeish had, as Celebration chairman, given the reception speech, but politically, I had to allow Griswold to do *something*. He was the chair of the Committee after all, and his wife would make my life a total nightmare if I slighted her husband.

I'd given Griswold a comprehensive list of people that needed to be thanked from the podium. Each senator was to receive a Swarovski crystal Capitol building; the donors would be given engraved sterling silver boxes. Senator Griswold decided to recognize only those senators he considered friends and totally blew off the donor gifts. People were furious. I was furious. Kelley could see it in my face; I needed a real drink. "Let's me and you take the gang out for shots."

All the staffers headed for Tequila Grill, where Kelley bought the first round. I did deserve a toast in my honor; the night had been a raging success. The RSCC had raised $9 million and was now, thankfully, over budget. Best of all, Kelley was the cat's meow. He absolutely owned the room. Sorority Row—my delicate, WASPy, young, pretty female junior staffers—was in a complete tizzy, the girls falling all over themselves to catch his eye. But Kelley only had eyes for me.

Netta pulled me over to the table she was sharing with Prudence and Jamie. Franklin had opted out of attending Senator Griswold's dinner, the wounds still a bit too fresh. Netta fanned herself with a cocktail napkin. "Three words: Hot, hot, hot!"

Jamie salted the back of his left hand, prepping for his next shot. "I told you he was unbelievable."

Prudence smiled but said nothing. I wanted to hear what she thought about Kelley. "You two were talking for quite a while."

Prudence nodded. "He's nice to look at, that's for sure."

Jamie tossed back his shot with an "Amen," then squinted hard against the burn. "Wooh!"

Prudence was holding back. It worried me but I smiled through my question. "You don't like him?"

Prudence glanced over at Kelley ordering drinks from the bar. She lowered her voice. "Intellectually, he can't push you. You need a man with a point of view, a man that does the *Times* crossword puzzle over breakfast. In ink." I knew Prudence was looking out for me but it felt like she'd just punched me in the stomach. "You two are from completely different worlds. Where's it go from here?"

I couldn't answer her question. Yet. All I knew was being with Kelley was like being on the boat with my family. Easy and comfortable, things just flowed without me having to lift a finger. For days after his visits, I found Post-it notes on the dryer, on the dishwasher, and in the cabinets. "I love you." "Are you smiling today?" Kelley wanted to marry me. He wanted blonde-haired babies running up and down the beaches of Mexico. He wanted to teach a son to surf. He wanted us to have a nice life together.

That's what he wanted.

{ *Seven* }

Strength Feels Like Weakness

*D*addy Gil had been at the Mayo Clinic nearly ten months when the doctors said he could finally go home. He'd made tremendous progress, enough that Mom was able to get him out of bed and wheel him to the hospital courtyard for fresh air and a change of scenery. He'd learned to use a walker and regained his upper-body strength quickly, though his legs were still weak. Doctors felt he'd soon be walking if he kept up his physical therapy. He would need nursing care and careful monitoring of his medications, but Daddy Gil would get to celebrate his seventieth birthday in St. Louis, in his own home, in his own bed. The worst was over.

We were beside ourselves with joy. I called Netta to share the glad tidings and let her know I had to extend my weekend. "Oh Temple, this is wonderful, wonderful news! I'll let everyone know!"

Mom and Nana began packing up the rented apartment while Sophia flew to St. Louis to oversee making the house wheelchair-accessible. Their absence gave me precious uninterrupted days to spend with Daddy Gil as he tottered through the hospital hallways on his walker. Daddy Gil had lots of questions. All of which were about me: my work, my friends, my parties, and most important, my love life.

"When's this Kelley going to give you a ring already?" Daddy Gil had been padding along in his hospital gown and booties for over half an hour. "I need some grandchildren."

I hovered beside with the wheelchair. Just in case. "Hold your horses there, Mr. Matchmaker, let's get you completely well first."

Daddy Gil was slowing. "He loves you. You love him. What's the problem?"

"There's no real problem." I kept a steady gaze on his feet, anxious he might slip. "We're just, you know, from different worlds, so . . . "

Daddy Gil struggled to push the walker, but it barely budged. Undeterred, he dragged his right foot forward. "Ah, I see. You want someone perfect. Tee, honey, nobody's perfect."

I squeezed the handles of the wheelchair tighter, nervous Daddy Gil might tumble any minute but not wanting him to feel badgered by my constant help. "That's not true. You and Mom have the perfect marriage."

Daddy Gil focused now on his left foot, a baby step that took herculean effort. "We had our awkward beginnings. We had growing pains. We weren't always tender and considerate of each other. We weren't always this in love."

"I don't remember those parts."

"They existed. Don't miss out because your Mom and I were selfish and spoiled you rotten." Daddy Gil was exhausted. "That's enough for now."

I flipped the brakes down on the wheels and helped him sit. I folded his walker into thirds and hung it from the back of the wheelchair. "Ready to roll?"

Daddy Gil gave me the thumbs up. "Ready."

I rolled him toward his room, his muscles so fatigued he almost drifted to sleep before we reached his bed. Under his breath, I heard him sweetly murmur, "I spoiled you rotten. Just rotten."

Sophia decided Daddy Gil's birthday could not pass uncelebrated. She'd filled the St. Louis house with birthday paraphernalia, hung balloons and Mardi Gras beads around his bed, taped a huge WELCOME HOME BIRTHDAY BOY banner to the walls, and hung colorful streamers from the ceiling.

We rolled Daddy Gil through the front door and were pleasantly startled to see Cecil and Hattie eagerly awaiting his arrival. Sophia had flown them in from Metairie just for the occasion. "Surprise!" Everyone burst into spontaneous tears of joy. Hugs, kisses, and love filled the room.

Sophia bought a sugar-free applesauce cake for our diabetic dad but splurged on full-sugar birthday cupcakes for everyone else. Our rendition of "Happy Birthday" came off like a rambunctious drinking song and our celebration lasted long into the night. It was more than a happy birthday. It was a miracle. Daddy Gil was home.

By Wednesday, I had to get back to work. The car came to drive me to the airport and it was my routine to give Nana a hug, Sophia a hug, and Mom a hug, then to kiss Daddy Gil and leave. But something felt wrong. I was scared to leave them. Scared to be alone, without my family. It was as if I'd been transported back to that bus in Italy with my double-strapped tourist purse. I could feel the thief coming to steal me away. I knew he would toss me under the tires and take all that I had. I knew something terrible was lurking just outside the doors.

I masked my hysterical paranoia by saying, "I'm just so happy," "I'm so thrilled you're home," but a deep, inexplicable dread ate at my stomach. What was wrong with me?

I returned to work to find a stunningly beautiful bouquet of magnolia blossoms waiting on my desk. The card was signed by Jamie, Franklin, Netta, and Prudence: "Little Sis, You are our steel magnolia. Blessings for your dad's continued recovery." In a town predicated on jealousy and competitiveness, I'd found the true cream of the crop. My friends protected and loved and cared for one another. I was a lucky girl.

Even if my job was driving me crazy. The races consuming my life were the same ones nagging at my conscience, the ones that caused my breakdown in the closet with the president. A breakdown I tried every day to forget. I'd done my best to keep the creepiest senators at bay but now it was all senators, all the time.

There was a group of gynecologists in Maine called Tastemakers Select who met twice a year for a wine-tasting. There were exactly one hundred men in the group and because Senator Sears was also a gynecologist, they wanted him to host their tasting.

The senator was decidedly younger than most, but already hiding his receding hairline with a heavily gelled comb-over. A little runt of a man with pointy teeth and troubled skin, his icky personality, violent homophobia, and constant paranoia made him just as ugly on the inside as he was on the out. I had no desire to help Senator Sears; he made my stomach churn.

I thought a smart way to make the Tastemakers Select tasting disappear was to require all their members to pay our $5,000 Patriot donor fee in order to attend. My plan backfired in a major way. Amazingly, all the men joined. They mailed me an envelope stuffed with a hundred checks totaling a half-million dollars and then I was stuck. Not only was the party on, but I'd have to attend.

Walking into the maroon-and-beige banquet hall of their local Marriot, the senator seemed inconvenienced and condescending. "I don't know what I'm supposed to do here."

Bull-pucky he didn't know what to do. He'd been a senator for a full term now. He knew how to shake hands and greet people. I bit my tongue and said politely, "Do you need me to staff you?"

That seemed to do the trick. The senator puffed himself up. "I know how to say hello to people."

"Then that's what you need to do, sir. They're all wearing name tags; it should be pretty easy."

We were escorted into the dinner and I was mortified to find they'd seated me next to him. What in the world was I going to talk about with this awful man? We took our seats. Because all the wines were red they'd pre-poured the tasting, affording each of the five wines the chance to breathe.

Senator Sears sat down and powered through the five glasses, one by one, and when he'd polished those off, he sucked the one little cordial glass empty as well. He turned to me and said, "They didn't fill those up, did they?"

"It's a tasting, sir." He stared at me blankly. "I'm sorry, sir, let me get you some more wine."

I flagged down the waiter. "Could we please have another set of the tasting for the senator?"

The gynecologists seated next to us shot their wives disapproving looks. These were five of the top wines in the world. The least expensive bottle of the bunch was $400.

The senator feigned ignorance to cover. "Was I supposed to drink each one with a course?" Now, come on. He's a U.S. senator; he's not that daft. What was his game?

Senator Sears liked to play the role of Simple God-Fearing Family Patriarch. It was a *Little House on the Prairie* mentality taken to the extreme. I wondered if the doctors around us fully understood Senator Sears's primitive, sexist, and fundamentalist philosophy. If they did, would they be at this dinner? And would they have brought their wives?

You can be assured that everyone sitting at a senator's table is listening to every word he says. I decided to pepper him with small-talk questions. "What does your wife do, Senator?"

"She homeschools the children."

I smiled brightly and made sure to project. "Is there much money in that?" The senator laughed, as did the dinner guests four deep on either side of us.

"No, and the hours are terrible." The ripples of laughter now moved six deep, then eight couples deep as guests shared the joke quietly among themselves amid the murmurs of "What did he say? What did he say?"

No matter the crowd, there is always *at least* one wife for whom the word "homeschooling" is like fingernails down a chalkboard. I surreptitiously scanned our growing audience for the woman who seemed to bristle. There she was. Three seats down on the senator's left. An attractive well-dressed brunette in her thirties, she was taller than those seated near her. She stopped slicing her filet mignon to address the senator directly. "And how many children do you have, Senator?"

The senator beamed with pride. "Eight. Three girls and five boys. I delivered them all myself."

All the wives were listening attentively now and with new ears. Not so funny to be the wife at home with eight children all day—five of them boys. The tall brunette was hooked. I could simply sit back and watch the show.

"Are you unhappy with the schools in D.C.?"

"My wife and I don't want our children overexposed to the world," the senator replied, sipping from his glass of $800 wine. "Homeschooling deepens the family bonds during the day, just like co-sleeping in a communal family bed does at night."

I froze my face into a carefully constructed, oft practiced facade of neutrality. I had a whole table of people watching and I was supposed to be working for the man. But the doctor to my right choked a little on his asparagus.

The senator continued like the star of his own show, blissfully unaware his ratings were plummeting. "American children grow up separated from their parents—especially if the mother works." The doctor beside me shifted uncomfortably under the penetrating gaze of his wife. "Siblings who sleep with each other and their parents develop an innate sense of trust, faith, and respect for family values."

I noticed the tall brunette's tightening grip on her steak knife as she protested, "As a pediatrician myself, I'd never advise a new mother to sleep with her baby, simply as a protective measure against suffocation."

The senator chuckled and finished off his tenth but not yet final glass of wine. "Oh, my children aren't babies. The youngest is six and my oldest just turned fifteen."

There was an awkward silence that washed over the table as the guests pictured the senator, his wife, and their eight children, some of them teenagers, crammed into the family bed.

I hoped against hope that Senator Sears would be defeated. I knew he'd just lost the sixteen votes at our table and maybe, as word spread through the room, all two hundred guests would speak against him to their friends and their friends' friends. It was a small victory, but I'd take it.

Phones that ring at 5 a.m. never bring good news. It was Sophia. I could tell she hadn't slept. "We're in the ER at Barnes-Jewish. Daddy Gil was running a high fever, he had chills, then he started acting really strange. He was confused and disoriented. They think he has an infection in his bloodstream. Mom's beside herself."

Groggy and unable to fully wake myself, I tried to understand what was happening. "He's going to be okay, right?"

Sophia paused, and the pause told me everything she could not bring herself to say aloud. "You need to get here."

I wafted through the airport terminal like smoke. Disconnected, out of body, one foot in front of the other but not feeling the floor beneath. Around me, people swirled with purpose, going somewhere, a destination, but my whole world was in upheaval. Daddy Gil was home. No, Daddy Gil was in an emergency room. I set myself to function and it took every ounce of energy inside me just to find gate 17A. Gate 14, Daddy Gil will be okay. Gate 15B, Daddy Gil will be okay. Gate 16 . . . an advertisement for the American Diabetes Association wrung my guts like a wet washcloth.

Finally, each step heavier than the last, I found my gate and an empty set of chairs where Goldie and I could be alone and not speak and not deal with life until absolutely necessary. We communed with one another. She sat on my lap as I petted her graying ears softly, distracted and in excruciating sorrow. We were a sad sight.

"What a good little friend you have there."

I looked up into eyes so full of compassion it took me a few seconds to blink and see the stunning man attached to them. He was breathtaking, an Asian JFK, with a flawless complexion and jet-black hair cropped close. I felt my heart lighten for an instant with just a twinge of hope. I tried to return his friendly smile and failed. "This is Goldie." The tears came quickly, full force, and would not be controlled. "My father's very sick."

He sat beside me then and just like Goldie, his very presence was enough to quiet my pain. It took several minutes but I regained control of myself, tried my best to wipe away the tears, and hoped my face wasn't blotchy red.

He smiled sympathetically. "Does Goldie like peanut butter crackers?"

I welcomed the change in spirit and laughed with relief. "Goldie loves peanut butter crackers."

He broke off a perfectly proportioned bite for her and reached across the arm rest to feed her. He had wide, flat palms and shortly snipped, clean fingernails. Goldie lifted her eyes as if to ask my permission and I egged her on. "It's okay, honey."

He broke off another small piece as he said, "How old is she?"

I cocked my head to one side. "Don't you know better than to ask a gal her age?" The beautiful man chuckled and we locked eyes for one delightful second. I muttered, "You're clearly a pet person."

"That might be an understatement."

"Few of your own back home?" I wanted to know where his home was and if there was a girlfriend there waiting for him. No ring on his finger meant anything was possible.

Why did I care? I had Kelley. Kelley who used the word "love." Shame on me! But technically, we weren't engaged. There'd been no promises made. Most of our relationship was spent on the phone. Plus, and this was a big plus, nothing else mattered except Daddy Gil's health. But Daddy Gil had pulled through before. He'd pull through again. I had to stop beating myself up for this instant attraction and instead, focus on the positive. The positively handsome man sitting in front of me.

"Actually, I take care of America's animals. All of them." He dug into the pocket of his jacket and opened a shiny metal cardholder. He handed me his card. Wilson Cho, President, The Animal League.

I looked him over with new eyes. His briefcase was made of canvas, his shoes were clearly synthetic. Wilson Cho was a lunatic radical, an animal zealot, hated and feared by my senators. He was PETA in sheep's clothing. I'd heard his name spat across conference room tables like a curse word. I had no idea he was so . . . fetching.

"*You* are famous." I handed him my card in return.

He read my title, his eyebrows lifting with a new respect. "I think you mean infamous." And we both smiled, knowing had we met in any other place, time, or situation, we would have been enemies.

He stayed with me for the full hour before his flight. And in the immediate intimacy that is created between strangers traveling, I spoke openheartedly about my love for Daddy Gil.

"He always tells me, 'When you walk into a room, you feel confident, because I'm always rooting for you.'" I let the tears roll unattended down my cheeks as Wilson carefully listened. "Knowing he's out there, cheering me on, keeps me brave."

"He's given you a wonderful gift." Wilson offered Goldie another small bite of cracker and she licked his fingers in thanks.

"He always tells me how lucky he is and how grateful he is for everything we have." Goldie was done with me. She crawled out of my lap and nestled into Wilson's, gazing up at him with adoring eyes. I had to acknowledge her crush. "As you can see, I try to instill that sense of gratitude in my own child."

Wilson smiled and his smile lessened the sorrowful nostalgia darkening my spirit. It was his turn to talk now. He talked about Washington, where he also lived. He spoke about his recent and painful divorce. He spoke about the pets that had graced his life and brought him such companionship in his own times of upheaval. He was a man of stirring passions, confident and articulate, a leader. I was more than slightly disappointed when he left us to board his flight.

I wondered, would I ever see this man again? We were on completely opposite sides of the aisle. We had no people in common. Was this a single firework of intimacy flaring bright, beautiful, illuminating, but only momentary?

He turned to wave goodbye and my heart seemed to break in half anew. I did my best to happily wave, lifting Goldie's paw as an extension of my own, but it must have been a pitiful display because Wilson only made it halfway down the gangway. He turned around and demanded exit from the gate attendants. I watched in awe as he walked towards me, his whole being glowing radiant with determination. I could not speak as he kneeled in front of me, took my face in his gentle hands, and said, "I'm going to pray for your dad. I'm going to pray that your mom, your sister, and you can find comfort in this scary time. You're going to be okay, I promise."

He kissed me softly on my forehead, a benediction, and hustled back to his plane. I was speechless, overwhelmed, and against all rational will, madly in love.

Walking into the Barnes-Jewish ICU with Goldie and my luggage, I felt my stomach fall to my feet. Mom and Sophie were nowhere to be seen. I swallowed back my panic and rushed to the nurse's island. "I'm looking for my family. My dad's name is Gil Matthews."

The nurse's calm demeanor helped settle my stomach. "You must be Tee and Goldie. Your mom and sister are in the chapel."

"Is my dad okay?" I could tell from the sadness in her eyes that something terrible had happened.

"Your dad went into septic shock. His blood pressure dropped, we lost his pulse, and he went into cardiac failure. His major organs have shut down."

"Is he . . . " I dared not say the word.

"We have him on life support. Your mom wanted you here. Would you like to sit with him?"

I could only nod my response. Yes.

The nurse began walking. "Goldie can come too."

Daddy Gil's bed was haloed by plastic. His chest rose and fell with the whir and click of his ventilator. Machines beeped and blinked. The nurse pulled back the plastic so we could approach the bed. He was so still and calm, he looked peacefully asleep.

Goldie struggled to get to Daddy Gil. I squeezed her tightly. "No, honey, no."

The nurse reached out to help me. "She can stay with him." She rested Goldie gently on Daddy Gil's chest. Goldie immediately quieted and looked up into his face with her sad, pleading eyes.

Mom and Sophia returned from the chapel. I'd never seen my mother so focused and strong. She hugged me tightly. "We need to say our goodbyes."

The four of us sat with Daddy Gil, Goldie on his chest and the rest of us seated around him. Mom was wholly present; not one tear escaped from her eyes.

"Do you remember, Gil, the night we met? You were coming off the stage from giving your speech and you saw me talking with your friend, Bobbie Jean. After I left, you asked who I was and she said, 'That's Hedy Sachet and she is very special and I'm watching out for her because she has two girls.' And you told Bobbie Jean that you wanted to meet me but she wouldn't let you until you told her you were going to marry me."

This was a family legend now confirmed. The way Daddy Gil had fallen in love with Mom across a crowded room, just like in the movies.

Mom stroked his hand and continued. "We stayed up all night talking and you proposed. You said, 'You're going to marry me and I'm going to marry you and that's it.' We flew to Las Vegas and you hired a driver and we looked at every chapel in that city."

Sophia and I sat very still, afraid to move, afraid to disturb Mom in any way. These were our parents' most precious memories, laid before us like diamonds.

Mom's face glowed as if she were that young bride again. "We saw the Little Chapel of the West. They were building the MGM Grand and relocating the chapel. They had it loaded on a flatbed truck. I saw it and I knew immediately that was our chapel. You jumped out and you convinced them to put the church back down on the ground and we were the last wedding in their old location. We got married there. And when I got home, Tee was so mad because she didn't get to be our flower girl."

Sophia and I laughed because it was true. I'd been saving a special blue velvet dress in case Mom ever decided to remarry. It'd never crossed my mind that she'd elope. I was more upset about not getting to wear the dress than the fact that I had a new dad.

"You are the love of my life, Gil, the love of my life."

Mom could not say another word. Sophia could only cry and hold Daddy Gil's hand. So I talked.

"Thank you for being our dad. Thank you for loving us and for letting us know you. Don't you worry, we will get through this. We'll never be okay, but we will always be fine."

The nurse entered and asked if we wanted to stay in the room. Mom shook her head no. I gave him a kiss, my sister gave him a kiss, and then Mom gave him a kiss. I tried to pick up Goldie but she held her little paws on him and wouldn't let go. Mom picked her up instead and Goldie relented. The four of us walked out of the room a family forever changed.

Daddy Gil had funded new stables for the St. Louis County Park Rangers, and they wanted to do a special tribute to honor him. The police shut down Lindell Boulevard for the procession as the mounted rangers followed behind a riderless horse. They led the way to Cathedral Basilica as the bagpipes played "Flowers of the Forest" and "Danny Boy." Mom, Sophia, and I walked slowly behind.

Thousands of mourners poured into the stunningly beautiful cathedral. Daddy Gil made many friends wherever he went. Walking the long aisle toward the high altar, I gazed up at the soaring ceilings, the grand arches, and elaborate, golden mosaics. I felt incredibly small. I was grateful when we slid into our pews and disappeared among the crowd.

Mr. Barrymore opened the service with a prayer, then Senator Ivy gave the eulogy. I listened but I could not hear until Mom nudged me, "Temple, can you do it?" Mom had asked me to say a few words on behalf of the family. I nodded and made my way to the altar.

So many of my senators had flown in for the service, I felt as if I were speaking before Congress. Scattered among the pews, I caught sight of my past. Girls I'd grown up with in Metairie, Brenda Charles and David Nichols from my first fundraiser, former mayor Gaffney, and yes, there was Elma towards the back. I hadn't expected those faces. It touched my heart profoundly to see them. I cleared my throat. "Daddy Gil had the unique ability to step outside himself to appreciate all that was beautiful about life. That perspective made him a generous man."

I glanced into the crowd again and with great relief saw Jamie, Franklin, Netta and Zack, and Prudence and Senator Olin scattered among the mourners. Prudence looked me straight in the eyes and just barely nodded her head, encouraging me to continue. That tiny gesture meant the world to me. It gave me the strength to go on.

"I remember one Christmas, we were opening presents and my sister had just come back from Mexico. She had this huge sombrero and she was dancing up and down the hall with it on her head. It was enormous. She had to turn sideways to move." The crowd appreciated the moment of levity.

"We were laughing so hard, we couldn't stop. And I looked over at Daddy Gil and he was crying. Mom asked him, 'What's wrong?' and he said, 'I love to see our girls laughing.'" My throat seized with grief. I had to stop. The memories washed over me in crashing, miserable waves.

That's when I caught sight of a familiar suit and tie. I'd seen that particular combination before, yes, at my Senate Celebration, but the man wearing them, looking into his face, I felt puzzled. I should know this man but something was amiss. Then it hit me. It was Kelley but his hair, his hair was gone. All of it. He'd buzzed his head down to bald. He was staring at me with eyes full of pity and I don't know why, but something inside me snapped. His pity infuriated me. Anger exploded through my muscles. I twitched to strike, the fight within me suppressed by reality. I had to get through this eulogy. Mom was relying on me.

"Daddy Gil literally counted his blessings aloud. We knew he loved us because he told us. He was a tremendous role model to me and my sister. He was a devoted husband to our mother. We will miss him always. We will always love him and keep him in our hearts and we will never be the same."

I wasn't the same, that much I knew. I could not tolerate Kelley and his hovering. He accompanied me back to D.C. after the funeral. In a time that should have brought us closer together, I just wanted him to leave. He tiptoed around my apartment wearing his needy empathy like a wet blanket. He handled me as if I might break. I couldn't stand it. I got in the shower and jumped up and down yelling, "It's too much, it's too much. Too much!" He thought I was grieving but in actuality, I was fuming.

Prudence was right. Kelley wasn't the right man for me. His life was a permanent vacation and I lived in the real world. Kelley was kayaking through life as if it were a crystal-clear lake. He left no wake and his skies were blue. My life rolled in on crashing waves in shark-infested waters. Two different worlds. In mine, I was drowning.

Mom called that night to check in on me. "Are you feeling lonely, darling?"

Although she knew Kelley had left the funeral with me, I didn't mention he was still in town. "The job will keep me busy. I'm more worried about Sophia. She has too much free time."

Kelley noticed my omission. When I hung up the phone, he said, "Why didn't you tell her I'm still here?"

I couldn't answer his question. I didn't know how.

He got very quiet. "Because it doesn't matter to you anymore." And then Kelley became very emotional.

I should have comforted him and explained that everything inside me had changed with a heartbeat—Daddy Gil's last. I should have assured him that he hadn't done anything wrong. That it wasn't his fault. It wasn't anyone's fault. But I couldn't because right then, in that moment, everything Kelley did was wrong. His love was wrong. His condolences were wrong. His vampiric caretaking, his needy affections, they were all wrong!

Kelley left the next day. He called to let me know he made it back to Mexico safely and said, "I'll let you call me, okay?"

But I didn't call him again.

{ *Eight* }

"Eccentric" Is Just a Polite Term for Crazy

I desperately needed a return to normalcy. Normalcy for me meaning insanity, angst, and distraction. Fortunately, the mother of all distractions was approaching: the Republican National Convention, the biggest party of them all.

In the past, the Convention had been a substantial money-raiser for the RSCC. You could charge donors $5,000 for a package, then get all the events underwritten by corporate sponsors. You could spend over a million dollars on a single party and still make money. But just my luck, I was running the first Convention affected by campaign finance reform. Suddenly, the Committee had to pay for everything. In Manhattan. The city of overhead.

I was trying to finagle how to make a party with coffee, iced tea, and no food when Prudence walked into my office. I bombarded her immediately with my complaints. "Why can't they just let the Conventions operate the way they always have and make them exempt for both the Democrats and the Republicans? The money doesn't go to campaigns, it's for parties! It brings in huge tourism dollars and all these laws are doing is making everyone even more sneaky and secretive about where they get their funding. The beast is insatiable."

Prudence sat down across from me. "You're preaching to the choir, Temple."

I mimicked pulling my hair out. "I can't ask my donors to pay $10,000 for an experience that probably wouldn't be as good the one they had four years ago for half that price!"

Prudence nodded. "I have a suggestion."

Prudence thought the Senate Committee could find a travel agency to sell donors a Convention package and that the agency, not bound by the laws of political campaign financing, could get companies to sponsor the big-ticket events.

"A donor can pay their annual fee to the RSCC, which will get them into the meetings and events at the Convention"—Prudence had given this some thought—"but the spectacular parties will be offered by the travel agency. They can legally get Coca-Cola to underwrite a party at the Met, no problem."

I was desperate for a solution, but not desperate enough to land in jail. "I can't be in direct contact with a travel agency."

Prudence smiled. "No, but I can."

I contracted Prudence's firm to handle the travel agency and paid her $50,000 up front—after going around and around a million times with our legal counsel, all of us paranoid about a paper trail. It didn't matter anyway. The donors just wanted to pay one price to us; they didn't want to deal with a travel agency. They were confused and called us about parties we weren't supposed to know anything about. It was a big mess and the whole thing fell apart. Prudence and Dominica moved on, contracted by Senator Ivy to run his Operation Shine benefit, while Netta, Jamie, and I took over the Senate Committee events ourselves. Essentially, we'd poured $50K down the drain.

Once we got to New York the chaos began instantly. We'd rented the Tupelo Grill across the street from Madison Square Garden and filled it with big-screen TVs and a twenty-four-hour buffet. It was meant to be the holding area for the Nut, excuse me, Upper House donors, but they would not stay put. They kept sneaking across the street into Madison Square Garden and into our Force GOP or our Team Victory hospitality suites.

The worst offender wasn't even an official donor. Remember harmless little old Mr. Kendt on his cane? Not so harmless anymore. Mr. Kendt had wised up and hired three gigantic bodyguards to roll him around in a brand-new wheelchair. He still hadn't donated a dime but now he had muscled goons wheeling his deflated little self all over Manhattan. He also had a tough-looking prostitute "girlfriend" calling the shots.

Netta called me crying. And Netta's not like me at all; she never cries. "That hooker yelled and told me they're going to do exactly what they want whether I like it or not! And those bodyguards are really big, Temple! I think they're Mafia."

"Calm down. I'll be right there."

It may seem silly. An old man wants to come to the Convention with his hooker and his goons; just let him be, right? But we only had two suites booked for our Major Donors and each room had only fifteen cushioned seats. We had scheduled the room so tightly that our members were literally being rotated in and out at assigned times. I'd already asked Mr. Kendt and his thugs to leave—had even threatened to involve Secret Service—but they kept sneaking around. As soon as they saw me coming, they rolled Mr. Kendt down the hallway. Jamie popped his head out of the Force GOP suite. "What's going on?"

"We've asked those men to leave fifteen times and they threatened Netta and made her cry!" Stupid, stupid me. I totally forgot how protective Jamie could be. As I watched him charge full-throttle down the hall, memories of his drunken, botched hit on Slick came flooding back. "Wait, Jamie, wait!"

I ran after him and into the Team Victory suite, which was chock-ablock with donors watching the vice president's speech on our streaming video feed. Even in such a small room, it was hard to see where they'd gone. As donors reacted to our abrasive entry, I flashed a tight smile and nervously giggled, then scanned the room. There was Ambassador Medici and his wife wearing her diamond tiara. Beside them, the hairy-legged, breast-feeding wife and her Internet whiz-kid husband, neither of whom had bathed since he cashed out his eBay stocks. There was . . .

"Aha!" Jamie cried as he leapt across the breast-feeder and jerked Mr. Kendt's wheelchair. Instant melee. Mr. Kendt's bodyguards and hooker jumped into the fray, and of course, all the donors were horrified to see Jamie roughhousing a wheelchair-bound elderly man. Ambassador Medici's wife swatted at Jamie with her purse. "What is wrong with you! Shame, shame!"

As security rushed the room and escorted Mr. Kendt and his entourage out, I tried to explain to our donors that Jamie was simply doing his job. Still they glared at him as we shrunk out of sight. In the hallway, Jamie straightened his tie. "I'm going straight to hell for that one."

I barely had time to catch my breath when my BlackBerry rang again. It was Franklin calling from the Operation Shine benefit at Rockefeller Center. "Can you get here quickly? I need you to escort Zoë."

I actually squealed. Aloud. Totally unconscious and completely out of character. Fame didn't impress me. Even if Zoë was the biggest rock star on the face of the planet. I was surrounded, every day, by history-makers. But my sister, with her wanderlust, always had these cool rock star stories. Me, I only ever met pickers, grinners, and cloggers. At every Republican gathering, country music, country music, and more country music. I'd finally have a rock 'n' roll story of my own.

Franklin was taken aback. "Let me just rewind, maybe I didn't just ask you that."

"No, no, no, I will be fine."

"Your voice is up twelve octaves. Are you actually going to be fine?"

I took a deep breath and calmed myself to assure him. "I promise." I jumped up and down like a teenager; Sophia was going to be so totally jealous.

As they say, politics makes strange bedfellows. Senator Ivy, being a former pharmacist, founded Operation Shine in order to fight AIDS around the world. Franklin now repped the companies researching and developing drugs to combat HIV, while Zoë had founded A2A (Aid to Africa) to save African lives from the same. Suddenly, a conservative senator, a gay lobbyist, and a rock star had something in common.

Prudence was working the door when I arrived. She was surprised to see me. "Aren't you supposed to be at the Garden?"

Sometimes Prudence had a tone that made me feel like a naughty daughter hiding a hickey. "Franklin needs me to staff Zoë."

"She has her own people."

"Franklin wanted me here just in case."

Prudence gestured behind her. "They're by the buffet."

I had to give it to Franklin. When he threw a party, it was done right. He'd completely transformed Rockefeller Center. The skating rink had been converted into a massive stage and the plaza was decked out as a swanky lounge complete with luxurious couches and a never-ending catered buffet. He'd even flown in a South African children's choir to perform for the event. Zoë was a strikingly beautiful woman, tautly muscled with not one ounce of body fat. A fashion icon and trendsetter, she'd dressed in colorful traditional African robes that hung like draperies from her bony collarbone. Somehow, she still looked gorgeous. Charisma oozed from her every pore and the smiling children surrounding her responded with gleeful laughter and incessant hugs. It was hard to tell who was having more fun, the kids or the rock star. I couldn't help but laugh out loud.

"If you think that's funny, have you seen the bird?"

I turned to meet the owner of the voice, a cherub-faced woman with cinnamon skin, perfectly coiled dreadlocks, and a sterling silver hoop pierced through her bottom lip. She offered her hand, every finger covered in colorful rings. She had a strong grip but not brutal. "LaSonya Neal. I work for A2A."

"Temple Sachet. Normally I work for the Senate but tonight I'm here for you guys."

"Oh, in that case, you have to have the full outrageous bird experience. Stay here for just one second."

When LaSonya returned, she was accompanied by a tuxedoed trainer carrying a ginormous American bald eagle on his shoulder. The South African kids went bonkers, jumping up and down with excitement at the sight of "Freedom," the flipping huge eagle wearing a tiny aviator hat, like Snoopy.

"Did I lie? That is one outrageous bird." LaSonya was beaming proudly, taking full pleasure in my amusement. I couldn't stop laughing long enough to answer her question. She gestured wildly to the trainer and flapped her arms. "Make him do the thing with his wings."

The trainer complied, instructing Freedom to first lift his right and then his left wing. Which doesn't sound nearly as impressive as seeing it first-hand. That eagle was so strong I could actually feel the wind from his movement. The trainer milked his fifteen minutes for all they were worth. "And for our grand finale, I will need an assistant."

LaSonya nudged me forward, yelling, "Temple will do it. Temple will!" And before I knew what was happening, fifteen pounds of Freedom was sitting on my shoulder while the trainer educated the gathered crowd.

"Freedom is tremendously powerful—his talons are capable of impaling and breaking a human arm. Show us your right hand, Temple." Now terrified I'd die a bloody death in front of the children, I gingerly lifted my right hand into the air. The trainer instructed Freedom to do the same and in my peripheral vision I could see his talons were the size of my hands. I smiled my pageant girl smile and tried hard not to picture my arm ripped from its socket. "He has a wingspan of nearly eight feet. Temple, will you hold out your arms?" And with great trepidation, I complied. "Freedom, wings!"

With a WHOOOSH, Freedom unfurled both his wings simultaneously. It truly felt like I left the ground for a millisecond. Freedom posed as if modeling for the Great Seal of the United States and everyone burst into applause. LaSonya pushed through the crowd to snap a photo with her camera phone. I did my best not to pee my pants.

The children's choir was called to the stage and Freedom and his trainer moved to another group of admirers. Zoë made herself comfortable on a couch as LaSonya and I moved to a nearby sectional, keeping our instinctive "staffing" distance—hovering inconspicuously but still in the line of sight. She showed me the photos she'd just taken. They were hysterical, well worth the terror. "My kids are going to love this shot."

What a totally different world LaSonya lived in. I'd barely known her for twenty minutes and already she'd mentioned kids. A person with a personal life, how completely refreshing.

"Boys or girls?"

"One of each." She scrolled through her phone photos, quickly blipping past the irrelevant to stop on a family shot. Her ivory-skinned husband hugging two beautiful toddlers. "That's David and that's Thando and Youssou. Youssou loves any kind of animal."

"Adorable. Your son looks just like you."

"Thank you. How about you, any kids?"

"Just my yorkie, Goldie Hawn." That got a good laugh out of LaSonya. "No, seriously, the Senate Committee is like working in an insulated cocoon. You never meet anyone outside of politics."

LaSonya corrected me. "Except tonight."

I liked her thinking. "Exactly."

LaSonya scrolled quickly back to my eagle image and showed it to me again. We couldn't stop laughing. "Give me your e-mail and I'll send it to you." We exchanged contact information, then my Black-Berry rang. It was Secret Service, and that's one call you can't let go to voice mail. I excused myself politely to find some privacy.

"We're holding a man and we need to confirm you have him on your registry."

"What's his name?"

"Bud Pittfield."

"Doesn't sound familiar. What's he look like?"

"Colonel Sanders."

"Are you serious?" The Secret Service is always serious. "You're sure he's one of mine?"

"He's wearing a Senate Committee lanyard."

"What color?"

"Green."

Because there were beaucoup people with credentials for the convention, we'd devised a series of four badges in different colors to represent each level of donor. They were bright, so if I was walking down the hallway and someone had on their lanyard, I'd know right away who they were and where they were supposed to be. Green meant Upper House, but all those guys were harmless. Weren't they? Why was Secret Service involved?

"We can't discuss this over the phone. We need a senior staff person from your office here immediately."

I frantically called Netta. "Netta, you need to go downstairs. Secret Service has a guy in the basement. You need to take escalator E and then there will be a staircase and there is a little office—" In the midst of my instructions, I heard what I can only describe as hootin' and hollerin' in the background. "Netta, did you leave the Garden? You are in a bar! You are having a beer and you are in a bar!"

I'm no teetotaler, that's pretty clear, but we'd made a very strict policy that no staff member could drink if they were hosting donors. If they were at a Lynyrd Skynyrd concert in some bar in the Meatpacking District and they decided to drink, as long as they showed up at 6:00 the next morning ready to rock 'n' roll, then it was absolutely none of my business. But drinking on donor time was verboten. Netta had apparently had enough of our no drinking rule and gone AWOL.

"You are drinking right now! I can hear you slurping!"

"No, I'm not."

"You are! You had better get your a-double-s into that Secret Service office and I'm not kidding."

Netta whined her response. "If I weren't so wrong, I'd talk back right now, but guess what?"

"I don't have time for this, Netta!"

"I'm drunk."

Clearly, Netta was in no shape to deal with Secret Service. I was going to have to handle this myself. I hung up, disappointed to prematurely end my time at Rockefeller Center. I didn't even have a good story to tell my sister.

LaSonya was sitting with Zoë now, the two of them joking with an ease that comes only from being a professional guest of honor. I donned my well-practiced air of casual disinterest as I approached them to say, "They're refreshing the buffet if either of you are hungry."

It was Zoë who answered. The first and only words I heard her say in person were, "I had a dog at the Garden."

I was shocked. I assumed Zoë was a vegetarian. Apparently not. That guy Wilson that I'd met in the airport would have been so disappointed. I realized that now I had something funny and specific to tell Sophia. It wasn't as exciting as running off to Rome with Goo Goo or Foo Foo whoever, but I thought it might suffice. Which is why, I guess, I chuckled and stood there like a bump on a log. LaSonya saved me with a "I think we're good for now, but thanks."

Her voice shook me out of my reverie. "Okay, well, I need to head across town. If you need anything, my dear friend Prudence is here to help."

LaSonya stood to shake my hand and give me her card. "I expect to see that picture framed the next time I'm in D.C."

I smiled brightly and sincerely. "I'll use it as my computer wallpaper."

It turned out the man held by Secret Service did look exactly like Colonel Sanders and had been on the Secret Service radar ever since he'd threatened Reagan's life. By the time I got to Madison Square Garden, they already had officers in his hotel room. They knew the flights he'd booked, they knew he'd taken a cab, and they had the cabdriver's number. They knew everything. It was a little scary. And it was all my fault.

I'd prospected off old event lists and he, at one time, had actually been a Patriot. I couldn't figure out why he'd suddenly stopped donating, so I included him in the Convention invitations. He'd rejoined at the Upper House level.

Secret Service was not happy with me. "He's been off every donor list for the past sixteen years. How did you find his name?"

I winced and shrugged my apology. "I'm industrious."

They were not amused. "You need to stop that."

Colonel Sanders was ejected and they took away his credentials. And that, I thought, was that.

Ha.

We were celebrating closing night of the Convention with an RSCC party in Griswold's honor held at the Rainbow Room. It was a party that almost didn't happen, thanks to Prudence's partner. I'd secured Clint Black to perform but when Dominica heard about my coup she had Senator Raines call Clint directly to get him to sing at their fundraiser instead. I let that one slide. But when she tried to steal the actual venue from underneath me, it was on. The Rainbow Room was A-list. And it was mine.

Before I hired Prudence (and indirectly Dominica), I'd approved a deposit for the Rainbow Room. When Prudence's firm hired the travel agency, they'd assumed the venue contract. When that fell apart, Prudence's company technically still owned the Rainbow Room booking. Dominica decided to keep the venue for herself and throw a closing-night party for Senator Raines.

I called Prudence complaining. "That Dominica is the most manipulative person. Can you talk some sense into her?"

But Prudence was completely distracted by the logistics of housing her Operation Shine donors. "I have all these rooms at the Essex House. Your Victorys and GOPs could all stay together. Do you want to swap Essex for Regency rooms?"

Prudence was clearly in no state to help and I knew Dominica underestimated me. She thought, because I giggled and smiled all the time, I didn't know the time of day. Which, normally, was fine with me. Better to let Dominica think she's in charge. As long as I end up where I need to be, it's not worth the argument. But when I stop smiling, it can get ugly real fast. And I was done smiling for Dominica.

Still, I probably should have taken a breather before I called. "What exactly do you think you're accomplishing by stealing my venue and upstaging Senator Griswold? He's in Leadership, remember?"

"I'm making sure the most popular senator in the country has the hottest party at the Convention."

"There will be resentment. Raines will pay for this party in four more years when he wants the presidential nomination. You're setting him up for disaster."

She said, "Don't try to turn this around on me. You're just ticked because I outmaneuvered you."

I felt my blood pressure pulsing against my brow. "Let's be clear on who's really turning things around. I got the Rainbow Room and I gave Prudence that contract, not you. You're not a genius strategist, you're a thief." And I hung up the phone.

Dominica returned the Rainbow Room to its rightful owner, *me*. I offered an olive branch, introducing her to friends who owned a restaurant near Union Square. Senator Raines happily hosted his party without ever knowing he'd had a shot at the big time. Raines could have Clint Black. I had a jaw-dropping panoramic view of Manhattan.

My Sorority Row staffers were dressed to the nines and I assured them they could have a drink and enjoy their final hours in New York. Jamie and I even decided to man the donor check-in table just to give the girls time to dance and grab some food. Thank the good Lord we did. I spotted the Colonel Sanders clone entering the lobby.

"Oh my gosh, Jamie, that's the crazy guy!"

Jamie was unfazed. "Nut House, huh?"

I was frantically dialing Secret Service. "No, Jamie, actually insane." I still wasn't getting a rise out of Jamie so I started screaming, "Dangerous! Violent! He tried to kill Reagan! Secret Service kicked him out of the Convention!"

That did the trick. Jamie yelled, "You are getting out of here, sir!" and in his beautifully tailored suit, he climbed onto the check-in table, leapt through the air, and landed on top of Colonel Sanders. All of our horrified donors scattered. Sorority Row had just returned with their fruity drinks and full plates of appetizers. They squealed and hid behind plants, frantic at the sight of Jamie attacking an old man.

And once again, Ambassador Medici and his tiara-wearing wife witnessed the whole hysterical fistfight. (Come on, a Colonel Sanders look-alike and a meticulously groomed pretty boy rolling around all macho on art deco marble floors. It can't get any funnier.) Rockefeller Center security held Colonel Sanders until Secret Service arrived. They'd already cleared out his hotel room and they escorted him to the airport.

Jamie was my superhero. As he and I helped ourselves to lemon shots, Jamie licked his sugary lips and said, "We have to start clarifying the exact levels of crazy."

After the Convention was over, I wanted to surprise Netta, Jamie, Prudence, and even Franklin and thank them for the support they'd given me during the most trying year of my life. They'd helped me run flawless events, given me fantastic advice, and just kept an eye out for me in a city where friendships were measured in favors.

The only reason I had to get out of bed each day, besides Goldie licking my face, was the support of my friends. I was completely fed up with Senator Griswold, utterly disgusted to be working for a hateful president, and devastated Daddy Gil was gone. But I loved, loved, loved my friends. They were my chosen family and I needed to let them know how much I cared for them.

The five of us met for dinner among the warm yellow walls, visiting Hollywood celebs, and Eurotrash of Café Milano, in Georgetown. Netta and Prudence had known me for years; they were used to my effusiveness. Jamie had witnessed a scene or two, had been the recipient of many hugs and voice mails of adoration, but Franklin was still relatively new to my heartfelt outpourings. I wasn't sure how he'd respond. I waited for a natural lull in our gossip before I sat up straight and clinked my water glass with my salad fork. Maybe I should have waited until we'd ordered, but I was bubbling with emotion. I wouldn't be able to eat if I didn't say what I needed to say. My four friends quieted and smiled at me, expectantly.

"Since Daddy Gil got sick in Italy last year—" I had to stop already and place a hand on my heart.

Netta lightened the mood with her "Shake it off, Sachet, shake it off." I shot her an appreciative smile, then I tried again.

"The four of you have been there for me. Netta, from the White House to Iowa and back again, you've been by my side every step of the way. I'd be lost without you." Netta actually teared up a bit, which gave me the courage to continue.

"Jamie, after seeing you jump those elderly men, I loathe to think what would have happened if you'd gotten your hands on Slick." Jamie air-boxed as Franklin feigned elderly terror. "You're the big brother I never had." Jamie nodded his affections for me in response.

"Prudence, you're always an inspiration. I wouldn't even be in D.C. if it wasn't for you. You've taught me everything I know and I love you like a big sister." Prudence cast her eyes downward and smiled slightly to herself. I could feel her desire to disappear so I moved on to Franklin.

"And even though you tricked me into this job, Franklin, I love you for it because it's a fantastic opportunity. I owe you. For the job and for getting to meet Zoë!"

Franklin toasted himself with his water glass. "Yes, you do!"

I laughed because it was true. I did owe him. It was a remarkable job, no matter how miserable it made me. I'd work on something in the morning and that night, see it on the news. It was intoxicating. A most effective way to forget Daddy Gil was gone.

I continued with my speech, "If there's anything I've learned by losing Daddy Gil, it's that you never get life moments back." I dug underneath my chair and pulled out my bag of goodies. "I got each of you a little gift to celebrate our friendship and I'd be honored if you'd accept it from me."

There were short-lived, humble protests of "You don't have to do this, Temple," before they gleefully tore into their beautifully wrapped packages. For the boys, basket-weave cuff links in sterling silver with blue enamel from Tiffany's and for the ladies, silk Hermes scarves in black and blue. My friends were thrilled and I basked in the sunshine of their happiness.

"I have another announcement," Prudence offered, never quite lifting her eyes to meet our gaze. "Clyde and I are getting married."

It was only then I realized Prudence wasn't staring at the place setting in front of her; she was examining her engagement ring! There was much celebrating that night. A few too many flutes of champagne and I was giddy.

It didn't even bother me that after leaving our soirée I had to return to my office and get back on the job. Maybe it was the champagne or maybe it was the e-mail from LaSonya. She'd sent the hysterical picture of the bald eagle sitting on my shoulder. As promised, I turned it into my desktop background.

And that's the image I saw every morning after I crawled out of my sleeping bag and turned on my computer. Me, trying to smile with fifteen pounds of murderous Freedom digging his talons into my back. I could fly away or I could be killed. Either was possible.

From the Convention to Election Day it was a mad race to the finish. To make matters worse, *Time* published a list of the best and worst senators and to my astounding horror, Senator Griswold was named one of the ten best. The man's head swelled like a watermelon. Hard to believe any of his cowboy hats still fit.

One of my favorite people, poor Senator Wade, ended up in last place. Such a sweet man, Senator Wade always had a hole in his suit. He was up for his second term and had barely won his first. But God bless him, Senator Wade would pick up the phone and make a call. I had senators so used to making pre-campaign finance reform $50K or $100K asks that they were insulted if I asked them to call people and offer two tickets to a dinner. But kindly Senator Wade never complained. He'd sit and make those $5,000 phone calls. Most senators, if they got a wrong phone number, would flip out on my staffers and yell, "Don't you fact-check?" Senator Wade would just try again. If the person answering said the donor was at their job in a Subway sandwich shop, Senator Wade would track them down at work.

But senators like Wade were being pushed aside while those like Senator Sweeney, a lifer with dementia who should have been counseled not to run, were still in the mix. Sweeney's Arkansas seat was hotly contested and the Party had spoken: The seat was needed even if it was filled by an insane, incompetent candidate.

Sweeney was asked to speak at the University of Arkansas and in the middle of his prepared speech he spotted a woman in the front row and said, "Those are beautiful breasts. I'd like to see those." Then he rubbed himself. You know where.

Someone pulled him offstage, and after it happened a second time (yes, a second time!), Sweeney was no longer allowed to make any live appearances. His chief of staff went so far as to pre-script a debate via teleprompter. His staff came into our offices bawling and crying, convinced they would soon lose their jobs.

To face the final push, I needed a whole new attitude. Prudence was marrying Senator Olin, Netta and Zack were applying to adopt a baby girl from China, Franklin had a new house and his new career, even Jamie and Denver were shopping for a vacation home.

Everyone else was moving forward and I was stuck, completely mired in a swamp of grief. Every morning a mourning. My legs so weighted down with gloom I could barely lift them out of bed. I needed a change. Quitting my job wasn't the answer. The job was a necessary evil. It kept me from pulling the shades, locking the doors, and hiding away from the world. But it didn't make me happy, and I needed happy. Even if I had to fake it until it was real.

"You need hair extensions." Sophia was just in town for the day, passing through on her way to London where she was meeting the guitarist from Big Toad or Giant Frog or some other amphibian-inspired alt-rock band. She was sprawled out on my sofa as I made coffee in the kitchen. "Thick hair is empowering. You need a little empowerment. Plus you've got big ears."

I touched my ears to see if they'd grown. They felt a little bigger. I scheduled an appointment. There was a new salon that shared lobby space with the Results Gym in Dupont Circle, a "he-ing and he-ing" place, a pickup joint for pretty boys. It was the only salon nearby that did extensions. My stylist had dyed pink hair and dressed like a goth Stevie Nicks. Layers and layers of black gauzy skirts, with combat boots. After a quick introduction, I sat down in her chair, eager to catch up on my *Cosmo*, *W*, and *People*. There was nothing but *Jane* magazine. The stylist whispered, "If you want to know who's doing who in this town, just listen."

She wasn't kidding. Who needed magazines when you could get this kind of gossip for free? I was completely distracted by the side talk. To my right, the uber-hip stylist was describing, in graphic detail, the sexual exploits he'd just had with a certain lobbyist in the gym locker room. To my left, the lesbian stylist was giving her client a sex-ed course, Girl-on-Girl 101. I felt like Rebecca of Sunnybrook Farm. Everyone was getting some except me. I hadn't sowed an oat in, seriously, years! In the three months Kelley and I'd been together, we'd only revved the engine; we'd never taken a test drive. And here I was, a girl with a full tank of gas, ready for a road trip.

Lord, it took a long, excruciatingly graphic time to put in those extensions. I closed my eyes as descriptions of acrobatic positions I'd never even imagined, let alone attempted, swirled through my mind. How long had it been, really?

There'd been Justin with the engagement ring; I'd fallen head over heels for one of the guys at the Ray of Hope office but he'd never even noticed I was alive. I'd dated a guy briefly when I worked for Mayor Gaffney whom Mom called "le petit cochon"—the little pig—and she was right; he turned out to be a total swine. When I moved to D.C. for the Barrymore campaign, Netta and Zack had fixed me up with one of Zack's buddies, a lobbyist (I should have known better!) who ended up cheating on me with a slutty L.A., a legislative assistant, who wore maroon velour thigh-high boots. Donors had tried to parlay meetings into dinners, but that wasn't happening. And then I met Kelley at Mardi Gras.

Wow, seriously? The last romp had been the cheater? Almost four years earlier? The funny thing is, I hadn't even noticed the time passing. Work bled into every aspect of my day. The personal, if I could squeeze it in, was burdensome. It was beyond sad. It was pathetic. The situation needed to be remedied ASAP. And I knew exactly the cure.

My heart, my mind, and my libido yearned for Wilson Cho. His ebony hair, chestnut eyes, the gentleness with which he'd fed Goldie peanut butter crackers. Why hadn't he called? Had I even suggested that he could or should? That day had been so horrible, who knows what I said. I'd definitely scared him off with my torrent of tears. If I ever wanted to see Wilson again, I was going to have to kick the Southern-girl shtick and make the call myself. I had the perfect excuse: a sky-box party for the Prince concert. If the hair turned out hot, I'd call Wilson Cho and we'd make our own scandalous stories to be whispered not-so-furtively to a hairdresser.

We gathered for our weekly Bombshell dinner (which now regularly included Franklin and Jamie) and the gang went into a tizzy over my new look. Franklin asked the obvious: "Did you get extensions?"

I rolled my eyes and laughed. "I didn't just go to sleep and wake up like Rapunzel!"

Jamie squealed like a total girl, "Take it down! Stand up, so we can see!"

I did as I was instructed, unleashing my thick, luxurious mane from the ponytail holder so it fell past my hiney. Jamie and Netta clapped their hands with glee. Franklin whistled. I flipped and tossed my hair to their oohs and aahs.

Prudence said nada. As I sat back down she stood up and moved in for a closer inspection. It felt a bit like a school nurse was checking me for lice. Finally she said, "They used glue? On your head?"

"It's called bonding." I sounded defensive. "You can wash them," I went on, more gently, "and they send you home with this special nylon brush with the bristles spaced out."

Prudence still wasn't sold. "What do you think the senators will say?" She genuinely seemed upset.

I shrugged. "My hair doesn't crunch the numbers."

Franklin teased Prudence, "Stop acting like her mom and let's order."

Prudence snapped at him. "I'm not acting like her mom. I'm being a friend. We all know how people talk in this town."

Jamie, the quintessential smoother-over, jumped in with a "Let 'em talk—all they can say is how *hot* Temple looks!" then flagged down a waitress to put a fine point on it. Discussion about my hair was over. Final vote: Hot: 4, Inappropriate: 1. Time to call Wilson Cho.

Wilson said yes.

He came and picked me up from the office. He was even more handsome than I remembered. Out of his three-piece suit, in a fitted cotton sweater and Rock & Republic low-rise jeans, I could tell Wilson's physique was lean and taut. He had a vegan tummy, not an ounce of animal fat on him. On the drive to the Verizon Center, I figured I should warn him about the night's offerings. "Everyone in the box tonight will be Republican."

Wilson smiled as he circled the parking garage looking for an empty slot. "There's nothing Republican about a Prince concert."

"It's just the host is a billionaire rancher and an oilman so there will be meat. Lots of it."

Wilson processed this new information, nodding intently. "Who's the host?"

"Larry Tiegs."

"Tiegs!" Wilson hit the brakes. "He's an environmental criminal!"

My stomach clenched with instant anxiety. Would Wilson kick me out right then and there with a scathing lecture about oil spills and fertilizer? No. He'd only stopped to let three scantily clad teen girls scurry in front of his hybrid. Still, I was worried. "Maybe I picked the wrong first date?"

Wilson spied an open parking slot. "Don't worry, Temple. I'll be a good guest." He squeezed in between two gigantic SUVs.

I blushed pink, mortified that I'd offended. "That's not what I meant—"

Wilson yanked the keys out of the ignition. "Ready to go?" He was completely unfazed by my faux pas so I dropped it and let myself out of the car unassisted. Wilson was a native New Yorker; he didn't open car doors for ladies.

The glass-enclosed luxury suite offered an unobstructed view of Prince traipsing all over the stage in his platform boots. How that little guy jumped up and off his piano in those things was amazing. Of course, no one in the suite danced.

Netta, Jamie, and Franklin loved that Wilson knew everything about everything and was into the whole Washington scene. They loved his encyclopedic knowledge of lobbying and issues and agendas and the senators and their chiefs of staff. He was a brilliant man, articulate and outrageously, blatantly, aggressively liberal.

Netta pulled me aside, nearly breathless from my exhilarating scandal. "Your boyfriend is a total commie!" Her breath blasted me with warm, oaky notes of red wine.

"Shhhh!" I hushed Netta. I had to nip that kind of talk in the bud. This was just our first date. Wilson wasn't my beau . . . yet. But yeah, yeah, he was totally a communist.

Netta reveled in her tipsiness and my naughtiness. "You think Prudence is freaked about your hair? Good thing she's not here tonight. She'd have a stroke over Wilson!"

Out of sight of my new vegan escort, I plucked a rib from the steaming buffet. "She's just worried my hair might break off."

Netta nearly snorted. "She's worried because you look hot! You already have big boobs and those bug her too!" Netta had clearly had one drink more than her limit. I tried to shush her but a drunk Netta was a chatty Netta. "She'd take one look at Olin and one at Wilson and yell, 'SWITCH!'"

The suite was filled with donors, most of whom knew Prudence and Senator Olin personally. I really did have to calm Netta down. "Netta, that's not something you'd want her to hear you say." I scanned the room for Zack.

"You're too nice, Temple, you're too nice." There was Zack. "You need to pay attention to people who are not nice and stop smiling at them." I caught Zack's eye, tossing him a look that meant it was time for a Netta nap. He headed over. "I've been burned so many times I have scorch marks."

Zack slid his arm around Netta's waist. "Want some coffee, baby?"

Netta melted into him. Relaxed. Ever since she and Zack had filled out the adoption application, Netta'd been drinking more than usual. She said it quieted the pins and needles of not knowing when the call would come. But I thought Netta was grieving the loss of her own maternity. She'd finally given up on pregnancy and taken up red wine. "When Jasmine comes from China, you'll be her godmother, won't you? Won't you?"

I wasn't sure, given Netta's state, whether to take her question seriously, until Zack bobbed his head in affirmation. "Jeanette and I want you to be Jasmine's godmom."

My heart swelled with love. "Of course, I'd be honored." Netta started blubbering and even Zack's eyes reddened from the stress of holding back tears. Sloppy hugs were exchanged before Zack was finally able to cart Netta out the door.

I was so high from the euphoria of Jasmine love I didn't even care that Wilson walked in front of me on our way back to the car. Jasmine. I would be Jasmine's godmommy. The fact that my hot vegan commie turned out to be an awesome kisser with roaming hands was pure icing on the cake.

{ *Nine* }

Winning Won't Save You

The day of the election, I was in my third-floor office completely and totally alone. The $95 million we'd raised had already been parceled out to the campaigns. The young ones had worked so hard I decided to send all of them into the field for "get out the vote" rallies, door-to-door canvassing, and to run phone banks in key races. We'd raised enough to fly them to every corner of the country; given their pitiful salaries and exorbitant working hours this perk was the least I could do. But it left me alone in my office on the big day.

Mrs. Griswold insisted her senator husband not be in his first-floor office for the election returns but instead be located on the second floor with Research and Communications, drafting immediate responses to polling numbers as they came in. She had the building manager hang black drapes in front of the elevator so no one could see in and made it very clear no one was allowed on that floor. Why anyone would want to watch Senator Griswold watching television was beyond me, but I abided by Mrs. Griswold's wishes and stayed in my office with my own TV set and my computer screen pinging with poll returns.

The endless prattling of predicting pundits was interrupted by my ringing phone. It was Jamie and Franklin.

"We're getting beer and coming over."

The boys arrived with the promised hooch but our drinking only made the silent emptiness even more impenetrable. Franklin sighed. "This is terrible. Two years ago, it was a celebration. You should have made the staff stay here."

"They need the experience."

Jamie stood up. "Well, let's go downstairs."

I jabbed a pointy finger toward the floor. "We're not allowed downstairs."

Jamie sat back down, exasperated. "That woman! Isn't she terrible!"

It was all terrible. We were winning. In every state. The family-bed-sleeping Senator Sears was up in the polls and even Senator Sweeney, who hadn't been allowed to speak in public for the last three months, seemed to be keeping his seat. Poor kindly Senator Wade was a goner.

I was miserable. I'd worked so hard and I didn't feel a part of anything. I was not excited for anyone. None of it mattered. It was a horrible commentary on all of my work and on the purpose of my life. It was very clear somebody else should have been sitting in my chair.

Franklin was hurting too. These were wins he'd orchestrated but for which he could claim no credit, receive no glory. There would be no party for Franklin, no knowing smiles or hearty handshakes. Senator Griswold and his new staff would shine like stars.

We finished the beers and suffered through election coverage to the bitter end. Franklin and I slipped deeper and deeper into melancholy as the night ticked down. Jamie teetered toward ecstasy. By 2 a.m. the results were in: the Senate majority was ours. Jamie grabbed me in a huge, effusive hug. "Congratulations, Temple!"

"For what?"

"For the election! You won!"

I was aggravated with Jamie now. Couldn't he see I was unhappy? Couldn't he see the hurt on Franklin's face? I licked my wounds a little. Just for show. "I'm sure Senator Griswold is very happy and everybody worked very hard, so I don't deserve the congratulations."

Jamie tried to smooth over the tension: "Don't be modest. We know how hard you worked."

Franklin sensed my anger. "Are you upset with us, Temple?"

I looked at them, these two boys who'd roped me into the most demanding job of my life, and I had no idea what to say. I was mad at the world. I'd been beaten up, worn out, and used up. But it wasn't their fault I was depressed. I was the one who stuffed down my emotional core, my personal life, my values and integrity, so that I wouldn't let the Party, Senator Ivy, Senator MacLeish, Mom, Daddy Gil, Prudence, Netta, Jamie, Franklin, and even useless old Senator Griswold, down.

"I'm just disappointed about how I feel about this whole day." I knew Franklin and Jamie probably thought I was a witch but I was too tired to care. It was over. It was all finally over. I just wanted to crawl into my own bed and have one night that wasn't spent in my sleeping bag on the office floor.

I just wanted to go home.

Jangling my keys to let Goldie know Mommy was home, I unlocked the door and was alarmed when she didn't run to greet me. No matter how late my arrival, Goldie always met me at the door. Goldie was always underfoot.

I searched every room and found her curled up under my bed, as still and quiet as a stone. "Goldie, baby, what's wrong?" I carefully pulled her out and was horrified by how lifeless her tiny body felt in my hands. She was barely breathing.

I frantically dialed Wilson and could not contain my hysteria. "It's Goldie, she's sick and it's so late, what am I going to do?"

"Wrap her in a towel, get her some water, and meet me at the Dupont Animal Clinic in thirty minutes."

It's good to be the girl dating the president of the Animal League. I gently wrapped Goldie in a fluffy towel and placed her water bowl on the car seat beside her. "Drink some water, please, for Mommy?"

But Goldie barely opened her eyes. During the maddeningly slow drive to the animal hospital, she seized, convulsing and shaking. I tried my best to keep my teary eyes on the blurring road while I petted her head and whispered everything was going to be okay, though I knew in my heart it was not.

Wilson was waiting for us in the parking lot in front of the clinic. He opened the passenger side door, carefully scooped Goldie into his arms, and ran.

I threw the car into park and sat there, gripping the steering wheel, my knuckles white with fear. Yes, Goldie had gotten slower, older, and grayer, but she hadn't been sick. I begged and bargained aloud. "Not Goldie too, please, not my little Goldie." I could hardly bear the thought of going inside. I had to force every step from the car to the clinic door.

Wilson and the vet he'd woken from a sound night's sleep were leaning against the cold stainless-steel table where Goldie lay, still wrapped in my bathroom towel. Wilson spoke in hushed and soothing tones. "She's gone, Temple."

I rushed to swaddle Goldie more tightly into the towel, lifted her into my arms and held her like a baby. "I'm so sorry sweetie, I should have taken you with me today. I shouldn't have left you alone. Can you forgive me? I'm so sorry."

Wilson helped me into a chair where I cradled Goldie close to my heart. He knelt beside me. His voice was steady, calm, and reassuring. "She had a stroke. There was nothing you could have done."

"I shouldn't have waited in the car. I should have been here with her. She didn't see me. She thought I left her." I searched Wilson's face for some sign of forgiveness and found it in his soulful eyes.

He smoothed my hair, rubbed my back, petted away my guilt. "Goldie knew you loved her. She wasn't alone. I was here. She wasn't alone. She knew. She knew. I was here. It's okay."

Wilson kept repeating himself until I finally heard him. "Thank you. I'll never forget that."

Wilson stood. "You want some time alone?"

I shook my head no and kissed Goldie's tiny ears goodbye. "I need you to drive me home."

Walking into my house, it hit me hard. Goldie would never greet me at the door again. I clutched her petite crystal-studded collar in my right hand and reached for Wilson with my left.

I said, "Stay."

He said, "On your couch?" And he was serious.

"No, not on my couch." I could not hide my aggravation. I wanted a messy, sweaty flail in the sheets. I wanted a fumbling, awkward grope that tangled my long, long hair. To feel alive, to feel loved, to feel desired, to feel anything but what was coming: ravaging despondency. "I meant with me."

Wilson took a half step back. "Not tonight, Temple. It wouldn't feel right. Not after this loss."

I did not want him to kiss me lovingly on my forehead or make me a cup of tea, but that's exactly what he did. Then he left and I immediately picked up the phone to call Mom with a voice so small I could barely hear myself speaking.

"Goldie died."

Mom started to cry. "Oh honey, I'm so sorry."

"I have to pick up her ashes tomorrow."

"She was your baby."

"She was, Mom, she was. I can't take anymore. I miss Daddy Gil so much. This job takes every ounce of energy I have and now Goldie . . . " My voice broke. I could no longer speak. I could only sob painful torrents of misery.

I rushed into my bathroom, cradling the phone against my neck, and frantically tore into the tissues. I collapsed onto the lid of my toilet and wept.

The seven months since Daddy Gil's funeral had been an act of sheer willpower. I threw parties when I felt like hibernating. I smiled to cover the numbness in public, and in private, I surrendered to anguish with endless streams of tears. Nothing helped. I couldn't cry it out. I couldn't smile it away. All I could do was sob and sob and sob while Mom listened patiently through the phone. She waited until my heaving turned to sniffling before she offered, "Maybe it's time to move away from that city."

Those words reverberated through my entire body, shaking me with simultaneous joy and terror. I sensed just the tingle of my imagined liberation before the frightful realities washed in.

All of my successes were measured in dollar amounts, all of my status was derived from the politicians I knew personally, all of my friendships stemmed from my career. I was loved, envied, adored, respected, feared, and most of all *needed* as a fundraiser. D.C. was my identity. It gave purpose to my days. I couldn't just walk away from it. Could I?

"And do what, Mom? What would I do?"

Mom could tell her suggestion panicked me. Her tone softened into one of nostalgia. "Do you remember, about six or seven years ago, when we were down at the lake house and Papa called, out of the blue?"

I had no idea where this was going but I couldn't summon the energy to care so I played along. "Daddy Gil got jealous."

Mom chuckled, "He did, he did. I hadn't heard from that man in fifteen years but Gil was still jealous. And you were mad."

I remembered now. That call had ticked me off. It still did. My anger strengthened me. "He didn't have the right to know how we were."

"Tee, honey, we married very young and we knew how to push each other's buttons. We were a cancer to each other."

By this time, I'd fully depleted my Kleenex supply and had moved on to hand towels. "You think D.C. is like cancer for me?"

Mom weighed her words carefully. "I know there's more to you than that job. Just like there was more to me than that man."

My nose and eyes were rubbed raw, my cheeks streaked from the brine of my tears. "My whole life is here."

Mom was done with gentle persuasion. "You need a new life."

I did not sleep a wink that night. In my head, a constant loop of Goldie memories with a voice-over by Mom: "You need a new life, you need a new life." I did my best to wait until 7 a.m. before I called Prudence. It may have been 6:59. I stayed under my covers and pecked at my BlackBerry, not wanting to move but needing a savior. Prudence answered as alert and direct as if it were noon.

"What's wrong?"

I palmed my forehead and squeezed tightly against my pounding headache. "I need a new life."

"Today?"

"Right now." I pinched the bridge of my nose between my thumb and second finger. Oh, my thumping head.

Prudence hesitated. I could tell she was scanning her calendar. "I've got a breakfast with Senator Ivy and a lunch with Dominica—"

"Dominica can wait. Cancel that lunch and meet me at TenPenh instead. One o'clock."

Prudence paused to consider my suggestion. "Are you alright?"

I pushed my thumb along the ridgeline of my eyebrow. "I'm about one centimeter away from jumping off a cliff."

Peering through the windowed facade facing Pennsylvania Avenue, I could see TenPenh was packed with lobbyists and politicos. There simply was no place nearby to have a decent meal without the constant pressure of my position. Still, I allowed the hostess, dressed in her long silk tunic, to usher me into the main dining room.

I nodded politely at familiar faces and once seated, fingered the hammered bronze flatware nervously. Prudence wasn't late; she was never late. I was just anxiously early. Was Mom right? Should I leave Washington? Prudence would know what to do. Prudence always knew what to do.

She arrived exactly at our appointed time and before she'd even taken a seat I blurted out, "Goldie died and I have to quit my job. Today."

Prudence froze in place for a moment, glanced around to see if anyone heard my declaration, then sat calmly down. "Start at the beginning. Quietly. Remember where you are. The room is full of ears."

Choking back emotion, I explained everything that'd happened the night before. Prudence listened intently and studied my face for traces of doubt. The faster I talked, the more agitated I became despite my best attempt at a whisper. "The election is over. I did my job. I don't have anything else to give!"

I threw up my hands nearly knocking the bronze bowl and warm towel out of our approaching waiter's hands. The mini-collision broke the momentum of my tirade. I apologized profusely, "I am so, so, so sorry."

The waiter wisely backed away from me as Prudence massaged her hands with her warm towel. "Temple, if there's one thing I've learned from *you*, it's that you have to follow your heart. And your heart is telling you to get out."

It was such a surprising relief to hear that Prudence supported my overnight, no-sleep, emotion-based decision. Then she said, "I just think you need to give it one more month."

I scowled with disappointment. "I can't stand one more hour."

"Just hear me out." Prudence picked up her menu then put it back down. We both knew the entrees by heart. She always ordered the crispy fish and I always got the calamari salad. "The new chair will be elected in the next few weeks. A new chair means a new bean counter. You'll most likely be replaced anyway, that's just how it's done."

I didn't like where this was going. "So why stick around and wait?"

Prudence leaned in and whispered furtively, "Clyde says Senator Sears wants that chair and I know how you feel about that man."

I actually groaned aloud. The thought of Sears gaining control of Senate campaign finances was unbearable. "This country deserves better."

Prudence continued, carefully eyeing those around us to make sure we were being ignored. "Brogan will run against him. But she's going to have a tough time unless you're still sitting at that desk, answering your phone."

I didn't have to ask Prudence for clarification because I knew what she meant. Senator Brogan wasn't well liked by the Senate good-old-boys or the power lobbyists. Big tobacco hated her. Gaming hated her. And depending on the gender of the person you asked, she was seen as either ambitiously driven or abrasively pushy. I liked her. I'd liked her from that very first ride in the red convertible. And when it came to asking for checks, Senator Brogan had been one of my most profitable callers. I couldn't let Sears take the Committee without a fight.

All I had to do was answer my phone. I was the person who knew that Senator Williams needed a typed-out script to make donor calls, that Senator Mayfield loved jelly beans and if you left a jar of them by the phones, he'd come over all the time. I knew that Senator Honor's wife, Jill, was an alcoholic who got wasted at donor parties. I knew that Senator Noth's chief of staff had a bad habit of cleaning out hotel minibars and sticking the Committee with the $600 bills. I knew that Senator Stiebel showed up to events with his hair looking like a bunch of cotton balls pasted to the top of his head. I knew that Senator Rolent had the audacity to behave rudely with junior staffers. I knew that Senator Bevin had the worst halitosis in America and that Senator Raines had everyone fooled—he wasn't a good guy. He was downright mean and he'd do and say anything to screw you in the end.

I also knew which senators behaved with integrity when nobody was watching. Like Senator Smith, who forgot to pack shampoo and insisted I take his $5 bill to cover any costs incurred as a result. Or Senator Young, who refused to task anyone with a job that he could do himself, like framing the pictures for his office or vacuuming the floor. I knew that after forty-five years of marriage, Senator Donavon was still madly in love with his wife. They looked like two little Keebler elves walking together, always holding hands. You could just picture them in striped T-shirts baking cookies.

I also knew that during one of my Upper House conferences, Senator Sears had insulted our lower-level donors by announcing he was "not staying for dinner because these people are crazy." Of course, on our trip with the lobbyists he had a grand old time. He was playing golf with the Big Guys and joked, "I was going to join a country club before I became a senator. I'm so glad I didn't. I saved myself a whole bunch of money because now I can just let you guys pay for me." He actually said that out loud.

Would I bluntly announce these truths to senators when they called for my opinions about their colleagues? No, absolutely not. But you better believe I'd let them know who raised what, how much time each senator had given to the Committee, and whether or not I liked them personally. I had the ear of every senator and more important, Majority Leader Ivy had become a close family friend. As far as I was concerned, with me on her side, Senator Brogan was a shoo-in.

Prudence felt the same way. "You need to leave the Committee in good hands."

I sulked. The finish line had been in sight, the marathon nearly over when ha, ha, just kidding, four more miles to go. "Another month of nightmares."

Prudence unsuccessfully attempted to flag down our waiter. "Go ahead and write your resignation letter today. Sign it, seal it, put it in your desk, have it ready. Trick yourself into feeling like you've already quit."

My mood brightened. "That's a fantastic idea. Writing that letter would be so liberating."

Prudence finally caught the waiter's eye. She beckoned him to the table. "Just don't give it to anyone until you're 100 percent sure it's time to go."

I returned to my office with every intention of doing exactly as Prudence suggested but found there was an unexpected visitor waiting for me. Specifically, Senator Brogan's chief of staff, Ian Conley. Sorority Row was hot and bothered by his presence. They popped up from their cubicles like alarmed prairie dogs.

Ian was young, probably my age, and a looker. He had a clean-cut, all-American Tom Cruise kind of look with a big smile and twinkling eyes. I recognized him from the Convention's closing-night party at the Rainbow Room. He'd congratulated Jamie on his successful takedown of Colonel Sanders and I thought he was kind of cute. A little short, but cute. I'd mentioned that to Jamie who, despite his clear membership on the pink team, had an endearing way of becoming jealous when I expressed interest in guys he knew. Maybe it was a protective brother kind of thing or maybe he had a crush on Ian, but Jamie never officially introduced us.

I greeted Ian with a quizzical smile and a firm handshake. "Did we have an appointment?"

"Weee did nooot." Ian was Deep South. He pulled vowels like taffy. "I was hopin' I could steeeal a minute of your tiiime."

"Sure, come on in." As I closed my office door, I caught Sorority Row rushing to the water cooler for a drink and a dish session. I had to smile.

I instantly knew he liked me. His body language was relaxed and playful. He sat slightly too close to my desk and every so often, he blushed bright red.

"Teeell meee 'bout yoourself."

There was that pesky phrase. In this case, it meant one of two things: either (1) Ian was actually considering keeping me on as finance director or (2) He wanted me to believe I had a shot so I would work to install Senator Brogan as chair.

For just a millisecond I daydreamed of answering Ian's inquiry with an unabashed look at my brutal reality. "Well, Ian, I'm a sexually frustrated single girl who spends most of her lonesome nights curled up on the office floor in a sleeping bag. I shower at the office, I eat at the office, and even if I have a date, I wind up back at the office. I keep two suits hanging on the back of that door and there are currently three pairs of undies in my desk. I haven't sowed an oat in years. In other words, I'm a mess."

Instead I said, "I was on the Phil Barrymore presidential campaign, then I moved over to PAC director for Senator Ivy—"

Ian interrupted me, clearly dissatisfied with my jumping to a list of names. "Actuaaally, I'd liiike to heeear 'bout you peeersonally."

I was so thrown I sat there blinking with confusion. "Like what?"

"Liiike do y'allwaaays tell the truuuth?"

In all the years I'd been raising money, nobody had ever asked me that question. I looked this Ian character over with new eyes. This guy, at this level, was still a believer. I was impressed. "Yes, Ian, I try to."

He squinted as if to see into my soul. "Tryyy to?"

"Sometimes I say something thinking it's the truth and later, I find out it wasn't. That's definitely happened before."

"Yessir, that suuure does happen sometiiimes." Ian slapped his knee. "Well Teeemple, I'm hopin' you'll throoow your suppooort behind Senator Brooogan. And if we wiiin, I'm hopin' you'll staaay."

I'd just looked this earnest cutie in the eyes and told him I didn't lie. I absolutely would not commit to another cycle with Brogan when I knew full well as soon as Ian left the room, I'd write my resignation letter. But Prudence's words rang through my ears: "Just don't give it to anyone until you're 100 percent sure it's time to go."

I stood up and extended my arm for a jovial this-meeting-is-over handshake. "I will do everything I can to help Senator Brogan be successful." If Ian sat across my desk for too much longer, I'd blab about quitting and now that I'd met him, my threatened exit seemed premature. Ian Conley was still a believer. What if Senator Brogan was too? What if everything I hated about the job and my harried life in D.C. could be remedied with one simple fix . . . a new chair? What if?

Senator MacLeish was the first to solicit my opinion. "Will Brogan travel?"

I'd picked my pony, now it was time to lay down the bets. "The woman's a machine. She could fall down, break both her arms and her hip, conk her head, and still get on a plane to Russia."

Senator Ivy made the next call. "Is she high maintenance?"

"No sir, she's high energy. She went out on the road for other candidates, did commercials for them, and lent her own donor list to our Committee."

The calls kept coming and I had an answer for every one of them.

Q: "Does she make calls?"
A: *"I can't keep the lists coming fast enough for her."*

Q: "Who has done the most to help?"
A: *"Senator Brogan's at every party we host. She gets the job done."*

Q: "Who do you like, who do you like, who do you like?"
A: *Brogan. Brogan. Brogan.*

It was decided by one vote. Senator Brogan took the chair and in a move that only a woman could pull off, she marched over to Sears's offices and gave him a big hug for the cameras. He smiled and shook her hand but there was no love lost between those two, believe me.

Love. That's what I felt for Wilson. He was officially under my skin. Wilson had seen me at my most raw, my most vulnerable, and he hadn't flinched. I wanted more and more time with him but our schedules kept us orbiting around one another. To a certain extent, every date with Wilson felt like the first. Netta feared we were flatlining.

She and I met for drinks to discuss Prudence's bridal shower. After details had been ironed out and two rounds of whiskey sours had been downed, Netta laser-beamed her life-planning spotlight on my relationship.

"Sachet, it's been six months. What's up with this Wilson, is he dating other people, is he gay, or what?"

I just about choked on an ice cube. "He's definitely not gay."

Netta eyed me over the rim of her tumbler, skeptical. "How do you know? You're not sleeping with him."

I blushed as bright pink as the silk scarf I had draped around my neck. Still, I defended myself. "There's been plenty of kissing and heavy petting."

Netta stared at me blankly. "You know what the problem is? That boy's passions move on four legs and you're a biped."

"We're both busy people."

Netta shook her foot to the beat of the ambient music. "Sachet, you need to determine whether he's in or he's out. Otherwise, you're gonna end up with your heart broken."

I heard Netta loud and clear. I just wasn't ready to admit defeat. "He's coming with me to the wedding."

Netta nodded her approval. "Maybe there's hope for him yet."

Walking proudly into the church with Wilson on my arm, I gasped with shock. Standing at the end of the aisle was Senator Olin wearing Daddy Gil's signature look. A blue-and-white seersucker suit with a pink tie.

Against my will, I was transported back to our sitting room in Metairie, that first day Sophia and I met Daddy Gil. I remembered the way Mom's eyes sparkled when she looked at him. I remembered that his silver hair glowed like a halo. I remembered shaking his fingers because my tiny hand couldn't hold his palm.

Seeing Senator Olin, in that suit, standing by the altar, my whole body ached. Daddy Gil wanted so much for me to change my mind about marriage and find the right guy. He'd wanted so badly to walk me down the aisle. Now here I was in a church with Wilson, the man for me, and I would never be able to introduce him to Daddy Gil. My heart felt as if it might burst. I quickly took a seat.

Wilson slid into the pew beside me. "You okay?"

I nodded and smiled and said nothing. Fortunately, tears at a wedding are expected. I managed to hold off the waterworks until Prudence emerged in her ivory off-the-shoulder gown. My upset only worsened when a bagpiper emerged to play as the happy newlyweds marched down the aisle. He was playing the Irish lullaby from Daddy Gil's funeral.

It'd been nearly a year but I was still in a fragile place. I was shaking and physically unable to walk out of the church, so Wilson sat with me, holding my hand, as one by one the pews emptied.

In a still, small voice, I tried to explain to him why I couldn't move. "The bagpipe. Clyde's pink tie." I knew he didn't understand but I wasn't capable of a fuller explanation. All I could manage was, "I really miss my Dad."

Wilson wrapped his arm around my shoulder and held me until the church completely cleared. He nestled his nose beside my ear and I listened closely for the romantic, strengthening words he would offer to soothe my soul. Softly he said, "You need a drink."

I cackled so loud, it rang through the rafters. "I totally need a drink."

We skipped out on the reception and found the nearest bar. Fully dressed in our wedding finery, we slammed back shot after shot after shot until we were nicely sloshed—then realized neither of us had any money or credit cards on us. We'd both assumed we would be eating and drinking for free at a wedding.

We had to sneak out and make a mad dash for my apartment in the rain. It was pouring buckets and I am not a fast runner. My feet were killing me, my toes bleeding—the heels were gorgeous but deadly. I bellowed at my shoes, "Why must I be so vain?"

Wilson stooped and yelled over his shoulder, "Hop on!"

"What?" I didn't get it.

"Piggyback, come on, before we get caught!"

I hiked up my dress, oh so ladylike, and jumped on Wilson's back, hugging tightly around his neck.

He gasped for air, "Choking! Choking!" I released my stranglehold and held across his shoulders instead. He took off.

Lord, he was fast. He zipped down sidewalks as we passed another one of D.C.'s innumerable black-tie affairs. I hooted and hollered at the line of black limos, penguin-suited men, and women convinced sequins meant they sparkled as people. "Look at my limo! Giddyup limo!"

Wilson took the corner violently and I held on for dear life. My apartment was in sight, thank God. We staggered through my front door. I dashed into the bathroom, slamming the door behind me, and quickly tried to remedy the mess that was my hair and makeup. Tonight was the big night. I could feel it. I washed my face, brushed my teeth, tended to my bleeding toes, stripped off my soaking clothes, and wrapped myself in the only thing hanging in the bathroom: my terry-cloth robe. It wasn't sexy but I couldn't walk out naked. Could I?

Actually, I could have. Wilson was sound asleep, face down on my living room sofa. He'd stripped down to his boxer briefs and for some drunken reason, had managed to fold his soaking-wet clothes neatly in a pile. Which he left on the floor.

"Wilson?" I tried to gently shake him awake but no response. I kneeled on the floor beside him. His smooth back was irresistible. I ran my fingers down the length of his spine. "Wilson?"

Then he snored.

I turned off the lamp beside his head, covered him with a blanket, and threw his clothes in the dryer with mine. They were the only thing getting a good tossing that night.

Senator Brogan turned out to be the real deal. She and Ian worked harder than anyone I knew, which was saying something. My phone began regularly ringing after 11 p.m. Senator Brogan wanted to know every detail of every event, every appointment, every donor. She never allowed a second to pass her by. Leaving one appointment on our way to another, she'd get in the car and ask for the call sheets. She'd power through those phone calls even if the drive was just a few blocks. She never took a moment to relax.

Senator Brogan's confrontational fundraising approach was such the antithesis of Griswold's do-nothingness that I had to completely rethink my strategy. I did not want Brogan asking for money across a table. It was tacky and donors would feel pressured. I had to nip this in the bud.

I commandeered one of Senator Brogan's mornings to present my new plan of attack. I knew I had one shot to sell her on my approach and it had to work. I hadn't been this nervous about pitching an idea since the day I asked Daddy Gil for a $10,000 check to sponsor the opera gala.

"These meetings, Senator Brogan, they should be a chance for people to connect with you personally."

The senator was skeptical. "So you don't want me to ask for a check?"

I pulled out two FedEx envelopes to visually support my argument. "As we leave each meeting, I'll call my assistant and tell her to mail these envelopes. The first one will be a purely personal letter directly from you. It will say 'It was lovely to meet you, I'm so happy to hear your daughter is getting married,' or whatever they told us in the meeting."

Senator Brogan could not wrap her head around this concept. "I'm still not asking for a check?"

"No, ma'am. I will. They get a second FedEx package from me the same day they get your letter. My letter will have their contribution history, information about our donor membership levels, and of course, a return envelope so they can mail their check directly to me. That way, they know the request is coming from your Senate Committee but if they can't give this year or they have to decrease their contribution, they won't be embarrassed."

Senator Brogan was quite impressed and seemed hugely relieved by this idea. She smiled at me warmly. "You always make me look so good, Temple."

"Why in the world are you still in that job?"

"I thought you said you resigned?"

Sophia was staying with Mom in Metairie and the two of them had called to, apparently, bombard me with simultaneous questions.

"Sophia, I like Senator Brogan, and Mom, I didn't actually resign, I just wrote a resignation letter so I would feel better. It's still sitting here in my desk."

"Well, give it to somebody and come with us on safari!" That was Sophia. After months of nagging, she'd finally talked Mom into continuing Daddy Gil's Sail-to-Somewhere tradition. None of us had been able to set foot on the boat in over a year, not since our last trip to Italy. I couldn't even bring myself to think about boating without Daddy Gil on board, but Sophia had convinced Mom that the Sail-to-Somewhere tradition needed to live on. To honor Daddy Gil's memory and to keep us all connected. Sophia was lobbying for South Africa.

"You can bring Wilson. He likes animals, doesn't he?"

"Uh, yeah, that has to be the understatement of the year."

Mom butted in. "Good, maybe then I'll actually get to meet him."

"You'll meet him eventually, Mom." Eight months without introducing my beau to my Mom. That was a Sachet family record and not one I cared to continue.

Mom wasn't crazy about it either. "When exactly?"

"How about after Boston?" I was escorting Senator Brogan to Boston the following week but after that, things were a little slow until the President's Dinner. "When I get back here, you guys can fly in and we'll all have dinner."

Mom wasn't buying it. "I won't hold my breath."

Boston. I'd set up a meeting with a man who'd started as a concession worker and then made a fortune in carnival games. This was the type of meeting I loved. A self-made guy, genuine, self-deprecating, and so completely honored he was getting to meet Senator Brogan that he agreed to come to her suite. Senator Brogan was nervous because I'd never actually met the man face-to-face; we'd only spoken by phone. But at some point, you have to go on instinct and meet new people.

He was a big, burly Irishman who grabbed me in a tight bear hug. "You're the little gal I've been talking to!"

I liked him right away. They sat down and he was so relaxed that he relaxed Senator Brogan. She became deeply nostalgic and sweetly sentimental. She'd gone to school in Boston, so they talked about Harvard Square and how she used to take the train.

He had a hearty, infectious laugh. "Do you remember that song, 'Charlie on the MTA'?"

Senator Brogan began to sing.

> *Let me tell you the story*
> *Of a man named Charlie*
> *On a tragic and fateful day*
> *He put ten cents in his pocket*
> *Kissed his wife and family*
> *Went to ride on the MTA*

The Irishman was thrilled the senator remembered and joined her for a rousing chorus, their voices cracking.

> *Did he ever return?*
> *No, he never returned*
> *And his fate is still unlearn'd*

He may ride forever
'neath the streets of Boston
He's the man who never returned.

Senator Brogan was absolutely radiant as she sang. I said aloud, "I wish I had a camera."

Senator Brogan joked, "I wish you had a bottle of red wine!"

As our Irishman hugged and kissed us both goodbye, he remarked, "This is such a different experience than I expected to have."

Senator Brogan winked. "I'll take that as a compliment."

The rest of our week went beautifully. Senator Brogan was a true pro. I was so used to Senator Griswold and that constant state of crisis management; I didn't know what to do with myself. There were no kicked-over priceless vases, no dripping Cokes, no shady legislation phone calls to our research department. This trip was truly a pleasure.

In the plane on our flight back to Washington, the senator said to me, "I'm so glad you stayed on as my finance director."

"I am too, Senator."

Against my very strict policy of not drinking in front of politicians, I announced I was having a beer. Senator Brogan kicked off her heels, saying, "I'll have one with you." And then she began to sing:

Charlie's wife goes down
To the Scollay Square station
Every day at quarter past two
And through the open window
She hands Charlie a sandwich
As the train comes rumblin' through

Sometimes you're in a moment and you know it's an extraordinary event. I knew right then and there. Being barefoot, drinking beer and singing with Senator Brogan, was going to be my best memory of D.C. We belted out:

> *He'll never return,*
> *No, he'll never return*
> *And his fate will be unlearned*
> *He may ride forever*
> *'neath the streets of Boston*
> *He's the man who never returned.*

Senator Brogan and I made a fantastic team.

{ *Ten* }

You Will Be Betrayed

I made it back in time for our weekly Bombshell dinner at Café Milano. I was disappointed Franklin couldn't join us but the rest of the gang was there, as was half of the Republican Party. The former adulterers Lila Weinstock and Senator Nayland were holding court at a nearby table. Nayland, the cheating preacher, had been reelected by a landslide and as a result had gained more power within the good-old-boy network. Lila was feeling her oats; she was very pumped up.

Netta stabbed at her insalata di rucola and whispered about Lila's peacockery. "When she was a lobbyist, she drank her beer out of bottles, but now that she's a senator's wife, her lips will only touch Cristal."

Jamie had already polished off his carpaccio and was slicing into his pizza. "I don't think Nayland's golf tournament will be using the Astroturf room anymore. Lila will want the carpeted ballroom."

Jamie and Netta were in rare form but Prudence had barely said a word since entrees were served. She seemed sullen and her eyes kept dropping away from me. I thought maybe I'd done something wrong. I tried to engage her by making fun of Ian's crush on me. "You have to read this e-mail Ian sent before I left for Boston. He found these two stray kittens and he wants to find them a home. I swear the e-mail is like five pages long. He's worse than Wilson." I scrolled through my BlackBerry e-mails. "Where did I put that thing? Ah, here it is!" Then I looked up.

Now I'd done something really wrong, it was clear. Neither Jamie nor Netta would look me in the eye and the mood stiffened. Something terrible had happened and I was the only one not in the know. I swallowed hard against the news. "Is Ian sick or something?"

Prudence spoke into her dinner plate. "I've been talking to him about taking the job."

I was confused. "What job?"

Prudence twisted her wedding band nervously. "The finance director position."

I heard the words but they didn't connect. "You mean my job?"

Netta shifted uncomfortably in her seat as Jamie reached for his water glass. A wave of hot embarrassment washed over me. Netta and Jamie already knew what was coming.

"I'm going to take it." Prudence watched me carefully now. She'd dropped the bomb in the middle of Café Milano surrounded by my supposed friends because she knew I wouldn't make a scene. I got a big pit in my stomach and said, "But Prudence, I haven't resigned."

"Actually, you have. Ian has your letter."

Prudence stole a momentary glimpse at Netta and the severity of the situation dawned on me. This wasn't a matter of confusion. The two of them had done this purposefully. Prudence pushed me to write the resignation letter, and beyond my sister and Mom, was the only one who knew it even existed. And Netta, Netta was the one with access to my desk. This was an orchestrated betrayal.

My whole body tingled as if thousands of tiny needles were digging into each and every nerve. I vibrated with an undercurrent of hysterical panic. How could my friends—? Why would my friends—?

Oh my God. My friends weren't actually my friends.

Jamie leaned forward and placed his hand on mine. "It's for the best, Temple. You've been so unhappy. Consider it an intervention."

I pulled my hand away and stared into the face of the stranger speaking to me. He was a man who resembled someone I used to love. I scanned around the table seeing only the familiar outer shells of people I had once held dear. They were empty cocoons. The friends who once inhabited those bodies were gone. Dead to me.

The one I'd once called Ms. Whipley had trained me well. She'd drilled the political into my bones. Restraint coursed through my veins instead of blood. I would no longer share the tiniest sliver of my heart.

I smiled Mom's scary smile, the one that meant I could order for myself, the one that meant Justin wasn't the man, the one that meant it was time to sever all ties, and said, "It's the perfect job for you, Prudence. You'll be fantastic."

I rose from the table and left. I knew it wasn't the healthy choice but I also knew I wasn't going to fight to save us. It was best to just close the chapter and walk out the door. Without offering to pay my portion of the bill.

I made it home just wanting to curl up in my cozy pajamas. No such luck. I'd run out of clean flannel jammies and all that was left was a negligee I'd reserved for Wilson. And reserved and reserved and reserved.

It would have to do. I slipped into the nightie in eager preparation for a prodigious crying jag. Then the doorbell rang. Squinting through the peephole, I saw Franklin brandishing a bottle of Jameson. "I've got the good stuff."

I opened the door but Franklin took one look at me in the negligee and hesitated before crossing the threshold. "Hot date?"

I swiped the bottle. "Get in here and get me blottoed."

Franklin had cigars. Cohiba Esplendidos directly from Cuba. I got dressed and we bundled up in blankets to brace against the chill of spring. We made ourselves as comfy as possible on the cold metal of my garden chairs. I had to ask. "Did you know?"

Franklin sliced the cap of his cigar with a guillotine cutter. "Jamie told me while you were in Boston. It's why I skipped the dinner."

I tried to wrap my brain around the evening. "Jamie and Netta both knew?"

Franklin shrugged. "Netta's ordered a baby from China. Jamie needs the Committee for Ivy. They made a job security choice."

The whiskey warmed my core from throat to tummy. "But none of this makes sense. Why would Prudence want the stress? That place is not a place to get rich. It's a public service job. She probably makes five times my salary consulting."

I tried to wait patiently as Franklin positioned the end of his cigar just above the tip of his flame and began puffing. I couldn't contain myself. "I mean, why is Dominica letting her do this? I wouldn't let my fifty-fifty partner take off for another job and leave me with all the responsibilities. I bet Prudence still expects to reap the rewards."

The outer rim glowed as Franklin spun his cigar and the smoke began to easily draw. Satisfied with his work, he leaned forward and offered me the black-banded beauty. "It's a night of change." I protested but Franklin insisted, "One won't kill you." I took the cigar as he instructed me to "pull and rotate. Don't inhale, just taste and let it go."

The smoke had a mellow, spicy languish. Smart, smart Franklin. With my mouth full of smoke, I had to stop grumbling and simply sit. Between the whiskey and the smoke, those frigid garden chairs were feeling much cozier.

"Prudence is married to a senator." Franklin began his second ritualistic lighting with a slice of the guillotine cutter. "A senator who has very little power." Franklin flicked open the flame of his lighter, then snapped it shut to finish his thought. "A finance director oversees campaign funding for every Republican senator. She or he is supposed to be completely impartial. To work for the Party, not a person. But you and I both know, Temple, the finance director only has so much money to hand out." Franklin popped his cigar in his mouth and fired up his lighter.

I finished his thought for him. "Suddenly, Senator Olin's a player again because his wife rules the roost and everyone needs his good graces." Franklin, busy with the puffing and rotating, pointed his index finger as affirmation. Through the haze of our smoke, things were actually more clear. The words floated out of my mouth, riding the blue swirls of Cohiba decadence. "My God, Prudence is unethical."

My eyes widened in fear. I'd said that out loud. But Franklin did not flinch. It was a profound truth, the kind that caused memories to fall like dominoes, toppling one facade onto another, racing to create an entirely new image of a woman I'd considered more than a mentor—a woman I'd idolized.

My brain clicked faster than my tongue could flap. "That whole travel agency business for the convention was her suggestion and she knew I'd contract her company. She knew it would fall apart, that if anyone went to jail it would be me, and she'd walk away with fifty grand."

Franklin stood to pour me another two fingers of whiskey; I motioned for three, make it four. "She works with Dominica, who is trouble with a capital T. And Calina, my God, Calina! She brought that criminal into the Barrymore campaign. And she still talks to her!" I was completely worked up now, the calming influence of smoke and liquor destroyed by these revelations.

Franklin waited until I'd had a few more sips and puffs before he offered his evidence. "The IRS is looking into her consulting fees for Operation Shine."

I was quite certain my ears were going to burst from my head. "Get out!"

"They were deemed excessively high." Franklin paused for dramatic effect. "Close to a mil."

I just about fell out of my chair. "Go to bed!"

"Mark my words, Operation Shine will lose their tax-exempt status because of her."

I was beyond scandalized, beyond disappointed. Seeing Prudence as she really was, I felt like I'd been tricked. Used. Manipulated.

I was confused all over again. "I tried to quit that job after the elections and she told me to stay. If she wanted my job, why would she tell me to stay?"

Franklin kicked his feet up on the edge of my chair. "Sears can't stand Dominica or Prudence. He never would have hired her. She needed Brogan as chair."

I sighed. "Wow, I've been totally played." I finished off my second whiskey, poured a third. "How could I have been so blind?"

Franklin pulled a long drag off his cigar, allowing the smoke to linger on his lips. "I say this with love in my heart so please hear it that way."

"Uh-oh."

"With all your family obligations, you've been in a walking coma. Prudence treated you like crap from day one." Franklin wrapped himself more tightly in his blanket. "Your career eclipsed hers and she was used to being in charge. That's why she controls your love life—because she can't run your career anymore."

"She doesn't run my love—"

Franklin interrupted, "You have no idea how many times Jamie and I tried to fix you up. Prudence vetoed them one by one."

This was news to me. "Like who?"

"Well actually, Ian Conley for one."

"That's why Jamie never introduced us!" I pouted. "She just can't stand it when anyone has one ounce of fun. That's why she spoke so badly about Kelley and tried to force Jamie to come home from Mardi Gras."

Franklin threw up his hands. "Don't get me started about Mardi Gras! The day that blogger ruined my life Prudence and Netta were nowhere to be found."

I shook my head vehemently. "They tried to call you."

"No, they did not. I tried to call them one hundred times and the only reason they got back in touch after my guy fired me was because *you* called every lobbyist on God's green earth. My party was the hottest ticket in town. They *had* to deal with me again."

It was enough. I'd had too much to drink, too much to smoke, had heard too much, had speculated beyond comprehension. It was time to call it a night. "I'm freezing. It's bedtime."

Franklin was still wild as a turkey. There was no way he could drive home. I gave him Goldie's side of the bed and the two of us spooned to warm away the remnants of chill. Never in a million years did I ever picture it would be Franklin sleeping over in my bed. Never in a million years would I have guessed Franklin would turn out to be my most loyal friend.

I wanted to believe that his visit was an act of bravery and loyalty, but after what I'd just witnessed at Café Milano I had my doubts. Franklin felt he owed me. Still, most D.C. insiders would now abandon me to the wolves, and see if I lived, before offering a helpful hand. Those that rallied around prey during a feeding frenzy were few and far between. Franklin had picked a side and for now, it was mine. As I drifted into a deep sleep, I heard him mumble, "The circles just get smaller and smaller."

I wasn't sure if it was my head or my BlackBerry buzzing at 7 a.m. I blinked against the morning light and had to remind myself that, yes, actually, that was Franklin on the other side of the bed. The BlackBerry continued buzzing and I let it pass to voice mail. My tongue tasted like a little man with poop on his shoes had stomped through my mouth. I was afraid my rancid breath would waft through the phone and melt the caller's ear. I stumbled out of the smoky blankets to the bathroom and splashed warm water on my face, brushed my whiskey-coated tongue, and gargled for good measure. Maybe I could deal with the new day. Maybe.

Senator MacLeish left a frantic message. "Senator Brogan roped me into the President's Dinner and now I hear you've resigned. What is going on? I'm not doing this without you! Come back, Temple!"

The next message was from Ian. I could tell he was peeved. "Weee've got us a situuuation here, Miss Sacheeet."

Prudence had completely screwed me. Senator Brogan and Ian now thought I'd lied to their faces. It looked as if I'd promised them my ongoing commitment while simultaneously resigning. I looked like a liar and I'd promised Ian I wasn't a liar.

I certainly didn't want to put Senators Brogan and MacLeish in an awkward position with Prudence or Senator Olin. But Ian was a different story. I called him back and told him everything, full disclosure. When I was done, I said, "I understand you'll need to keep me at arm's length."

I could hear Ian processing my story on the other end of the line. I waited for him to speak. "I should neeever have accepted that leeetter from anyooone buuut you direeectly."

"You are not responsible for the way grown people behave." I didn't want Ian burdened by my confession. "Prudence is a fantastic fundraiser and she'll raise beaucoup money for you. You'll hit all your goals."

Ian cut me off. "I still neeed you to do the President's Diiinner. MacLeish has refuuused to chair unless you're invooolved. He says you're the queeen. He's a big faaaan of yooours." I could almost hear Ian blushing through the phone as he complimented me. "We aaall aaare."

So I hadn't been entirely booted. "Ian, if you and Senator Brogan still want my help, I'll give it."

"Problem iiis, I've gotta hooouse y'at the Committeeee. You'll seee your ooold friend ev'ry daaay for the next six months."

"I'm a professional. You know I'm good at what I do. I won't let you down."

Eleven

The Only Way Out Is Out

*P*rudence so resented my continued involvement that she not only kicked me out of my second-floor office but moved me to a tiny cubicle on the first floor. Which was disrespectful, but I kept my mouth shut. Then she took away my assistant. The dinner was my swan song, my last hurrah for the Senate Committee. I was going out firing all my bullets. But I needed help to do it.

I burst into my old/her new office and confronted Prudence directly. "If this dinner's a failure, it happened on your watch. You're sabotaging your own success, not just my name."

Prudence feigned exasperation. "Temple, you continue to be nothing but a burden to me."

I'd never seen the outright hateful side of Prudence. Manipulative, yes. Backstabbing, unfortunately, yes. But hateful personal attacks? I stared in amazement as she continued.

"There's always some disaster, always some crisis. Your dad, your dog, some guy. You're a wounded bird and I don't need the project."

My mouth actually dropped open and before I knew what I was saying, the words tumbled through my teeth, "Wounded bird, my ass."

Prudence's face flushed scarlet. She sat straight up in her black leather chair. "Excuse me?"

I held my ground. "Yeah, that's right, I said ass. As in you are a giant one."

Prudence stood behind her desk. "I don't appreciate—"

I interrupted her, at full voice. "In my most heartbroken, betrayed moments of trying to understand why you've done what you've done, I never once imagined you pitied and patronized me for our entire friendship."

Prudence swallowed hard and her discomfort emboldened me to continue. "I thought friends stood by one another in the bad times. I thought, stupid me, that even though you stole my job, you still respected me as a person and deep down under all the, the, the shit, yes, I said shit, that is this city, you loved me as your friend. I could not have been more wrong."

Prudence dropped her eyes to the floor and I thought I recognized that small gesture as her shame. I was mistaken. She lifted her face toward mine and whispered, "I'm the boss now. Get the job done and don't expect me to baby you anymore."

Picture, if you will, the tasting.

The convention center's in-house catering had set a long table with linens, silverware, centerpiece options, and four different selections for every course. Since the President's Dinner was a joint effort between the two branches of Congress, both the House and the Senate planning committees had to agree on the menu.

We absolutely could not allow a repeat of last year's House disaster: the dreaded frozen chicken debacle. In their defense, the House was dealing with the aftershocks of campaign finance reform. The Cattlemen's Association could no longer donate steaks. The National Beer Wholesalers could no longer donate the beer or wine, and they weren't allowed to ask for corporate underwriting. The dinner turned out worse than a fifty-foot trough with a sneeze guard at a steakhouse. They literally put big bowls of Fritos at the entrance to the VIP reception. I mean, what Team Victory donor is going to grab a scoop of Fritos and then shake hands with the president?

Matters went from Fritos to freezo at the sit-down portion of the meal. The House staffers were running around screaming into their walkie-talkies, "Section 798 does not have chicken! Repeat, I need chicken at 798!" Two hundred people were served frozen, raw chicken. Seven hundred others didn't even see a plate. People were paying $1,500 for that chicken, they wanted their daggone chicken. It got ugly.

Which was why my tasting was so important. Normally, each Committee's finance director attended and brought their event person and that was it. But my tasting more resembled Da Vinci's crowded *Last Supper*. Complete with a Judas.

Prudence brought her den of collaborators: Netta and Dominica, whom she'd hired to do ticketing and seating. The job used to be an arduous process, worse than longhand accounting, and when done the old-fashioned way, yeah, it was worth some bucks. But the Stone Age had long since passed and now there was software that meant a monkey with a laptop could do it in an hour and a half. But Dominica was still charging 15 percent.

In other words, Dominica's contract was worth about $250,000, which meant, indirectly, Prudence was paying herself a consulting fee of $125,000 for work she would not be doing. If I'd had any doubts as to her integrity or her ethics, they were gone now.

Battling Prudence over Dominica was a lost cause. I had my hands full enough handling the House coordination team. They wanted Jessica Simpson to sing the national anthem. I absolutely could not have Daisy Duke showing up in short shorts and overshadowing the president on his big night. I hired the Harlem Boys Choir instead.

Repping the House at our tasting was their finance director and her highly overpaid team, Nina and Ellen. Nina and Ellen were a couple—though they were not "out" per se, they were inseparable—and had paid for their first, second, and third mansions with President's Dinner paychecks. They'd had the market cornered for years and came with a six-figure price tag, which I'd cut in half. No one on the House side was happy with me.

Ian Conley was so unnerved by the tension surrounding the planning he'd decided to show. Then I arrived, flanked on one side by Franklin, who had volunteered to handle all the moving parts. If there was anyone in D.C. who could transform a cattle call into a hot-ticket party, it was Franklin. On my other side was Hudson Emetaz, my event uber-manager, who'd staged the fireworks for the Statue of Liberty Celebration and ran the pope's schedule when he visited the United States. The guy was a pro's pro. Top-notch. My boys had my back.

At the last minute the president's office decided to send someone over as well, even though the president never ate; he just came, gave a speech, and never even bothered to sit down before he left the dinner. Attending the tasting was a "connected thing" and the honor was often handed to the most connected lobbyist in D.C., which meant Franklin's hubby, Evan Vaughn, walked through the doors and joined us. On top of all the seething animosity, now we had to pretend that Franklin and Evan weren't a couple.

The convention center's in-house caterers placed four different salads in front of us. Poor little dishes never had a chance. The mood in the room was on-edge hostile—the women just looking for a fight, the men completely in over their heads. Our hatred manifested as acerbic food criticism worthy of the *New York Times*.

Prudence pushed her first plate away. "These greens are over-dressed." The first punch thrown. A dig at my style.

I smiled oh-so-innocently. "Really? I find them bitter."

The tasting went downhill from there. The men at the table ate. The women did not. We were pecking and prodding, sneering and snide. Prudence felt the risotto was "too rich"; I countered by describing the beef as "past its prime." By the time desserts were offered, I was sick to my stomach. The thought of swallowing cold dishes of jealousy, venom, and rivalry for eight more weeks of planning was enough to turn a binger into an anorexic.

In terms of the actual food, it was apparent I'd have to hire an outside caterer. We'd all been so brutal, I had no other choice. But in terms of my emotional well-being, there was no company I could hire to save my soul. That was a contract that couldn't be jobbed out.

Life had an outrageously miserable way of reprioritizing my upsets. Prudence was diagnosed with a malignant tumor and a nasty storm was bound for New Orleans. Our petty squabbles no longer mattered one iota.

Sophia was in Metairie hunkered down with our next-door neighbors, Cecil and Hattie, and their menagerie of five cats, three dogs, and a bird. Cecil'd fired up their generator and the three of them were throwing a "bring it on" party instead of flying to Mom's house in St. Louis as both Mom and I had begged them to do.

"It's headed for the panhandle, we'll be fine." Sophia was unconcerned by the escalation of the approaching tropical storm and the declaration of a hurricane watch. "We'll call when it's blown over."

From the safety of my apartment in D.C., I watched CNN's coverage ceaselessly. The hurricane was named Katrina and continued to gather strength, building from a Category 1 to a Category 3 then to a Category 5, until finally a press conference was called and Mayor Nagin, in his short-sleeved polo, stepped in front of a mass of microphones, his face so full of worry it filled my gut with dread.

"I wish I had better news, but we're facing the storm most of us have feared." The mayor was flanked by city and state officials, all of whom looked as if they might burst into tears. "This is very serious. This is going to be an unprecedented event."

Mom called me, flustered and going to pieces sitting in St. Louis, now unable to reach Sophia by phone. "Why didn't she listen to us?"

"Mom, when has Sophia ever listened to anyone?"

By her breathless delivery, I could tell Mom was pacing. "I've got to get there and find them. I'll take the plane down tonight."

"Mom, Mom, no! You are not flying into that storm. You don't even know if they're still there. They could have evacuated."

I was somewhat successful at keeping Mom calm, until the levees breached in St. Bernard Parish and the news began reporting that people were hacking through their roofs with axes in order to be rescued. We had no idea if Sophia, Cecil, and Hattie were okay. We had no idea if our house, three blocks down from the Lake Pontchartrain levee, was still standing. I was on the phones nonstop, unable to eat, sleep, or think straight. There was little to no helpful information coming out of any parish. The only thing we knew for sure was that all airports in the region were open only for humanitarian and rescue operations.

Mom wasn't going to let that stop her. "I'll load up the plane with food and clothes. People need help and I have to find your sister!"

There was no talking Mom out of her mission. "I'm going with you."

"No, no, one of us has to stay where there are phones and banks and electricity in case they try to reach us."

I was out of my mind with worry. My stomach was in knots and burning with hot fear. Cell phone service was sporadic and it took four terrifying days to hear from Mom.

"Oh thank God, are you alright? Where's Sophia?"

Mom was trying to keep it together. "I found Cecil and Hattie. They made it to Arkansas but they were separated from Sophia in the chaos."

I could not stop myself from screaming, "WHAT DO YOU MEAN? WHERE IS SHE?"

"Temple, Temple. We'll find her. We will."

And we did. Thank God, we did. Sophia called me from Baton Rouge, where she was sleeping on the floor of a friend's house, physically safe but furious at what she was seeing. "People have no money, the banks in Baton Rouge won't cash FEMA vouchers, and the Red Cross is turning away food from restaurants and hotels and brand-new clothes from retail stores and handing people smelly unwashed T-shirts and fruit roll-ups. There's no leadership."

Cecil and Hattie were equally frustrated. "FEMA moved five hundred trailers out here and stuck them in swampland. They sunk like stones. That's American tax dollars sitting in the mud when people need houses!"

Mom, being Mom, had taken matters into her own hands. She was holed up in the original offices of Sachet Connections, located in Jefferson Parish. She was calling every major rental property owner from Texas to Florida to figure out the entire open inventory in the

South. She had addresses, contact names, and phone numbers for every available apartment. She knew square footage and number of bathrooms and had negotiated rent breaks for relocated renters. Mom had mobilized her employees and sent them into the field all over the South, one representative to every Red Cross receiving shelter, where they could help the refugees (did I ever think I would use that word about Americans?) find a new home near their families and loved ones.

All her work was for naught.

She called me, crying from frustration. "The Red Cross won't allow us to sit at their tables and hand out information. They keep saying FEMA's handling housing but FEMA is shipping parents to Utah and sending their kids to Idaho. It's beyond stupid. It's a travesty."

This, this was how I could be helpful! All those soul-draining months finally meant something. I knew people at Homeland Security. I had friends at the Senate. I'd accumulated favors. I had direct phone numbers. I could be of service!

I told Mom, "I'll get the senators down there if you can show them firsthand what's happening."

I put the President's Dinner on the back burner to organize tours of New Orleans. My first tour, only Senator Brogan signed up. I was outraged by the response—or more accurately, the total lack of response. You would've thought New Orleans was on the other side of the world. D.C. had insulated itself and was looking the other way. There's not a word for how disgusted and demoralized I felt.

I pulled out my BlackBerry and I started pecking. These senators couldn't ignore me. I'd done my part for the Party, now it was time for these men to step up to the plate. I decided I couldn't give them the chance to say a polite "no" over the phone. I showed up at their offices, hat in hand.

My first visit was to Majority Leader Ivy. "Sir, I need the entire Senate to get on a plane and see New Orleans. Armageddon has hit my state and I need your help."

"Problem is, Temple, it's become a partisan issue." Senator Ivy stopped examining the itinerary Mom and I created to expose senators to the worst-hit areas in the Ninth Ward and St. Bernard Parish. "I can pull from the Republican caucus but between you and me, we've got a senator who views this situation as an opportunity for self-promotion. He wants to be the face of Congress during the recovery efforts. He won't be happy you're stealing his thunder."

I no longer held my tongue in front of Senator Ivy. After his benevolence with Daddy Gil and his bailing me out with Senator Griswold, the man was family to me. "This is life or death, Senator. It isn't political."

The senator sighed mournfully. "It's always political."

Ivy pressured twenty-four of his colleagues into our tour, a very different tour of New Orleans than my last trip for Mardi Gras. No Happy Bus, no genteel balls, the streets turned to rivers, muddy with sewage and the floating dead.

Seeing it on TV and being there were two very different experiences. Everything seemed to move in silent, slow motion. I could not catch my bearings. Buildings half-submerged were unfamiliar, landmarks had been swept away. Mom would point and say, "This used to be . . . " and I heard her words but they had no meaning. I peered out the windows of the yellow school bus Mom secured for our tour.

Water. Water. Everywhere.

Was that the roof of the school where I'd run for Little Miss Valentine? Was that the hospital that held the gift shop where Mom had worked long hours so she could open her own business? Where was the hotel where Kelley and I first kissed?

Water. Water. Everywhere.

My efforts were the equivalent of patching a band-aid on a severed arm. When Daddy Gil had fallen ill in Italy, I'd felt powerless. But Hurricane Katrina rendered me useless. It was a feeling I'd tried to avoid my entire life but now, here it was. Smacking me in the face. Useless.

Over and over, I was reminded that the controlling grip I thought I held on life was in fact a tenuous grasp, feathers in an open palm. The faster I swatted to keep them nicely stacked in a pretty pile, the farther they blew away. My city had blown away.

Miraculously, our house was still standing. The nearest levee had held even though none of the trees, power lines, and windows in our neighborhood had. Walking into our front yard, I reached for Mom's hand. We stared up at our stubborn old house, grateful beyond words.

Lucky, we were so lucky.

I returned to D.C. to finish what I'd started: the President's Dinner. Sophia joined Mom in New Orleans and for the next five weeks, they ran a free apartment-finding service out of Mom's office while their parking lot began to fill with locals offering clothing, food, and money to whoever showed up in need.

Hope returned to Mom's voice. "I've got a man in my parking lot handing out $50 bills. There's a woman who's a seamstress; she brought her sewing machine and she's here sewing clothes for survivors. The country needs to see that strangers are helping strangers. Not everyone is looting and killing."

New Orleans was decimated and I was spending my energy orchestrating the biggest, most lavish party in the country. The seven-thousand-person event stretched the length of the entire convention center floor, two football fields long. It was costing us over $3 million to run and we'd hired six hundred waiters just to get everyone fed. We'd raised over $25 million for the Republican Party, which paled in comparison to the $100 million raised prior to campaign finance reform. Still, it was a ton of money. Money that could have been rebuilding my hometown.

I needed my family around me. Though Mom had been a Team Victory member for years, she'd never come to any of my D.C. parties. She hated seeing me stressed out, frantic, and overworked, but I was really proud of the dinner I'd managed to program in spite of seemingly every possible obstacle. I knew my last hurrah in Washington would be beautiful and I wanted to share it with Sophia and Mom.

My day began, sharp-suited, at 7 a.m. as I zipped through the convention center on my final run-through. Franklin was handling the Big Bad Voodoo Daddy sound check while Hudson oversaw the installation of the laser light equipment. I trusted them implicitly, which gave me the freedom to brief the catering captains on accommodating our VIP guests.

When everything at the convention center was good to go Secret Service emptied the building. For the next three hours they swept every inch for bombs. That was my cue to check in on Mom and Sophia. I called Sophia's cell phone and caught them sitting down to lunch at the Four Seasons.

Sophia asked, "Can you pass by?"

"Uh, no, I'm working on this tiny little event here at the convention center. It's called the *President's Dinner*, you've heard about it, right?"

Mom grabbed the phone away from Sophia. "You can't stop and have a bite?"

Clearly, Mom and Sophia had no understanding of the magnitude of the event. "I'll grab a hot dog on the street. Now remember, you two need to get there early because you have to be magged at the door."

"Magged?" Mom hurled the word like an insult. "What do they think I can fit in a tiny little beaded purse?"

"It's like airport security, Mom. You've got no choice. They have to walk you through the mags and then wand you. Y'hear me? Get there early, okay?"

My old office, which had a shower and room to sprawl on the floor, was a bad memory but would have come in handy. Instead, I was relegated to using the first-floor bathroom to slip into my formalwear. My Upper House donor the Baroness of Brazil was already stationed in front of a mirror, half-naked, with her homemade beauty products strewn all over the sink. I had the unfortunate task of buckling the Baroness into her bustier. The image of her breasts smashed flat against her ribs scarred me for life. Once the Baroness was tucked in and on her way, I scurried to beautify.

I'd fallen in love with a gorgeous vintage YSL cocktail dress on eBay and had it shipped express just for the occasion. The dress was fantastic: with sheer, black blousy sleeves, a plunging neckline caught up in an empire waist and bow, with layer upon layer of sheer black fabric cascading down my thighs. I loved the way it felt and moved, even if I was strapped across the hips with a walkie-talkie, wearing flats, and burdened by a ten-pound logistics binder. All of it was necessary. I had to have on hand every possible contract, seating chart, ticket number, and scheduling breakdown that might be needed. I even managed to slip a comb and lipstick into the side pocket. I took one last look in the mirror, then headed back to the convention center.

My BlackBerry rang en route. The president was running late for the VIP click line. His chief of staff informed me we'd have very little time with him before the dinner started. Great. My Team Victorys were going to be ticked from the get-go.

I instructed my driver to pull up to the Senate entrance, where the senators and their wives were arriving by car and driver. The House members, in sharp contrast, had been loaded onto a Greyhound bus in front of the Capitol and shipped over like a bunch of sixth graders on a field trip.

I found Majority Leader Ivy standing with his wife on the line to be magged. I gave him the play-by-play. "The president is running late so if you don't mind, I'd like you to meet and greet the VIP click line until he shows. We can grab some candids."

"Whatever you need, Temple." I could always count on Senator Ivy. I fast-forwarded him and his wife through security, then led them into the VIP Mainstage Reception, where cocktails and hors d'oeuvres were supposed to be passed while our elite donors waited in line for their presidential click. I walked into the curtained-off VIP area and discovered there was nobody was in the room. Our head Senate table, donors who'd each raised $100,000, were missing. Our $250,000 president's table people were missing. Our honored dais people were missing! The waiters were standing around talking to each other.

This was a disaster in the making. I knew Secret Service and the president's press team would shut down the click line if I didn't have donors in the room when he arrived. I smiled and quickly ushered Senator Ivy and his wife over to the bar. "Have a drink and I'll be back with the donors in two seconds."

Safely out of earshot, I grabbed my walkie-talkie and quickly SOS'd Franklin. "We've got no donors in VIP."

Franklin was already on it. "Dominica's people created some convoluted way of checking people in. The names are organized by ticket number and not alphabetically. We've got gridlock at check-in. I need you here."

I took off at a full run. Every party-planner knows, you always have an alpha list and a table list and a company list so you can move people along. What was wrong with these women!

I burst into the lobby, where all my donors were being herded through the mags like cows to the slaughter. Most of the Senate donors were in suits and cocktail dresses but the House donors had taken it to an entirely new level of tacky with tuxes and full-length, sequined mermaid gowns.

Our zany cast of Upper House characters gave them a run for their money, arriving bejeweled and pre-lubricated. Kindly Mrs. Houghton was already swooning in a nonexistent breeze. Brookie Judge had her leaking personalized pens and our Asian Mafia were escorting wives with eyes so heavily lined with black kohl they resembled Goth vampires. Our sheet-wearing lady had opted instead for a Little Bo Peep ensemble complete with a hoop skirt and matching umbrella.

All of them were grabbing at my arms, wanting to air-kiss hello, waving and trying to get me to give them a hug. I could not linger. I pushed through the sea of tulle and sequins to see three women with pencils behind their ears, scratching their heads, flipping through papers. The VIP check-in line was at a standstill.

Franklin commandeered the lists and quickly handed me a clipboard. He and I ran up and down the line, providing donors with their tickets and table numbers. We cleared the line out in ten minutes, then swiftly ushered the lot of them through security and directly to the

VIP reception where Senator Ivy began immediately to shake hands and work his magic. The president arrived shortly after and his press team quickly propped him on his toe mark. The click line pushing and pulling began. Crisis averted.

Franklin laughed with relief. "Man, we're good."

I wasn't ready to relax yet. Big Bad Voodoo Daddy started their opening set and Mom and Sophia were still nowhere to be found. I had not told them they'd be seated on the dais because I wanted to surprise them, but now I was regretting that decision. If they didn't show up soon, I'd have to give those seats away to another donor.

Given the incompetence of Dominica's check-in staffers, I was worried they'd been directed to the wrong pre-dinner reception by mistake. I first checked the Congressional Reception where my Upper House donors were posing in front of huge standing logos for the RSCC and the RCCC as well as the presidential seal. Franklin had set them up as if it were a prom and it was clearly a big hit, just hokey enough to be right up their alley. I did my best to ward off the sex-starved mamaw in her sequined mini-skirt and once I was convinced Mom and Sophia were not in that reception, I ran to the Leadership Lounge area.

Once again, Franklin had outdone himself transforming the loading dock of the convention center into an elegant, almost cabaret-like atmosphere. Lobbyists mingled with high-level donors as senators and congressmen posed for candid photos by the open bar. But still, no Sophia or Mom.

Guests were being ushered to their dinner tables where their *beautifully dressed* (if I do say so myself, and I do) salads were pre-set. By the time Hudson cued our video tribute to the American flag on the enormous wraparound surround-sound IMAX screens, I was truly panicked. Where were Mom and Sophia? I could not have empty seats on the dais.

I scoured the lobby, searching for their faces. They breezed in just as the Harlem Boy's Choir began the national anthem. I didn't even say hello. I started running them, as fast as their high-heeled tootsies would go, to the Mainstage holding area. "Where were you two?"

Sophia hiked her skirt up so she could hit full stride. "We were having champagne."

I was panting as I ran. "You realize we have champagne here, right?"

Mom tried to slow to a walk. "Is all this running necessary?"

I grabbed her by the elbow and sped her up again. "Yes, yes, it is!"

We made it to the VIP holding area just as the overhead announcement blared, "Welcome to the annual President's Dinner." I pushed Sophia and Mom in line behind my senators as the spotlight hit the curtain in front.

Applause rose up as Majority Leader Ivy led the dais honorees onto the stage. Mom and Sophia finally realized what was happening. They had ringside seats for the extravaganza.

Delighted, Mom turned to me as the line inched forward, "Temple, we get to be in the front of the whole room!"

"You've given enough money as a Team Victory donor. You deserve some special treatment."

Sophia was awestruck. "You totally rock."

It was their turn to step into the spotlight. "Hug me later, go, go!"

Mom and Sophia walked out into the white light and finally, the dinner was underway.

The speeches started. Speech after speech after speech. Finally, Senator MacLeish introduced the president, who talked for forty-five minutes (these were his peeps after all) while guests chowed down on their perfectly cooked beef Wellingtons. Not a frozen chicken in the room. I made my way to the back of the convention center, safely out of earshot of all the congratulatory brouhaha. I may have thrown the guy a dinner but I didn't have to listen to him.

As Gray wrapped up his pep rally, Hudson took over with a laser light spectacular that had the whole room clapping and cheering along. It was a hard act to follow, but Big Bad Voodoo Daddy took the floor again as the revelers spilled onto the three dance floors. That was the staff cue to run for the hills.

For the first time that night, I had time to track down Wilson. The Animal League had written a $15,000 check to the RSCC, something it'd never done before, which entitled him to a ticket. Wilson and my family were finally in the same room. Their meeting was long overdue. I could feel the butterflies caged and fluttering in my tummy. Would Mom and Sophia like him?

I searched everywhere for Wilson and found him at one of the bars badgering a visibly perturbed Senator Sears about gestation crates legislation. "Wilson, come. I want to introduce you to my family."

"Now? The senator and I were just discussing . . . " But the senator had wisely seen his out and taken it. Wilson put down his drink, offered his arm, and walked with me toward the dais.

I bounced along happily beside him. "I should warn you. Sophia's probably going to ask you to come on safari with us."

Wilson scowled. "Safaris are a perverse subculture. A bunch of wealthy elites, shooting at the world's most beautiful animals. Just to show off trophies."

I felt the hair on the back of my neck lift. "Well, we don't want to shoot the lions, Wilson, we just want to see them."

Wilson's eyes scanned the room, darting back and forth, his own internal facial recognition system. "I thought you were going to seat me with Senator Inhoff. I need him to get behind our post-Katrina neutering initiatives."

"I put you at the same table. He didn't show?"

"Ah! There he is." Wilson unwrapped himself from me. "I need to grab him." He blew a kiss in my general direction. "Call you tomorrow."

I stood there like a dejected Cinderella, the light bulb finally clicking on. Wilson Cho had absolutely no desire to meet my mom and sister. He wasn't recovering from his divorce. He wasn't being respectful of my grief. He wasn't honoring my losses. Wilson was flat-out using me for my contacts!

Being with me gave Wilson unprecedented access to Republican senators who otherwise would have seen his face and hightailed it. Good God. I'd been in the dumbest relationship ever. It wasn't even a relationship, it was a joke. A wave of regret washed over me. And it had nothing to do with Wilson.

Kelley. I'd seen Kelley through Prudence's eyes and decided he didn't measure up. I'd thrown away his love and his loyalty to chase after a man from "my world," someone Prudence couldn't condemn. And then, out of fear she'd still disapprove, never even introduced Wilson to her.

I watched as Wilson cornered Senator Inhoff like a hound with a coon. How wrong I'd been. Prudence would have loved Wilson. He was just her type.

I owed Kelley a huge apology. And it couldn't wait one more second. I ducked back into the empty VIP holding area and called his Mexico number. His surfer friend, Shade, picked up the phone. "Bueno."

"Shade? This is Temple, is Kelley around?"

There was a long pause and I assumed Shade needed a reminder. "I'm the girl from D.C."

Shade finally spoke. His tone was protective and angry. "I know who you are. Kelley's not here and I'm going to do him a big favor and not even tell him you called."

"Wait, wait, don't hang up. Can't you please tell him I'm sorry?"

"Lady, unless you're moving here to marry him, he doesn't need your 'sorry,' okay?" And then he hung up on me. Which is exactly what I deserved, even if it felt like crap.

I had no time to recover my wits. Mom and Sophia had tracked me down. They were smiling like I hadn't seen them smile in ages. Sophia hugged me first. "You're a total superstar. We had the best time."

Mom hugged me proudly. "Tee, honey, it was absolutely beautiful. You've come so far from that little opera gala! Remember how scared you were back then?"

Sophia and I both laughed out loud. I corrected Mom's memory. "You mean how scared *you* were for me?"

"Okay, yes, you're right." Mom held up her hands in defeat. "But Tee, this was extraordinary. You really outdid yourself."

Sophia freshened her lipstick without the assistance of a mirror. "So are we going to meet Wilson or what?"

Now it was my turn to throw up my hands in defeat. "Actually, no. That's done. Hup!" I quickly pressed my index finger against Mom's parting lips. "And I don't want to talk anymore about it tonight."

Mom quietly nodded her agreement to my terms as Sophia snapped her cocktail purse shut. "So, where's the after-party?"

My Sorority Row girls had organized a "shhh, don't tell Prudence" goodbye gathering for me at a bar called Zaytinya. The whole Senate Committee posse (minus Netta and Prudence, of course) had already gathered and was well on its way to intoxication. Franklin was passing out tequila shooters like they were water. Staffers blubbered their well wishes and hugged me. Ian Conley even showed up for the fun. He pinned me against the bar, whispering cautiously about Prudence's health. "She's doing better but she's lost all her hair. Have you seen her?"

I'd done everything in my power to stay out of Prudence's way the last six months. Our relationship had deteriorated to a series of "chemo-calls," Prudence calling me with long lists of complaints as she sat, I.V. in arm, getting her dose of salvation. It had been unbearable but you can't yell back when someone is suffering. At least, I couldn't.

The last thing I wanted to talk about was Prudence. Tonight was the first night of my full freedom and I wanted to feel good. The job was history. Wilson was history. And by God, I was going to sow an oat whether anyone liked it or not. The perfect candidate, Ian, was standing right in front of me: a man with a crush and a sweet Southern drawl. Done and done.

Franklin interrupted, pushing a shot of tequila in front of my nose. "Drink up, Temple!"

I wanted to be stone-cold sober for my Ian rendezvous. I didn't want to miss one moment. "Give it to Mom. She'll drink it."

Franklin was shocked. "I'm not pushing a shot on your mother."

"Mom!" I yelled down the bar where Mom and Sophia were entertaining anyone within earshot. "Franklin's going to make me drink this unless you do."

She waved the glass her way. "Hand it to me!" The shot was passed down the bar, picking up spectators along the way, until it reached Mom. She saluted the crowd then tossed it back like a pro. A deafening cheer and applause rose up.

Ian's eyes were wide as saucers. "Your Mom's the coolest."

"Yes, yes she is." I glanced back down the bar and Mom shot me a quick wink. I winked back.

We shut the bar down, all of us tripping into the street, laughing and singing under the full August moon, red in the sky. A full moon meant transformation. A full moon meant the end of the old and the beginning of the new. A full moon meant . . . Wolf Blitzer?

I spotted him first, gazing not at the red moon but at a red light, stopped and waiting for the go. I howled as loud as my lungs allowed, "Awwwwwooooooooooooooooo!" I wasn't drunk; I was giddy with my hard-won freedom and continued to howl "Awwwwwoooooooo!," pointing at the moon then the Wolf, the moon then the Wolf. Everyone thought I was crazy; nobody knew what I meant—until Wolf Blitzer got out of his car, cracking up laughing and clapping for me. Finally, my party realized who he was, what I was doing, and joined the Wolf in his raucous applause. I took a deep bow. "And a good night to us all!"

Ian caught up with me and took my right hand in his left. "I can drive you and your mom and sister home."

What a sweet guy. We'd never even been on a date and already he was taking care of my family. More than Wilson had ever offered. I squeezed Ian's hand in mine. "They're big girls. Let's go to your house instead."

Which we did. And thank heavens to Betsy, I finally, *finally* sowed myself an oat.

And an oat.

And an oat.

Hee hee.

I jumped awake at nine the next morning. Oh my God, oh my God, oh my God! Had I really? Yep, yep, there he was, Ian Conley with his bare legs tangled in the sheets of my, nope, nope, this wasn't my bed, it was his. Those were my shoes, that was my dress and bra, but this was definitely not my bedroom. Oh my God, oh my God, oh my God, I had to go, go, go.

I flew out of bed and like a Tasmanian devil spun around the room redressing and searching for loose pieces—my shoes, a purse, that burdensome binder, my earrings, too many pieces. Really, all this crap was mine? Now?

Ian woke and smiled, scruffy haired and adorable from the long night. He watched me from the comfort of his bed, amused by my frantic spinning. "You don't have to go."

"Sophia and Mom are going to be at my apartment in like twenty minutes." Where in the flipping world were my undies? "I promised we'd have breakfast before they left."

Ian unwrapped himself from the sheets and began dressing. I averted my eyes, blushing like a freshman on her walk of shame. "I'll drive you home."

"No, no, I'll take a cab."

"What kind of guy would I be if I let you take a cab home?"

Ian insisted on driving me home. As we neared my block, I spied Mom exiting a cab in front of my door. I slinked down into the seat. "Pull over!"

Ian laughed but obliged. "Does your mom still think you're a good girl?"

Peeking over the dashboard, I said, "I am a good girl." Ian put the car in park, a little too close for comfort. Mom was in sight. I attempted to open the passenger-side door from my prone position.

Ian leaned down to kiss me. "Call me, okay?"

There was no way in heck I was going to call Ian. This was a one-night stand, the only one I'd ever had in my life, and I wanted to leave it that way. I kissed him anyway. "Okay, bye-bye." I gathered my things and tried to ooze out unseen. No such luck.

Disheveled and wearing last night's dress, I shuffled toward Mom, trying hard not to drop everything in my hands. Mom cocked an eyebrow but before she could open her mouth to say a word, a black Lincoln Town Car with tinted windows pulled up to the curb. Sophia emerged, only slightly less inebriated than she was the night before. Both Mom and I craned our necks to catch a glimpse of the Big Bad Voodoo cutie tucked inside. Sophia and her musicians . . .

Sophia and I stood before Mom, who just shook her head and tried to look stern. "You two are a fine mess." She couldn't hold it together and laughed right in our faces.

"Let's get inside before all of D.C. starts yapping."

Shoes, purse, and binder in hand, I somehow managed to get my keys in the door. I just needed a quick shower and then we could eat. Starved, I was starved.

We paraded into my living room but something was off. No, wrong. Completely and totally wrong. Everything I owned was gone.

The living room was stripped bare. I could see through my curtainless sliding glass door—no patio furniture; the porch lay empty. I dropped everything. My keys crashed to the wooden floor. No rug to break their fall. I ran to my bedroom. No bed, no clothes. The bathroom, no towels. The office, no computer. The kitchen, Nana's silver gone. My heart wrenched and I ran for the fireplace mantle. Goldie's ashes, her urn—everything was gone. Everything.

I spun in baffled circles. Sophia fell to her knees. Mom sat beside her on the floor. We were all speechless, overwhelmed, and frozen with shock. Seeing them there, the two most precious people in my world, in the middle of that empty shell I called my life, it all became very, very clear.

These two women, my sister and my mother, they were my soul. I saw them as if I were standing slightly outside myself, from the perspective Daddy Gil taught me: looking and appreciating and feeling all at once. If he'd been standing beside me—which I felt, perhaps, he was—he would have held the moment to the light like a diamond. To gain clarity. To examine its colors.

If I could have, right then and there, gone back in time and done one thing over, I would have stopped Daddy Gil from getting on that boat. I would have taken him to a hospital and I would have thrown out all his candy bars and I would have saved our family. I would have brought us all together again, because losing him, I lost myself. I was lost and blind to who I was, what I was doing and why. I'd lost a vision beyond my own sorrow. I wanted so desperately to bring him back and that desperation had skewed my internal moral compass. Daddy Gil had been my due north. Without him, I'd been lost at sea.

I saw now the faint lines of sorrow circling Mom's eyes. She was still a beautiful woman, the source of my integrity, my determination, my spirit. But she was lonely without Daddy Gil. Beside her sat Sophia, my stunningly gorgeous, driven-by-passion sister who taught me independence, self-reliance, and courage. Suddenly, she looked like a frail little doll. I wanted to wrap her up in a warm blanket. A surge of protective, territorial fury rose in me. Nobody had the right to scare my family like this.

"Somebody wants you gone." Sophia was spooked. I saw it in her eyes.

I shivered with the creepy-crawlies. "We've got to get out of here."

"First, you need to call the police, Temple." That was Mom. But I shook my head no. I wanted out of that chilling, empty place as fast as possible. And I wasn't talking about my apartment. Suddenly, D.C. was the most desperate, manipulative, and terrifying city in the world. I wanted out as fast as humanly possible.

"The boat, Mom. Let's get on the boat."

A Spirit Will Rise

*D*addy Gil once told me, "When you hit rock bottom, that's good, solid ground." Fleeing D.C. cut me down to bedrock, but I still needed a firm foundation on which to rebuild the new, improved me. I found it in Africa.

What started as an awe-inspiring safari adventure complete with elephants, lions, hyenas, and giraffes extended into Botswana then Tanzania then Kenya. Africa affected me deeply. I'd seen poverty in Appalachia, I'd seen New Orleans in a state of emergency, but I'd never, in the face of such extreme deprivation, seen joy. The African spirit was indomitable.

The country did more than inspire me. It sent me on a new life journey. Zoë was in Kenya, visiting the AIDS Prevention Project, her charismatic rock-star presence making her the hot topic among tourists.

Sophia's innocent question—"Didn't you meet her?"—spurred me to text LaSonya. Sure enough, she was with Zoë, and I met up with them in the coastal town of Mombasa. When I returned to the States, I became an official employee of A2A.

I moved to New York, where my time was spent rounding up and engaging the talented, the intelligent, and the famous to lend their names and influence to the A2A mission. My energy and my work actually helped people instead of lining the pockets of overpaid advertisers, pollsters, spin doctors, and God forbid, other fundraisers.

Three years passed quickly and another November ushered in sweeping change for my old colleagues. The Democrats ousted the Republican majority. Senator Sears was outed as a gay man and Senator Griswold, despite his eleventh-hour begging appeal for Franklin to save his campaign (which Franklin happily declined), was handily defeated. Senator Ivy opted not to run after the IRS began investigating his charity and Senator Olin, who'd "conveniently" replaced Brogan as the chair of the Committee, was bearing the full brunt of the fallout.

Jamie was now in charge of the Team Victory donors, replacing Netta, who'd finally become a mother. I'd been invited then disinvited to Jasmine's baptism. Prudence was named her godmother.

Christmas brought with it the usual parties and since Mom was still a Team Victory donor, she was invited to attend Senator Brogan's holiday bash at Essex House off Central Park. The night's host: the meat-eating oilman who loved Prince, Larry Tiegs.

Mom happened to be staying with me in New York but did not want to go. "I don't want to see that woman." Mom no longer referred to Prudence by name. "I might say something unpleasant."

"Mom, if you're not going to go, you have to call them and tell them that you're not coming."

"Why are you still watching out for them?"

"Because I adore Mrs. Brogan and Ian's not so bad either."

"Fine. I'll go. But you're coming with me."

So, the two of us went. First people we see? You guessed it, Senator Olin and Prudence. Senator Olin had aged in a way that caused my heart to skip a beat. He looked pale and weak. Prudence had survived breast cancer and was, as usual, perfectly coiffed, her blonde, sleek hair grown back and chopped into severe bangs once again. She was wearing the blue Hermes scarf I'd given her after the national convention and she looked exactly as I remembered her from that first meeting on the airport tarmac. Tightly polished—and, I now realized, terse and mean. Cancer had not softened Prudence in any way. She shot over an icy glare then crossed to the opposite side of the room.

Mom smiled her scary smile. "I'm a donor. She should, at a minimum, make sure I have my name tag and a drink!"

I placed a calming hand on Mom's arm. "That was for me, not you."

Everyone else was thrilled we'd shown. Our arrival was heralded by donors and staffers who hadn't seen hide nor hair of me for over three years. Mom spotted Nancy Reagan sitting beside Tony Bennett and Larry King, and headed for their table.

I was bombarded by hugs and questions, because nobody, and I mean nobody, ever completely walked away from those jobs. Maybe they stopped fundraising, but only to take an even more lucrative lobbying position. The fact that I'd walked away from D.C. entirely and was working for a nonprofit was incomprehensible.

Sorority Row wanted to know all about Zoë. Senator MacLeish urged me to "come back, the Party needs you," while Ian Conley pulled me aside and whispered in my ear, "We miss you in Washington. I miss you."

Thankfully, Senator Brogan interrupted us. She just about knocked Ian over to get to me. "Oh, Temple, I was hoping I'd see you!" As Senator Brogan nearly strangled me with a bear hug, I spotted Jamie standing at a distance and smiling directly at me. Jamie, wow, I hadn't had an actual conversation with him since that awful dinner at Café Milano.

After Senator Brogan and I caught up and she headed off to schmooze my mom, Jamie shyly approach with a shamed smile. "Temple. You look amazing."

I scowled at his handshake and grabbed him in a hug instead. "So do you, darling."

What did it matter anymore to hold that anger? I certainly didn't trust Jamie any farther than I could throw him, but harboring anger only hurt me. Still, Prudence wasn't happy about our little make-up session. I could feel her eyes boring holes through the back of my neck.

I leaned forward, conspiratorially. "Somebody's angry with you."

Jamie sing-songed his secret. "Somebody's being indicted."

There it was. The reason why Jamie no longer feared Prudence, the reason why Netta had left the Committee: Franklin's prediction had come true. Prudence was under federal investigation.

Hearing those words, my heart softened for her. What lay in store for Prudence was worse than her battle with cancer. It was misery I'd never wish on an enemy. I turned around and walked straight for her.

Maybe it was my overactive imagination, or my inherent sense of drama, but it seemed to me that time slowed and every eye in the room focused on me. Senator Olin saw me coming and his nervous expression caused Prudence to turn around. I caught her by surprise, which was, given her constant stoic demeanor, an accomplishment in and of itself.

I reached out and took both her hands in mine. I spoke sincerely. "Prudence, the party is fantastic. You always do such a beautiful job. There's nobody better."

Prudence blinked hard against my compliment, unsure how to respond. Her mouth formed the words "thank you" but her mind was still spinning.

As I started to walk away, I said, "I'm so glad you like the scarf. It truly is stunning on you."

Three days later, Mom and I were headed to another Christmas party on the Upper East Side when a FedEx package was delivered to my apartment. Even though we were already running late, I opened it immediately because it was from Prudence.

Inside the padded envelope was the blue Hermes scarf. I lifted and shook it, searching for a note, an explanation. Nothing.

Mom saw my hurt expression. "Were all those Chanel purses you gave her in there too? That's something that woman could've sent back."

"Mom, you're terrible."

"It's the truth. You would've taken those back." Mom cinched her coat closed and slipped on her gloves. "Are you ready to go, Tee?"

I wrapped that rejected, opulent square of silk around my own shoulders, the brilliant blue framing my face, a reminder of those first days when I'd fancied myself the next "Brenda Charles," a woman with purpose. That lavish, decadent scarf, fifteen pounds lighter than a murderous eagle. This, this was Freedom.

"Yes, Mom. Let's go."

The End

Acknowledgments

Nicole and Susan would like to thank: Each other (of course!), Marty Richards and Producer's Circle for bringing us together; Maura Teitelbaum and Vanessa Mickan for helping us find our way; Tom Walsh for helping us keep it real; Scott Watrous and Ronnie Gramazio for believing in our dream. And Lara Asher, Inger Forland, Gary Krebs, Susan Blond, Carol Klenfner, Eric Wielander, Alison Daulerio, and Steve Moore for helping us shine.

Nicole would also like to thank: My sister, Tracy, for being my wings. My grandmother, Maye, for being my roots. My best friend, Karen, for my childhood and every supportive day since. All those who have ever hired me or dared to work with me. All of my cherished friends who have given me so much laughter and wonderful memories especially the girls from D.C. who inspired me to write this book, and finally Coco, who I miss every day. I adore you all!

Susan would also like to thank: Julia Cho for writing and life advice; Ed Chung for medical advice; Celia Johnson for those first notes; Eric Loo for the last-second looky-loo; Andrea Wachner for the vegan rules; Anthony (Tony, to me) Watts for his impeccable style; and Maria Headley and Sally Robinson for "how to deal with the biz" pep talks. Special shout out to my Wednesday Ladies (you know who you are) for your constant laughter and cheerleading. Under-the-chin scratching goes to Harley, my neighbor's cat, whose daily visits made the empty, white pages seem less daunting. (Thanks, Rob, for letting me steal your boy.) But mostly, I send much love to John Williams for his unflappable patience and his enduring belief in me as a writer and a person.

NICOLE SEXTON worked as a Republican fundraiser for fifteen years and served as the Director of Finance for the National Republican Senatorial Committee from 2002 to 2005, where she helped to regain the Republican majority in the Senate. She currently works for the ONE Campaign helping to raise awareness of the crisis of AIDS and extreme poverty around the world. She splits her time between New York and Washington, D.C., with her beloved yorkies, Eloise and McKenzie.

SUSAN JOHNSTON is a native West Virginian and five-time published playwright who received her MFA from NYU's Tisch School of the Arts. She's been the recipient of a MacDowell Colony residency and a Jerome Fellowship and was a Fulbright nominee. Susan's written for *Interview* magazine and A&E's popular *Biography* series. She lives in Santa Monica.